BEFORE HIGHLAND SUNSET

SPECIAL OPS SCOTS
BOOK 1

KAIT NOLAN

TAKE THE LEAP PUBLISHING

ONE

ALEX

I stared down at the final signature line on what felt like a mountain of paperwork and wondered if I was signing my life away. Not that I regretted going into business with two of my best mates, but buying property felt like a huge commitment when so much of my life had been lived for the short-term. Especially as I hadn't even seen the place yet. But I trusted Callum Quinn and Finley Patterson with my life. We'd survived far worse than purchasing joint real estate during all our years together in the Royal Marines. All of us were retired now, and this was the first real step in putting down roots. If I came to regret it, it wouldn't be because of my friends. I had unfinished business here in Glenlaig that they knew nothing about.

Resigned, I scrawled my name one last time.

Alexander Conroy

"I reckon that's the last of it."

Hamish Colquhoun, the local lawyer who was overseeing the paperwork and title transfer, flipped through the contracts to verify all three of us had signed and initialed in the requisite spots. "Aye, everything seems to be in order, gentlemen. My office manager will see that everything is filed appropriately and copies are made for each of you. You're welcome to stay here while she does that, or you can take the keys now and pop back by later."

Finn predictably shoved to his feet. The man waited for nothing unless he had to. "I'm for picking up the paperwork later."

As Theo Gordon, the seller, had already done his bit earlier, in order to get back to a job site, it was Hamish who handed over the keys. "Congratulations. We're all very excited about your outdoor adventure company."

Callum paused, fingers clenched around the keys. "We havenae said what sort of business we're opening."

Hamish's eyes crinkled in amusement. "Ewan mentioned it at poker night a while back. And, well, it's a small village, aye?"

Ewan McBride—aka Sentinel—aka our former section leader, who'd retired before all of us and come home to buy the local pub. He was most of the reason we'd chosen to settle here instead of elsewhere in the Highlands along more typical tourist routes.

Callum grunted in a tone I knew meant annoyance. As the last of us to retire, it would likely take him the longest to acclimate to civilian life, especially since he'd had no intention of giving up his career for years more. I knew what that was like, though it hadn't been injury to put an end to my service.

Three years into my own retirement, I was still finding my way, feeling almost as untethered as I had the day I'd walked away. There'd been a moment when I'd had another choice. A shot at a very different life. But I'd chosen the familiar instead and botched that chance beyond belief. I'd been waiting for it to bite me in the arse all this time. By moving to Glenlaig, the wait would be over. I just didn't know exactly how soon I'd have to face the consequences of that decision.

"We will actually have to advertise, ye ken?" Finn prodded. "There's no business without customers."

Callum's grey eyes narrowed.

I pushed back from the table. "Aye. Right. We'll be going then. Thanks, Hamish. C'mon, lads. I want the full tour."

The village itself wasn't large. Our new building was easily within walking distance of the law office. But as it was currently pelting rain, we elected to drive. I was fine with that. From my position in the backseat, my head stayed on a swivel, scanning the street and buildings beyond the water-streaked glass. Few people were braving the weather, though I expected that to change after working hours. For many, the warm, inviting pub on a rainy evening was just the thing. I fully expected my business partners to suggest we head that way for a toast after the tour, and I was already trying to come up with an excuse. I wouldn't be able to put them off long. In truth, it was pure cowardice that had prevented me from dealing with this years ago. But I just wanted another day to find my footing before I faced what—or rather, who—potentially awaited me inside Ewan's pub.

Finn turned off the high street just past the newsagent and onto a tree-lined road that wound away from the village proper. A quarter mile down, he pulled to the kerb in front of an unassuming building that disappeared back into overgrown trees. The sign out front read Furry Friends Highland Haven.

I leaned forward. "What exactly did this place used to be?"

Finn shut off the motor. "A pet spa, apparently."

"Seriously?" I squinted at the red brick facade and tried to picture it. "I can't imagine there'd be much need for such a thing somewhere like this."

"Aye. Which is why the building's been for sale for more

than a year." With that pronouncement, Callum got out of the car and rounded the bonnet.

Finn and I followed, reaching the door just as Callum got the lock open. We stepped inside, out of the chill autumn rain. Someone switched on the overhead light. A half-dozen anemic fluorescent bulbs flickered madly for a few seconds before finally deciding to stay on. I looked around the front of the shop, which contained only a dusty counter set on peeling linoleum tiles. It was clearly meant to be a reception area of some sort. The bulk of the building presumably lay beyond the door on the back wall, but I suddenly had grave trepidations about what they'd gotten me into.

"Really? This is what we just paid for?"

Finn swung an arm around my shoulders. "Just wait till you see it. It's got lots of potential."

"Lots of work, he means," Callum grumbled. "But it's the best pre-existing building in the village that can be converted to suit our needs. It would've been a lot more expensive to buy land and build from scratch."

As I noted a wet spot on the ceiling that needed addressing in short order, I hoped he was right. I'd spent most of the last three years working for my brother's construction company, doing restoration work and additions. I well knew how much rot and ruin could be hidden behind walls and beneath floors. We wouldn't know for sure what we were in for until we started ripping things out. At least I had the skills to do something about most of it.

I followed Callum through the door into the back. Again, we were met with fluorescent lights. The back of the building was fairly massive for a village this size. The walls were lined with empty chain-link kennels. Most of the center portion was covered in artificial turf that had, presumably, been the play area during snowy winter months and rainy days. I appreciated the fact that it had been cleaned and there was no lingering odor of pet waste. Small mercies. As I walked around, Callum began talking about what needed doing.

"Obviously, we'll need to do a facility build-out to better suit our needs."

I was only half listening as I scanned for signs of impaired structural integrity or other major issues. It didn't look too bad on the surface, though I wouldn't know for sure until I had a look at the foundation outside and checked the beams and joists in the attic. This part of the building had clearly been added on to a previous structure at some point in the distant past. There was no guarantee it had been joined correctly, so we'd want to make any necessary repairs there before we got too far down the list on Callum's build-out.

"—split our time between renovations and exploring the area for adventure opportunities." Of course, Finn would want to get out in nature immediately. The man would probably never come inside if not for inclement weather.

"Aye, that's grand as a plan," I interrupted, "but before we get started on any of that, I've got to find a place to live."

Finn blinked. "I thought you were bunking with me."

He'd rented a cottage on the outskirts of the village, within a stone's throw of the nearest trailhead. The best descriptor of the place was cozy—which was fine for one person. But for two —well, I'd done my time in small spaces with my former team- mate. I didn't relish the idea of sharing with him, or anyone else, for that matter.

"For the short term. But much as I love you, mate, I want my own space." Not least because Finn was a nosy bastard, and there were things that would come up from being here that I didn't want to talk about.

Unconcerned, Finn just crossed his arms. "I'm sure we'll find you something in a week or two. Now, what do you think about converting these kennels into individual storage for equipment?"

As the two of them continued discussing the potential of the space, I added more items to my mental to-do list. I wondered just how much of it I'd be able to accomplish before running into the one person I'd been avoiding for the past three years.

TWO

CIARA

The problem with being bottom of the pecking order at work was that I drew the short straw by default. Not that being the official errand runner was a bad thing, and, God knew, I was ecstatic to have been hired on full-time as a staff member at Ardinmuir Event Planning. Being able to quit my second job as a server at my brother's pub had been a fine day indeed. But the last thing I wanted to do today was make this trip to the neighboring village of Braemore to pick up lamb chops from the butcher there for our event tomorrow.

Really, it was my own damned fault. If I'd told my bosses—one of whom was also my cousin, Kyla—why I didn't want to go to Braemore, they'd have made other arrangements. But telling them would inevitably involve the news leaking to their significant others, who were all bonus protective big brothers on top of the one I already had. No doubt they'd get it into their fool heads to give my ex, Brodie Drummond, some kind of threat or ultimatum if they knew he wasn't leaving me alone. He was harmless, really. It was just that he was having a hard time accepting that I really meant it when I'd broken off our relationship.

It would've been easier if he'd been a jerk. I'd have told him off without compunction. But it had been a classic case of "It's not you, it's me." I just... didn't love him the way I needed to love him. Instead of acknowledging that sucked and moving on, Brodie had begun a campaign to win me back. Sending me gifts and assaulting me with puppy dog eyes on the regular were hardly crimes. But three months on from our breakup, I was moving past sympathetic and into exasperated.

The anxiety I felt at simply turning onto the high street in Braemore annoyed me. As a rule, I didn't mind confrontation. But I hated hurting people's feelings, and it seemed like that's all I'd been doing lately, whenever I'd seen my ex. I'd started changing my habits to avoid the possibility of seeing him, and that was ridiculous. While he didn't live in Glenlaig, this area of the Highlands was one big community. Our paths would inevitably cross. Unfortunately.

But I was a grownup, and this was my job, so I'd pull on my big girl pants and do the thing. It was the middle of the workday, anyway, so the chances of running into him were lower, right?

Parking was at a premium, with the weather being what it was. Not that rain was remotely unusual in Scotland. I tugged up the hood of my red rain slicker and slipped out of the car. By the time I made it the two blocks down to the butcher shop, I was wishing I'd put on my Wellies this morning. My feet squished inside my sodden socks, and my toes were already starting to cramp from the cold. As soon as I got back to the castle, I was hunting up Angus and begging a cuppa and whatever sweet he'd baked today.

Behind the counter, Ross McFarlane looked up with a smile. "Och, good day to you, Ciara. Here for the chops?"

"Aye. You're saving our event, you are. I can't believe they wanted to change the menu the *day* before."

"It's no trouble. These just came in this morning, and they're gorgeous. I'll just get them all packaged up for Afton, aye?"

"Perfect. Thanks, Ross."

He disappeared through the door to the back, and I moved to the refrigerated cases to browse his other offerings. Cooking wasn't my best skill. With the wide variety of food offerings in Edinburgh, where I'd gone to university, there'd been little impetus to cook for myself. Since I'd moved home, my saint of a mum was prone to popping by to stock my wee freezer with my favorites because she knew I often worked long hours. But I wasn't entirely useless in the kitchen, and Afton Colquhoun, our chef at Ardinmuir Event Planning, had been teaching me a thing or two. Maybe I'd pick up a roast or pork loin to put in the slow cooker this week.

When the shop bell jangled, it was instinct to turn toward it. The moment I caught sight of the newcomer, I wished I'd done anything else because, of course, it was Brodie.

His face brightened at the sight of me. "Ciara! It's so good to see you."

Politeness was too deeply ingrained for me to say nothing and ignore him. Especially as the shop wasn't large enough to hide. "Brodie."

"How have you been?"

"Good. Busy." It was the truth, if not the detailed version.

"Business is clearly good. There have been cars up by the castle every time I've been by."

A prickle of unease trailed down my spine. You couldn't just see cars at the castle from passing by on the road. You had to actually drive up to the castle to see that. How often had he "been by" since we'd broken up?

"Wedding season is slowing down now, I'd guess, what with autumn arriving."

That unease shifted to a full-on knot in the pit of my stomach because I knew where he was going with this. The busyness of work had been part of my reasons for breaking up with him. He'd begun resenting the fact that I simply wasn't available most weekends and quite a few evenings because of events we were running. If he believed that was going to change, it would just add fuel to the fire for his win-back campaign.

"It's not really slowing down that much. We're booked out solid almost all the way to Christmas." It wasn't a lie. We were booked up that far, just not entirely with weddings.

A flash of... something darkened his expression. Frustration maybe. "I know you love your job, but it's important for you to have a life. To take time for yourself."

I struggled to hang on to my patience. This was just more evidence that we truly didn't suit. "Brodie, I have a life. I do take time for myself. And I'm sorry that doesn't include you. But I already explained I just dinna think we're a good fit."

For just a moment, his lips flattened. Then he was back to the hang-dog expression that had become his norm around me. "How can you just up and decide that after more than a year?"

In truth, I'd known it pretty early on, and I'd deluded myself into thinking that it would be okay. That I'd grow to feel what I needed to feel for him. But there was another part of me that knew that was horse shite. If I was going to feel it, I'd have felt it straight out of the gate. I knew from previous experience that was how I worked. And that wasn't what I'd had with Brodie. I'd let our relationship go on way too long because I'd been lonely. It felt like everyone around me was falling in love, getting married, having kids. Not that I was ready for all those things, but I wanted someone to share a life with, and I'd thought Brodie could grow to become that person.

Instead, I'd hurt him by not acknowledging the truth, even to myself.

"Brodie, I am sorry. I should've made the call a lot sooner than I did. I didn't set out to lead you on. But let me be as transparent and clear as I possibly can to save you from further grief: we are not getting back together."

"But if you'll just give us another chance, I—"

In that moment, Ross stepped back out front. God love him. "I've got your order here."

Desperate, I turned back toward him. "Thank you so much. These will be perfect."

I felt Brodie's gaze on me as I finished paying for the food, but he said nothing. Feeling ten kinds of awkward, I grabbed the bag and dared to meet his eyes. "I have to get back to work. Take care, Brodie."

Without waiting for a reply, I rushed back outside into the rain.

He didn't follow me this time, and I counted that as a win. Maybe this would be the end of it. Maybe he'd finally listen. I hoped so, because I was so over having to tiptoe around male feelings.

As I slid behind the wheel of my car, I wondered briefly about what might have been if things had actually worked out with the man I'd felt that instant flash of connection with all those years ago. Where would I be now?

Before my mind could even conjure his face, I shook my head. What use was it wondering? My instincts couldn't be trusted because what I'd believed was a mutual connection had turned out to be nothing more than a one-night stand with a man who'd made promises, then ghosted me.

With him and Brodie in my past, it was fair to say my personal radar was broken, and I ought to resign myself to staying single for a while.

THREE

ALEX

"I'll take it." Relieved to have sorted out my own place so quickly, I turned to shake Hamish's hand.

When we'd stopped back by the law office at the end of the day on Friday to pick up our copies of the sale contracts, I'd told his office manager, Marsaili, that I was looking for somewhere to let, and she'd mentioned that Hamish and his wife had just recently finished renovating the flat above his office. He'd already gone for the day, but Marsaili had called him and arranged for me to see the place late Saturday afternoon.

It wasn't huge. One bedroom, one bath, with a surprisingly spacious main room that made up the kitchen and lounge area. I didn't have need of much, and the location couldn't be beat. Right around the corner from the pub, it was also within easy walking distance of work. Unlike Callum, who'd bought a house in what felt like the middle of bloody nowhere, I didn't mind being right in the heart of the village. I could have continued to stay with Finn, but I wanted my own space. Eventually, if everything worked out, I'd buy something. Put down some real roots. For now, this suited. Best of all, it came mostly furnished, so I wouldn't have to waste time or money on that myself. I traveled pretty light. I had things in storage down in Dumbarton where my family lived, but I could make a trip down to get it when it was convenient, rather than rushing.

"Fantastic. How soon are you wanting to move in?"

"As soon as possible. Tonight? Tomorrow?"

If Hamish was surprised, he didn't show it. "We can make that happen. Let's just step downstairs to sign the lease."

I followed him down to the office, skimming through the paperwork and signing on for a year. If I ended up needing to break it, I'd only be out a month's rent and my deposit. I wrote out a check.

Hamish handed over the keys and a business card. "We've just finished renovations in the last few weeks, so everything should be set, but if you have any trouble with anything, just give me a call, and we'll get it sorted."

"What about the utilities?"

"Och, Monday will be soon enough to get them switched over. Welcome to Glenlaig, Alex."

"Thanks." I followed him outside so he could lock up the office and waved when he got into his car.

For a moment, I simply stood there, soaking up the quiet of the autumn evening and debating with myself. I could go straight to Finn's and begin packing my things to bring over. It wouldn't take me long. I'd been living out of a duffel bag for the few days I'd been here. But I'd promised him and Callum that I'd meet them at the pub so we could have the celebratory drink we hadn't gotten around to last night. I couldn't really beg off again without rousing sufficient suspicion from them both to spark an interrogation.

The truth of it was I was being a coward.

I'd chosen to move to Glenlaig with my mates, knowing that *she* was here. It wasn't a large village. We'd inevitably cross paths sooner rather than later. I just hoped that whenever that happened, I had some genius idea for what the hell to say. Three years hadn't been enough time for me to figure it out, so I was relying on the pressure of being under the gun to get me out of this mess of my own making.

But it was Saturday night. Given her line of work, she probably had a wedding today. She'd either be working or too tired to come out after wrangling clients all day. Right? Surely, I'd have a reprieve and get more than two days before I had to face the consequences of my past?

Decided, I pocketed the keys to the flat and strode around the corner and across the street to The Stag's Head Pub. A roar of sound greeted me as I stepped inside. It was a good place Ewan had here. When he'd left the Royal Marines, he'd bought it from the younger generation of a family who hadn't wanted to continue the business. Other than adding a few more televisions for coverage of the various sporting events his clientele enjoyed, he'd changed little. With its tartan wallpaper and dark wainscoting, The Stag's Head looked like what it was—a friendly neighborhood pub.

The latest Premier League football match was on the two screens I could see. Patrons clustered around them, pints in hand. More were shooting pool at the table in the back. I wove my way through mostly full tables toward the bar. Ewan moved behind it with the same fluid ease he'd once used for infiltration on missions, but he no longer wore the shadows of the things we'd done in the name of duty.

Credit for that went entirely to Isobel Donnchadh, the world-renowned violinist everyone else knew as Elizabeth Duncan. When she'd gone on the run to escape her controlling and abusive manager, Ewan had been the one to rescue her and give her a place to hide out until the legalities could be disentangled. He'd fallen arse over teakettle for her, as had she with him. I wouldn't have believed it if I hadn't seen it with my own eyes. But Finn and I had joined them as security on the last leg of her final concert tour, so we'd gotten to know her well. She was a total sweetheart, and our former section leader was a lucky bastard. He'd taken the lot of us ring shopping a while back, but so far, he hadn't worked up the nerve or found the right time to ask her to marry him.

I bellied up to the long stretch of polished bar, where Finn and Callum perched on stools.

"Decided to join us, then?" Ewan asked.

"I said I would." Never mind that I'd had to talk myself into actually following through. "Where's your better half this evening?"

"She's visiting with my mum, but said she planned to stop by later."

Callum pivoted on his stool. "Did you find a flat?"

"Aye. I ended up leasing the one above the law office."

"Close enough to stumble home," Finn declared. "Though I dinna ken why you had to move out so bloody fast."

In the way of old friends, I lightly shoulder checked him. "Because you snore like a bleeding freight train. I had enough of that on missions, thanks very much."

Finn clutched his chest like a heroine in one of the historical period dramas my mum liked to watch. "I'm mortally offended, sir."

I grinned at him. "Your ego needed some deflating." Turning back to Ewan, I slapped a hand on the bar. "What's a man got to do to get a pint around here?"

"We're drinking to business. That calls for whisky," Callum announced. "The good stuff, McBride, aye?"

Ewan pulled out three glasses and poured. We each picked one up.

"To Highland Hooligans Adventures," Finn proclaimed.

Callum and I stared.

"We're no' calling it that," I insisted. "What about Caledonian Quest Adventures?"

"That makes it sound like we'll be taking clients on a hunt for Nessie or some shite. No," Callum vetoed. "To the business, the name of which is to be determined. There's no one I'd rather trust my future to than you lot."

Finn faked blinking back tears. "That was beautiful, mate."

Callum scowled, which only served to highlight the scar that ran through his left eye. "Shut yer puss and drink."

We clinked glasses and did exactly that.

The whisky slid down my throat like warm, smoky butter.

As we'd talked, more and more people had come inside, raising the noise level and with it my own twitchiness. I was back to wanting quiet. I finished off the whisky. "I think I'm going to call it an early night. I want to go back to Finn's and start packing."

Finn draped an arm around my shoulders. "Come on! It's Saturday night. We're here to celebrate. You can move tomorrow."

I opened my mouth to make excuses again and glanced back toward the door. Whatever words had been on my tongue simply died as *she* walked into the pub, surrounded by other women.

She was even more gorgeous than I remembered, with all that rich, dark hair I itched to sink my fingers into and those lips I still woke up convinced I could taste. My tongue promptly glued itself to the roof of my mouth, and I knew I was well and truly fucked.

FOUR

CIARA

Some of the tension slid off my shoulders as we stepped inside the pub. The Stag's Head was my brother's place, and so far, it was the one location Brodie had avoided since our breakup. Probably because he was afraid of my brother.

Justifiably. As a former Royal Marine, Ewan was a certified badass.

Beyond that, I'd worked here for my first two years after uni, so it felt like home. Even so, I was relieved not to be carting drinks and meals around the room. After the day we'd just had, I was too damned tired to even lift a tray. The wedding, which was the first time the bride's divorced parents had been in the same room since their split, had gone off, if not without a hitch, at least without bloodshed, and that felt like a win we were all here to celebrate.

It was crowded tonight, and I found myself grateful for the room in the back that Ewan habitually kept roped off for family and close friends or private parties.

As we collectively moved in that direction, Sophie MacKean, who'd married my cousin Connor, Kyla's brother, laid a hand over the gentle swell of her baby bump. "I've been dreaming all day of Dom's cottage pie. Do you suppose anyone would look at me funny if I ordered two?"

Dominic Bassey, the genius in the pub's kitchen, had a tendency to father the entire staff and a love of feeding people that transcended boundaries and endeared him to the entire village. He was also the reason I'd added more than a few curves to my figure since I'd moved home from Edinburgh. If the tradeoff for finally having cleavage was hips, I could live with that.

I looped my arm through Sophie's. "I say you're eating for two, so why should it matter? An order for each of you." Especially as she hadn't been able to keep anything heavier than rice down for the past couple of months. "For my part, I plan to sweet talk him into making me a steak and ale pie with a side of his famous garlic mashed potatoes. After which I intend to haul myself upstairs to my flat and fall face-first into bed. Maybe for the next three days."

Kyla pressed both hands to the small of her back and stretched. "Getting off my feet sounds heavenly."

"I'm grateful to work back of house so I can at least wear comfortable shoes. Nobody cares what's on the chef's feet," Afton declared.

I mock glared at all of them. "At least you lot have partners who will offer up a foot rub at the end of a long day."

It was bad enough that I spent most of my time planning other people's nuptials. But all three of the owners of Ardinmuir Event Planning were disgustingly, happily married, with babies already here or on the way or actively hoped for. Not that I was ready for that. At twenty-five, my biological clock still had years to go. But I missed sex and intimacy. The dating pool here was small, so there was no such thing as a casual hookup that wouldn't lead to complications. And after what had happened three years ago, I'd been soured on the idea, anyway. Nothing like having the most mind-blowing night of my life, only to find out that crazy chemistry didn't equal a future.

Brodie and I hadn't had crazy chemistry. He'd been... adequate. We'd been comfortable. For a long time, I'd let myself believe that I could have one or the other. In the grand scheme of things, I wanted comfort and stability. A partner to share my life. That was more important than chemistry.

Except I needed more.

It was just one of many reasons I'd ended things. I had to believe there was more out there. That I'd find someone I didn't feel like I was settling for.

Of course, that would be far easier if I didn't have a completely unrealistic standard in the back of my brain. The man I'd let into my bed, and far too deep into my heart, hadn't been real. He'd played me, and I'd learned my lesson. But I still hadn't been able to let go of the dream he represented.

It was probably just because I'd gotten no closure. He'd been an open wound for so long, and I hadn't been able to move on properly.

Eejit. You've already wasted too much time and brain space on the likes of him.

"I say we get company-wide pedicures this week," Kyla suggested.

Grateful for the save from my own spiraling thoughts, I grinned at my cousin. "You're on."

"Ciara, Kyla." My brother's voice rang out over the din. "Come meet my mates."

I tensed, everything in me going on alert for reasons I

couldn't name. Then I promptly lost my breath as my gaze met familiar brown eyes that I'd once seen across a train car.

Alex.

I'd guessed back then that he was military. But I hadn't known he'd served with my brother. I'd heard stories about these men that Ewan had served with for years. But he'd always referred to them by their last names. Not until Isobel had come along had I found out that Conroy was Alex Conroy. Even then, I hadn't imagined that his squadmate was the same Alex Conroy I'd known so briefly. I hadn't been able to bring myself to try to wheedle information out of my brother. Not when I had no reason I was willing to share as to why I was asking. Not when it wouldn't change what had happened.

But here was the confirmation I let myself seek out.

I'd wondered for years what had happened, wasted so much time pining over this man. And there he was, big as life, as if he had a right to be here. Seeing him was an absolute punch in the gut. He looked even better than he had three years ago. Civilian life hadn't made him soft. That body that had once ranged over mine was still fit as hell, and my fingers itched to touch, as if he hadn't stomped all over my heart. Heat flushed my body from head to toe.

He didn't appear shocked to see me, which meant that, at some point in the past three years, he'd put two and two together about who I was. Had that been why he'd ghosted me? Because he'd realized he'd slept with his mate's little sister?

Or had he always known? Had he taken me to bed knowing exactly who I was?

God, I hadn't ever thought of that. I'd always assumed that *if* he was Ewan's squadmate and *if* he knew who I was, he'd found out after. But if he'd known from the beginning, that made all of this worse.

My friends carried me toward him in a wave I was helpless to resist.

I barely heard Ewan's introductions to Callum and Finley. Handshakes and nods were going round. When Alex came to me, he said only, "Nice to meet you."

I stared at him, searching for some hint of recognition. Some spark. Either this man was an award-winning actor, who didn't want my brother to know we knew each other, or he... didn't remember me.

The flush of heat faded to a chill. Meeting Alex had been a life-altering moment in my life. Had our time together meant so little to him that I hadn't even made an impression?

There was a distinct possibility I was going to be sick.

"—so nice you're all here for a visit," Kyla said.

"Not a visit," Finley announced. "We're opening an outdoor adventure company here."

"Here? In Glenlaig?" They were the first words I'd managed to speak.

"Aye. We thought it would make a good base," Callum said.

They'd moved here. *He'd* moved here, to my tiny village, where I wouldn't be able to avoid seeing him. Not only because it was small, but because he was one of my brother's best friends. He'd be a part of the circle of people I saw all the time.

I physically felt my world shrink around me. I was already avoiding places and people because of Brodie, and now I'd have to do the same because of Alex.

Abruptly, my temper kindled.

What was wrong with me? I wasn't going to change my life because of some man. I shouldn't have changed it because of Brodie. I sure as hell wasn't going to waste another moment on the likes of Alex Conroy.

Fuck him.

It was my village. My people. I was here first.

I'd avoid him when I could, and when I couldn't, well, it was fine. Because he didn't matter. I wouldn't *let* him matter anymore.

I turned to my brother and forced a smile that was probably a little feral around the edges. "I need a drink, brother. I've had a real pisser of a day."

God knew I was going to need one to get through the next half hour.

FIVE

ALEX

So much for the pressure of being under the gun.

Faced with an older, wiser, more beautiful Ciara McBride, I hadn't been able to come up with a single bloody thing to say.

I was a bawbag of the highest order, falling back on my training not to react. Just so I didn't have to admit to her brother that we'd once shagged each other's brains out. He'd beat me to a bloody pulp, and I would absolutely deserve it. But I hadn't missed the flash of hurt in her bonnie blue eyes when I'd pretended not to know her.

Fuck. *Fuck.*

I hadn't really expected to run into her like this, in front of Ewan and all these other people. All these years, I'd hoped for a chance to speak to her privately. Not that I had any better idea of what to say to her now than I had when my life had gone completely off the rails. If I hadn't already known that I owed her an apology for my behavior, the carefully neutral but still frosty look she'd shot in my direction as she had a drink with her friends—coworkers?—certainly would have told me.

I had reasons for going back on my word. Unfortunately,

she didn't have the security clearance to allow me to tell her what most of them were, which just made the whole damned thing worse. I couldn't regret the countless lives and careers saved because of what I'd done, but if I'd known what would happen when I'd gotten that job offer, I'd have turned it down flat. The things I'd lost because of it were a far higher price than I would have been willing to pay.

If I'd followed my heart instead of my pride—if I'd chosen her—everything about my life would be different now.

But I hadn't. And here we were.

I didn't know how to make it right, only that I had to say or do something. So when I spotted Ciara pushing back from the table and heading for the door after finishing the drink she'd ordered, I turned to make my own excuses.

"Okay, I really am done for the night. I want to head back to pack. That way, I can do whatever I need to do to settle in tomorrow so we can dive into work on Monday."

My mates made a few more ball-busting remarks but didn't try to get me to stay. I made for the door, stepping outside just in time to see Ciara rounding the corner of the building.

I rushed to catch her. "Ciara."

She stopped in her tracks, halfway down the alley. Her shoulders rose and fell, as if she were breathing hard.

"I'm sorry." It was the only thing I could think to say, and it wasn't nearly enough.

Ciara swung around, and there was no careful neutrality now. Every line of her lovely face was dialed to livid. "You're sorry? What exactly are you sorry for, Alex? Why dinna you spell it out for me?"

I'd known this was coming, and still, I didn't know the right thing to say. "I'm sorry for disappearing on you. You deserved better than that."

Her hands curled into fists, and I wondered if she'd actually use them on me. "Why the hell did you even say you wanted to see me again in the first place? I never expected more."

Scrubbing a hand down my face, I thought back to that day in her flat in Edinburgh, when she'd filled my world with hope for a future brighter than the one I'd lost. When I'd refused to say goodbye and promised I'd see her soon. When I'd assured her that the moment I knew my plans, she'd be the first to know.

I'd wanted to remember her exactly as she was right then. Skin still flushed from a shower and the things we'd done to each other in it, lips full and rosy from mine. And I had. With high-definition clarity, I remembered every millimeter.

"Because when I made that promise, I had every intention of keeping it." This was one of the few pieces of honesty I could offer her.

"Then why didn't you?" Sarcasm gave her words a bite that said she didn't believe anything I was saying. But there was just a hint of vulnerability. Of hope that there was a good explanation that would take away the sting of what she'd no doubt interpreted as resounding rejection.

Because it wouldn't have been safe for you.

But that was part of the long list of things I couldn't tell her.

When I didn't answer, her expression hardened, her eyes glimmering. "Was I just some grand joke to you? Did you get some sick satisfaction from screwing your friend's sister?"

"God, no. I had no idea of your connection to Ewan when we met."

"Is that why? You somehow found out he was my brother and freaked out?"

It was a reason. Not a good one, but it was an excuse I could actually offer her that was the legitimate truth. But I didn't have it in me to pretend that was all it was. "That was part of it."

Again, she waited for me to elaborate.

When my brain continued to give me nothing but static, she shook her head, face twisting. "Did I mean so little to you that you couldn't even admit you had regrets or had changed your mind right after you left me?"

God, that look of betrayal was worse than a knife to the gut. "No. No, it was never that." Wanting to comfort, I took a step toward her, but she took one back. That, too, was a slap.

"You hurt me." Those three words shook with emotion I could see her desperately fighting back, and they made me bleed. "I waited for you a hell of a lot longer than you deserved because I didn't want to believe you were the kind of man who would sleep with someone and then just ghost her without a word." She gave a humorless laugh. "But hell, I've learned that I was wrong about all kinds of things."

What did that mean?

Before I could ask, her shoulders squared, and she lifted her chin in unmistakable defiance. "I know you're going to be living here now, and it's a small village. We're going to see each other. You're going to end up as part of the circles that I travel all the time. So I'll be polite, because that's who I am. But do me a favor and stay the hell away from me, Alex."

Turning her back on me, she walked away. I watched her go, wishing I could do anything to make this better. When she disappeared behind the building, I followed. Glenlaig didn't strike me as the sort of place with a lot of crime, but a woman alone in the dark was at risk anywhere. I made it to the corner of the building in time to see her climbing a set of stairs at the rear. Because apparently, she lived in a flat above the pub.

At least she'd made it home safely.

Lost in my thoughts, I headed back toward the law office, where I'd left my 4x4. I'd already felt like a clarty bastard for how I'd handled things—or not handled them—with Ciara. But now I could see that this wasn't just wounded pride or a woman scorned. I'd well and truly hurt her.

It was just one more reason on a very long list of why I hated myself.

SIX

CIARA

"What do you think of this one?" Isobel held something up in front of the mirror, but I wasn't really paying attention.

Our shopping trip hadn't been the great distraction I'd been hoping for. My mind was far too full of all the things I wished I'd said the other night. "Super cute."

The silence spun out way too long before I finally met her gaze in the mirror to find one blonde brow arched. I refocused to take in the neon-pink leopard print and faux-feather-lined monstrosity of a jumpsuit in her hand.

Busted.

"I mean, it would definitely make a statement at the release party." Not that Isobel would be caught dead in such an outfit. Every part of her professional brand as Elizabeth Duncan screamed class.

She hung the eyesore back on the rack. "Right. We're going for lunch, where I'm going to ply you with wine, and you're going to tell me what's on your mind."

What was on my mind was Alex. I couldn't very well tell her about *that*, given he was one of Ewan's closest friends. As

I'd predicted, I'd seen him around town three times in the past four days. He'd done as I asked and kept his distance, but that only helped so much. Just seeing him physically hurt. And when I didn't see him, it seemed like every bleeding person in the village was talking about him and his mates and their adventure company. Not that I blamed them. It was the biggest news to hit Glenlaig since Afton pulled a runaway bride on my cousin Connor and shifted the three-hundred-year-old marriage pact binding their families onto Kyla's shoulders.

I didn't fight as Isobel led me from the boutique. There was no point. Her stubbornness wasn't anywhere near as overt as my occasionally blockheaded brother's, but it was just as potent and a hell of a lot sneakier. By the time we'd settled in a cozy back booth in some upscale eatery, I still hadn't figured out what to tell her.

She smiled sweetly at the server. "Can you bring us a bottle of the house Cab?"

As the guy nodded and walked away, I went brows up. "A bottle? Is it going to be one of those lunches, then?"

"For one, you've been working your arse off and deserve it. For another, a glass might not be enough to loosen your tongue."

"So it's to be an interrogation? Have you been taking direction from Ewan?"

"I don't need special forces training to see that something is seriously bothering you. Is this to do with Brodie?"

"No." I appreciated not having to lie. Yet, anyway. The one good thing to come from all of this was that I was no longer wasting brain space worrying about running into him anywhere I went.

"Okay, then what is it?"

When I just stared at her, she sighed. "Look, you've been a friend to me from the moment we met. Give me the chance to return the favor. If you need to talk about something, whatever this is, it stays between us. Contrary to your apparent belief, I don't share *everything* with Ewan. I do know how to keep a secret."

That was true enough. She'd kept her identity under wraps for months when she'd hidden out in Glenlaig. For a long time, we'd known only that she was a woman in trouble. That had been enough for all of us to circle the wagons.

I wished my problem was as simple as hiding out from an obvious villain. But nothing about the situation with Alex was simple or easy. We shared too many other connections beyond our own. I'd never told a soul what had happened, and a part of me wanted to spill out everything to Isobel.

The server came back with our wine. We placed our lunch orders, and I sat back in the booth fiddling with the edge of the tablecloth.

She must've sensed me weakening. "Ciara, truly, I just want to help."

Maybe it would be better to talk it through with someone else. I believed her when she said she wouldn't divulge anything I said to my brother.

"You can't, under any circumstances, tell Ewan if you value him staying out of prison for murder."

Isobel blinked, her brows drawing together. "If this has to do with something that compromises your safety—"

"No, no. It's not that." I knew my physical person was as safe with Alex as it would be with Ewan himself. "Just promise."

"Alright. I promise."

To buy myself some time, I picked up my glass and sipped, hoping the alcohol would grant me a little courage. "Did you ever watch that old movie from the nineties, *Before Sunrise?*"

Her face brightened. "Oh, your mum had me watch it sometime last year."

"It's one of her favorites. Was always one of mine, too."

"Ethan Hawke really had a look about him back then."

"He did."

"What does that have to do with what's going on with you?"

"Well, right before I graduated uni, I kind of had my own personal version. I met someone on the train back from a job in London. Instant connection. Fireworks. The whole bit."

There went that brow again. "The *whole* bit?"

My brain helpfully flashed back to what it had felt like to come apart beneath his hands and his mouth. A flush worked its way from my hairline to my toes, and I took a bigger gulp of the wine.

"We had one incredible night. We were both in places of transition, so I didn't expect anything else, even though it felt like we had a soul deep recognition of each other. He was the one who said he wanted to see me again. He made sure to get my number, made sure that it had been typed in correctly. And he said as soon as he figured out his plans, I'd be the first to know."

Isobel leaned forward, both elbows on the table. "So what happened?"

I looked down into the deep red of my wine. "He ghosted me. I messaged him a few times, but he never replied. So I let it go. *Tried* to let it go."

On a soft sound of distress, she reached out to cover my hand with hers. "But it didn't work."

"No. No, it did not. I was still thinking about him when I started dating Brodie. I guess I thought if I threw myself into a real relationship, it would all go away. I'd get over it. But I

didn't. Which was only one of the problems with that relationship. But that's not the issue."

"So what's going on? Did you hear from him? Your train
affair?"

"Oh, it's so much worse than that. He just moved to
Glenlaig."

Isobel's eyes widened, and comprehension dawned. "Oh,
my God. Is it..."

I sighed. "It's Alex."

"Alex Conroy?"

"Aye."

"Now I understand the concern about Ewan going to jail
for murder. Definitely, *definitely* not telling him. Did you not
know who Alex was?"

"No. I guessed he'd been military, but we didn't talk about that.
We didn't even share last names until after. He didn't know Ewan
was my brother until sometime later." I paused as something new
occurred to me. "He was going to meet a mate in Inverness when he
left Edinburgh. Hell, he was probably coming to see Ewan then."

Jesus. If he'd gone essentially straight from my bed to
finding out that I was his friend's sister...

"Oh, well, I imagine that was a shock. You've seen him,
then. Since he moved to town?"

"Oh, yes. Ewan introduced us at the pub on Saturday
night."

"Oh God. What happened?"

"He pretended like he'd never met me before."

Isobel's shocked expression turned into a scowl. "Bastard."

Her instant defense made me smile, just a little. It meant
something that she'd taken my side, because I knew she really
liked Alex and Finn. She'd gotten to know them well when
they were acting as security for the end of her tour.

"You know, over the years, I imagined so many scenarios of seeing him again. I spent so much time thinking about what I'd say. I wanted to make it absolutely clear how little he mattered to me. To make him feel as small and insignificant as I did."

I hated the empathy shining in her eyes. Hated, too, the fresh burn of tears I felt in my own as she squeezed my hand. I'd been skating so close to an emotional edge for days, barely holding it together. I'd promised myself I'd shed my last tear over Alex Conroy.

Shoving my roiling emotions down deep, I pulled my hand away and sipped more wine. "None of those scenarios involved him moving to my home, where I'll have to see him all the time, and him giving some shitty, half-arsed apology, where he said he made the promise because he intended to keep it at the time, and then didn't tell me why he couldn't or didn't."

"You don't think it was finding out your connection to Ewan?"

"He made it sound like that wasn't all there was to it. Even if that *was* the reason, he could have texted me and said he didn't know who I was. It would have been pure mince, but at least he could have acknowledged *something,* instead of leaving me in radio silence all this time. The kind thing to do would have been giving me some bloody resolution instead of leaving me to wonder."

Isobel bit her bottom lip. "Maybe he had a good reason."

"If he had a good reason, why wouldn't he share it?"

Something flashed over her face that made me think she knew something. "I don't know, but I do know he's been through a lot in the past few years. None of which is mine to tell."

Damn if that didn't spark my curiosity. I didn't want to waste more time on this man. I didn't want to keep thinking about him. About the might-have-beens or the what-ifs.

The server came back with our food, and I took the opportunity to drain the last of my glass. "Well, it's resolved now. Not especially well, but he's made some kind of an apology, and it's time for me to move on. We've both just got to find a way to navigate around each other."

Isobel plainly thought that was a terrible idea, but she didn't belabor the point. "Okay. That's your call. I won't say anything to anyone."

The tension that had lodged in my shoulders as we'd talked drained out. "Thank you for listening. I do feel better for having told someone."

"Of course. And since this scenario is apparently not going to result in some sort of fabulous reunion sex, I'm springing for dessert."

SEVEN

ALEX

I gripped the next chain-link fence panel and unfastened it from the post, moving it to the pile with all the others. We'd elected to get rid of the old kennels rather than attempting to convert them into something else. As they were still in good shape, we were dismantling them section by section. Callum had already found a buyer who wanted the lot of them. It wouldn't be a huge sum, but every little bit helped offset the cost of lumber and other materials for the renovation we were planning.

It was methodical, repetitive work that did nothing to distract me from the frustration and anger that had been dogging me for days. I wished we were tearing out walls. I needed the physicality of swinging a sledgehammer to bleed off a little of the self-recrimination that had been on constant repeat in the back of my brain since Ciara had walked away from me.

As she'd predicted, I saw her often. A half-dozen times in the past week, at least. And as she'd requested, I kept my distance insofar as possible. But I didn't miss the hitch in her step whenever she spotted me. That hitch belied her otherwise breezy, casual confidence. Because every single time I crossed her path, she was reminded of how I'd hurt her.

I'd been a fool to think that some half-arsed apology would do anything to give her real closure. But I didn't know what more I could do, short of bailing on my mates and the business we were starting and leaving Glenlaig entirely. My guilt over how I'd let her down wasn't enough to overcome the debt of friendship and gratitude I felt for Finn and Callum. Ewan, too.

Which meant we were at an impasse.

Was there any possible scenario where she forgave me? If there was, I hadn't figured out what it might be. It wasn't even about wanting her back. How could I want someone back, who I'd never really had in any substantive way to begin with? The twenty-four hours we'd spent together had felt like Fate, but possibility wasn't reality.

Still, I missed her. Which was completely mental. She'd been a blink in the grand scheme of my life. And yet, our time together had fundamentally changed something in me. Maybe I was only just now realizing how much, when it was entirely too late.

I threw down the next panel with more force than necessary.

"Och, what did that fence ever do to you?" Finn asked.

"Sorry." I was already turning back to the last remaining kennel. Once this was done, we'd be ripping up the artificial turf to make way for framing in some new walls. I wouldn't actually get to break anything until we opened up the side wall for a rolling door to allow for moving large outdoor equipment in and out. That had to wait until a longer stretch of dry weather than we'd been having.

"What's crawled up your arse? You've been scowling for days."

"Nothing. Just twitchy is all." It was something we'd all experienced since we left the military, and I expected him to leave it at that.

"You sure there's nothing you want to talk about before Callum gets back from the bank?"

I didn't even spare my friend a glance as I began removing the nut and bolt holding on one of the last post clamps. "Since when do we ever want to talk?"

Finn took up position to the side, ready to grab the panel when it released. "I noted you left the pub right after Ewan's sister last weekend."

My considerable training was the only thing that stopped my hands from jerking at this observation. I'd thought I'd been more subtle than that. "Did I?"

He was looking at me with far more speculation than was comfortable. I simply kept at my task, as if it were absorbing my full attention.

Finn opened his mouth to say something more, but before he could, I heard a noise.

"Shhh."

"You cannae put me off that easily, mate."

"No, no. Listen. Do you hear that?" I held perfectly still, angling my head to try to catch the sound I'd heard before. A faint rustle and sort of squeak. "There."

Setting aside my tools, I took a few steps, then paused to listen again.

"It's probably rats."

"Well, if it is, we need to know so we can get rid of them. I think it's coming from over here."

I wandered over to a pile of wood pallets in the back of the building. We'd held off on doing anything with them in case the wood could be repurposed somehow. "Come help me so the mountain doesn't collapse on whatever's under here."

Together, we carefully began shifting pallets off the stack. And halfway down found the source of the noise.

"What the hell is it?" Finn asked.

I crouched down, carefully extracting the wee orange creature from a pocket between the pallets. "A wee kitten. It can't be more than a few weeks old. I guess she was stuck under there."

The tiny body shivered in my hand, so I unzipped my fleece vest and tucked it against my chest. It butted its tiny head against my shirt and mewed at me.

Finn scratched at his stubbled cheek. "How the hell did it get in here?"

"I don't know. Are there others?"

He poked around the remaining pallets, looking for any littermates, but the wee tabby beastie seemed to be the only one.

We were still debating where it had come from when Callum returned. "I thought you lot would be finished by now."

"We found a stowaway." I unzipped my vest to show the kitten.

A blonde woman in a worn puffer vest and mud-spattered Wellies followed him into the back room. Her gaze slid straight to me. "What have you got there?" Her voice was at odds with her appearance. Instead of the Scots I'd expected, her accent was straight from London. The kind of posh upper-class cadence that spoke of boarding school and money.

At the sound of it, I could practically feel Finn bristle.

"May I?" When I nodded, the newcomer reached out and gently lifted the kitten, who objected to the change in position by digging its little claws into my shirt. "Come here, little one. Let's look you over."

"You know something about cats, then?"

She glanced up with bright green eyes that glittered with amusement. "I should hope so, since I'm a vet. Saoirse MacGregor."

"Dr. MacGregor is the one buying the old kennels," Callum explained.

"I figure I can use them for boarding at my practice. Here now, little love." Saoirse ran her fingers over the creature, checking its limbs, its teeth. The kitten mewled its protest at a surprising volume. Something about her reminded me of Ciara.

"She's underweight, a little dehydrated, and most certainly in need of a bath. No doubt she'll need her shots, but she seems pretty healthy otherwise. I'd say about four to five weeks old."

I stuck out my finger, and the kitten batted it with a tiny paw.

"What are we supposed to do with her?" Finn asked. "She's not ours."

A flash of something that might have been disgust passed over Saoirse's face. Before the situation could devolve, I found myself opening my mouth. "I'll take her."

I hadn't intended to keep her. But maybe it would be good to have someone else to focus on that wasn't me or the woman I'd accidentally scorned.

My mates stared at me in shock, but Saoirse smiled. "You can come by my office, and we'll get the shots taken care of and see about getting her a bath and all the other things you'll need. She's underweight, so you might need to do a little bottle-feeding to supplement for a while. Since we don't have a pet store in the village, we keep the basics on hand to get people through until they can order supplies or go pick them up somewhere else."

"That sounds good."

"Here you go, Da." Saoirse passed the kitten back to me.

I held the wee beastie up to eye level. "You okay with being my new roommate?"

The kitten promptly batted my nose, but without claws.

"I'm taking that as an aye."

I settled her into the inside pocket of my vest, where she curled up in a ball and promptly began to purr.

"Well now, let's go find your new baby some water."

EIGHT

CIARA

"To the unquestionable success of the new album, and all of you who helped get me there! I absolutely couldn't have done it without you."

Like everyone else in the wall-to-wall packed pub, I raised my glass to Isobel with a cheer. We all had a vested interest in seeing her succeed. She'd been so afraid when she'd come to us, having been kept under her manager's controlling and abusive thumb from the time she'd been a teenager because of a predatory contract. In the years since, she'd taken a page out of Taylor Swift's book and had been rerecording all her previous albums. The effort had been a wild success among her fans. Tonight was a celebration of the latest release, and it felt as if the entire village was here.

The doors to the outdoor patio were thrown open, and for once, the weather was on our side. The crowd spilled out into the courtyard, kept warm by the crush and the strategically placed outdoor heaters. Inside, it was just shy of standing-room only. My friends and I were fortunate enough to have snagged a small table in the corner. Under ordinary circumstances, I'd have been thrilled to be here celebrating Isobel's success, but everyone being here meant *everyone*—including Alex. Not that he'd approached me. But I kept catching glimpses of him over by the bar, clustered around Isobel in a posture I recognized as protective. He had been part of her security team, and I supposed old habits died hard. He and Finn were both keeping close, while Ewan ran things behind the bar.

"Are you all right, Ciara?"

I dragged my attention back to find Saoirse watching me with concern. "Aye, fine."

Pippa Wallace blinked at me from behind the lenses of her glasses. "Are you sure? You look like you're about to jump straight out of your skin."

She wasn't entirely wrong. Evidently, I was failing miserably at hiding my own discomfort.

Skye Stewart, the fourth leg of our little group, leaned forward and lowered her voice, though no one was likely to overhear a word that wasn't bellowed. "Are you worried Brodie's gonna show up?"

It was a reasonable excuse. They all knew I'd been having some trouble with my ex.

"Not really."

"Has he finally left you alone, then?" Pippa asked.

"Maybe? We had a bit of a run-in at the butcher shop in Braemore a couple of weeks ago. I had to get a lot more direct with him than I have before. It felt incredibly rude, but I think it maybe, finally, sank in that I was serious. I haven't seen him since."

Skye settled back in her chair, fingers tapping on her nearly empty glass. "It sucks when you have to be rude to make people listen. I don't know how it is for y'all over here, but back home, we have courtesy drilled in from the cradle. Sometimes, though, there's no substitute for a clear, concise 'Fuck off.'"

There was something incredibly amusing about hearing the profanity in Skye's sweet Southern drawl. A fairly recent transplant to Glenlaig, she'd moved to Scotland from Mississippi to be with her boyfriend, Jason McKinnon, who was presently manning the opposite end of the bar from my brother.

"We all know that if such tactics were taken by a man, it would be called 'direct' instead of 'rude'. I say the world would work far smoother if we were all more direct," Saoirse announced.

I smirked. "You're just saying that because you dinna want to put the effort into curbing the first thoughts that come into your head."

Casually, she took a sip of her beer. "Well, you're not *wrong*. Animals are so much easier than people. People are such finicky creatures."

"Truth." Pippa clinked her glass to Saoirse's in solidarity. "I'd much rather spend time with my coos." A computer programmer by trade, Pippa's true love was making artisan cheese. She'd been making quite a name for herself in some circles, enough so that she was hoping to be able to switch to making cheese full-time in another year or two.

Saoirse propped one booted foot on her knee. "So, it's been —what?—four months since you broke up with Brodie? When are you going to get back out there?"

"You literally *just* talked about how finicky people are," I protested.

"Finicky, yes, but men still serve a purpose. You have needs, love."

I didn't need reminding of those needs. Practically every time I spotted Alex, it felt as if I'd been hit by a blowtorch. "I dinna have any intention of getting back out there right now."

Skye's dark brows drew together. "Why not? You weren't in

love with Brodie, so it's not like you're getting over a broken heart."

For a grand total of three seconds, I considered saying something of the truth. But the more people who knew, the more likely it was to get back to Ewan. And that was not something I wanted to deal with.

"There's the small matter of lack of available men. Which is what got me into trouble with Brodie to begin with."

Saoirse made a vague gesture toward the bar, where all of Ewan's mates were gathered. "Um, excuse me, we've had a fresh influx lately. Or have they been working you so hard at Ardinmuir that you hadn't noticed?"

Pippa absently twirled one of her myriad tiny, beaded braids around one finger. "Have you met them, then?" In some women, such a gesture would've come off as coy. In Pippa, it simply served as the closest available fidget toy.

"I have. Did a little business with them."

"Well, don't hold back. What are they like?"

Saoirse raised a brow at Skye. "Are you looking to trade Jason in for a beefier model?"

"No. Jason and I are fine, but I like gossip just as much as the next girl. So what *are* they like?"

"Callum is very gruff and brusque. He takes taciturn to an entirely new level, which I can appreciate in person. We managed to get through my purchase of the old kennels they were tearing out with only about half a dozen sentences. Finley seems to be an irresponsible ass."

It was my turn to raise a brow. "Based on what?"

Saoirse's shoulders twitched. "It's just a feeling. I went over there with my lorry to pick up the kennels I'd bought, and they'd found a kitten. He was quick to say it wasn't his responsibility. I've got no time for people like that."

I didn't know Finn beyond having met him a few times.

He'd struck me as something of a practical joker. The humor of the team. But I could see how that might rub my very serious friend the wrong way.

"What about the third one?" Pippa asked.

"Ah, Alex." Saoirse's lips curved in a smile that made it all the way to her jade green eyes. "He took the kitten. Tucked it right into his pocket after I gave her an exam. I set him up with a starter kit of food and such. If there's anything sexier than a big, burly man being gentle with a baby animal, I don't know what it is."

I felt queasy at the idea of Alex dating someone else. Not like I was going to date him, but I felt physically ill at the idea of any of my friends crossing that line. I couldn't say a word about it without offering an explanation, so I said nothing. Maybe him getting back out there was the kick in the arse I needed to get over him myself.

"If you think he is such a catch, why don't you go after him yourself? It's not like you've been exactly burning up the dating circuit since you got up here."

In the year and a half since Saoirse had moved to Glenlaig, I hadn't seen her go out with anyone.

"I don't have time to date. I'm too busy picking up the slack and convincing my grandfather to let me actually *run* the practice, not just pick up the slack." She'd initially come to help after he'd been thrown from a horse and broken his hip, and she'd stayed to try to keep him from getting hurt any further by being constantly overextended. "If you don't want him, maybe Pippa should have a go."

"Me? What?" She blinked owlishly.

"Oh, I think Pippa's still holding out for a guy with a sexy southern drawl and a cowboy hat," I teased. "I didn't miss how you looked at Raleigh's friend Zeke when he danced with you at the wedding."

Raleigh Beaumont was the Texas cowboy who'd won the barony of Lochmara from Afton in a poker game. He'd been the one in the hot seat to marry Kyla because of the three-hundred-year-old marriage pact, or they'd both lose their estates to the crown. But it had all turned out in the end. Raleigh and Kyla were perfect together, and their little girl, Lily, was the cutest wee thing.

Pippa flushed bright enough that it showed in her brown cheeks. "I dinna ken what you're talking about."

"Haven't y'all been emailing, though?" Skye prompted.

"It's just email. That's all. He's addicted to my cheese."

"Is that a euphemism?" Saoirse asked.

"No!" Pippa's blush deepened in a way that suggested she'd definitely thought about him being addicted to something other than her cheese.

"Hey, Jason and I started as virtual pen pals, and look where we are now. Cohabitating and co-parenting the world's sweetest sheepadoodle."

"Yes, you're a disgustingly cute couple," Saoirse sighed. "If you weren't so damned likable, I'd have to hate you on principle."

Skye blew her a kiss. "I love you, too. Now, I really don't have an opinion on this since I am, as you pointed out, already part of a disgustingly cute couple. But I say, if y'all want to date, date. If you don't want to date, then don't. Nobody should feel pressured to couple up if that's not their jam. But I agree with Saoirse that those are some very attractive options now swimming in our tiny dating pool. And that's all I have to say about that."

She wasn't wrong, and that meant that, at some point, Alex was going to date someone else. He'd be taking someone else to bed. Blowing someone else's mind.

I shoved back from the table. "It's so crowded, it'll take

forever for Zo to work her way over here. Who wants refills?" I might not sling a tray here anymore, but I could do my former coworker a solid by not adding to her work.

Everyone agreed, so I made my way toward the bar, intent on pulling my own drinks. I spotted Ewan out front with Isobel, making like they were about to leave. Would the party thin out after they headed out? Past experience told me probably not. I still needed a minute, so I changed directions and went to the loo.

When I came back out a few minutes later, I bumped into a solid form. "Oh, sorry, I—" The apology died as I realized it was Alex.

With the distance he'd been keeping, I wasn't prepared for this, and there was far more bite than civility to my tone when I asked, "What do you want?"

You eejit, he probably wants the loo, same as you.

I was so aware of all the people around and the fact that anyone could see us together. Was it obvious that we used to be lovers?

If my sharp words wounded Alex at all, he didn't show it. "Look, I know I promised to keep my distance. I just—I hate how things are with us, and I wanted to know if there is anything... anything at all that I can do to make this better?"

"Do you have a time machine in your pocket?" The words were out before I could think better of them.

His hand lifted automatically, covering one side of his chest that I now recognized was... lumpy. And as I stared, it moved.

"What the hell is in your pocket?"

"Just this wee one." He unzipped his vest and out popped a tiny, furry head. The kitten he'd rescued.

Do not soften. Do not.

"You have a kitten now."

"Aye. This is Saffron." He stroked her with one knuckle and the wee beastie pressed into the touch.

I didn't want to be interested, but damn if Saoirse wasn't right about big men with tiny animals. "Saffron? Why?"

"Because she's got a spicy wee personality."

I couldn't stop myself from reaching out to run one finger over the silky soft orange fur. "She's very cute. Good luck with that."

Disengage before this gets any worse.

I stepped back, hardening my resolve. "But I meant what I said, Alex. Stay the hell away from me."

The flash of pain across his face before I walked away was far less satisfying than I'd hoped. With a nod to Jason, I slipped behind the bar to get our refills. I could only hope that this would be sufficient fortitude to get me through the rest of the night.

NINE

ALEX

One consequence of impulsively acquiring a pet that I hadn't considered was that I couldn't just leave town on a whim. A week had passed since the launch party at the pub. We'd made good strides on the tear-out at our building, and my business partners had disappeared into nature to do some preliminary scouting for adventure opportunities in the area. Under normal circumstances, I'd have joined them, but I couldn't just leave Saffron. I didn't even leave her at home most workdays because I didn't want her to feel abandoned. She was content to hang out in my pocket, so she went more or less everywhere with me. Callum and Finn teased me mercilessly, especially as I'd ordered a folding kitty play pen to keep her corralled while we did heavier labor. But I'd caught them giving her wee head a scratch when they thought I wasn't looking.

"I'm crawling the walls, wee one. Ewan and Isobel are off to celebrate their engagement before they meet up with the rest of her crew to start recording the next album. Finn and Callum are off camping. It's just you and me here for the weekend. Why don't we go for a walk?"

I swished the feather on a stick that seemed to be Saffron's favorite toy, trying to entice her to come out from where she'd hidden in the corner past the bookcase. Her eyes gleamed, but she didn't move. She'd only just been allowed free roam of the flat a couple of days ago, and I suspected she was still intimidated by the space. I tried jiggling the bag of her favorite treats, certain that would lure her out. But she only meowed as if insulted by the offer.

"I'll go by Village Chippy," I sing-songed. Then I thought better of it. She was still so young. Probably even a wee bit of fried fish would make her sick. Best not risk needing an emergency vet visit with Dr. Saoirse on the weekend.

"Fine. I'm going for a walk. I suppose you'll be all right here on your own for a while. Don't get into any trouble while I'm gone."

I made a bit of a production of putting on my shoes and gathering my keys and wallet. All the things that would signal I was leaving and her chariot in my vest was waiting. When she still didn't come out, I was ridiculously disappointed.

"I'll be back." Before I could talk myself out of leaving on account of the cat, I stepped out and locked my door. Rescuing her was one thing. Becoming a hermit because of her was another.

With the postcard-perfect autumn weather, I expected the high street to be bustling, but I saw only a handful of people out. Perhaps most of the villagers had taken a page out of my partners' books and gotten out for some hill walking. It was a good day for exploring. I might not be able to go far without my little co-pilot, but I could check out more of the village proper. Since I'd gotten here, I'd seen little but work, the pub, my flat, and the market. Admittedly, some of that had been in an effort to avoid Ciara. I hadn't forgotten her order to stay the hell away. Though it went against every instinct I possessed, I was doing my very best to honor that request. But I did live here now, so it was time I expanded my horizons. Maybe I would stop by Village Chippy for a late lunch and find a park bench or somewhere to eat it.

I spotted the man first, clearly invading the personal space of some lass down in front of the market. Even from here, I could read the pressure in his posture and the stiffness in hers. I'd picked up my pace and made it another dozen steps closer before I realized that the woman was Ciara. I hesitated, wondering if I was reading the situation wrong. Maybe this was some new guy in her life. Ignoring the way my gut curdled at that idea, I took another few steps forward, debating whether I ought to cross the street. Then I watched the guy reach out, as if to touch her. Ciara backed up, straight into the side of the car. Trapped.

Whoever this wanker was, his advances were unwelcome. She and I could sort out our issues later. I was already hurrying in their direction when she saw me and called out, "Hey, Professor."

It was a callback to our past. A reminder of another time when she'd been in a similar situation with a guy who wouldn't take no for an answer, and I'd stepped in pretending to be her boyfriend. I could only assume from her use of the nickname that she'd prefer that sort of intervention to my physically hauling the guy off her and beating him to a bloody pulp.

Fine. I wasn't fussy.

Sliding easily into character, I closed the last of the distance. "There you are." As if it were as natural as breathing, I slid an arm around her, pulling her against my side. The stiffness I'd seen from meters away relaxed, and she melted into me in relief. For a moment, all I could register was the perfect way she fit and how something inside me finally unlocked at the contact.

"Who the hell are you?"

Adopting a mild expression, I turned toward the other guy. He stood on the pavement, all puffed up like a rooster, his stance aggressive.

Sliding my hand down, I curved my fingers over the perfection that was Ciara's hip. "The boyfriend."

"You are not."

This twat reeked of entitlement, as if I'd just laid claim to his favorite toy. It made me want to drive my fist into his face. As I didn't think Ciara would appreciate that, I drove in a weapon of a different sort.

"I assure you I am. Isn't that right, Hellcat?" My tone dripped with familiar intimacy. Because she had been a wee hellcat in bed, and those memories had gotten me through countless lonely nights.

Riding on memory, I shifted her around to face me, making no effort to hide how much I still wanted her. If I'd seen alarm or pain or worry, I wouldn't have done it. But what I saw reflected in those big blue eyes was the same wanting that was burning me alive. So I did the most inadvisable thing possible.

I kissed her.

I expected hesitation or some stiffness, though that would have blown this entire farce. Instead, her hands curled into my jacket, and she rose to her toes to press closer. I wrapped my arms around her, angling my head to take the kiss deeper, drinking in the taste of her like a man dying of thirst. The now and the then warred in my brain until the only clear thought left was a resounding *Mine*.

Dimly, I was aware of the other guy stalking away, but I didn't want to stop. Because after all the distance, all the antipathy, this felt good and right and perfect. But eventually, I forced myself to lift my head. Her mouth, that lovely, sassy mouth, was swollen and pink from mine, and her eyes were just a little blurred.

"Is he gone?"

"Aye. He walked away a few minutes ago." Shaking off the lust, I focused on the important thing. "Are you okay?" Clearly, that guy had been hassling her. I wanted to ask a million and one questions about who he was.

But whatever spell we'd temporarily been under had broken. Ciara stepped away, releasing her grip on my coat. "Yes. I've got to get back to work."

With jerky movements, she stepped to her car.

"Ciara."

She didn't even look back, just yanked the door open. At the last second, she deigned to glance over her shoulder. "Thank you for the rescue. This doesn't change anything. I still hate you for what you did."

Without another word, she got into the car and drove away.

I recognized a retreat when I saw one.

It was instinct and training that led me to analyze every situation for vulnerabilities that could be exploited. I understood that the harsh words were meant to put us back into the boxes she'd assigned. But regardless of how it had started, that kiss hadn't been an act. She was still attracted to me, and God knew, I still wanted her with every fiber of my being. Maybe... Maybe there was some opening here.

Because her continued refrain that she hated me was starting to feel like the lady doth protest too much.

TEN

CIARA

I stared at the enormous pile of white fur doing his best impression of a throw rug on the floor of my flat. "I know you've basically forsaken all others since Isobel came into your world, and that you miss her like crazy, but kindly remember that I am your favorite aunt, who brings you all the bacon-flavored dog treats you want."

Havoc, my brother's massive dog who had totally claimed Isobel as his person the moment he met her, gave a half-hearted thump of his tail and looked at me with big, liquid eyes, as if I could somehow make his people change their minds to take him up to the exclusive recording studio in the Hebrides where Isobel was starting the re-record of her next album.

He was staying with me until they returned in a few weeks' time. Honestly, I was surprised they hadn't taken him along. Havoc had even gone on the last leg of her tour and become utterly adored by everyone involved with the show. But I supposed it would have been a challenge to take him to Italy for the two weeks they were spending in Tuscany to celebrate their engagement before heading north. So, I had a furry flatmate for the foreseeable future. I didn't mind. I enjoyed sharing my space with another living creature. I'd considered getting a dog myself, but with the hours I worked during peak season, that hardly seemed fair. Plus, while my flat was plenty of room for me, it wasn't ideal for a long-term canine companion of anything but the purse dog variety.

No, thank you. I wanted a big warm body to curl up in the crook of my legs and drape over my feet.

Right, because that's a reasonable substitute for the adult companionship you're not getting these days.

That made my brain shoot to Alex and how it had felt to have him wrapped around me in sleep.

No. Nope. Not going there right now. Or ever.

"Listen, how about we go for a walk? Get a wee bit of exercise? I know it's not the same as tromping around the forest out back of the house, but there will be stuff to sniff, aye? And maybe we'll stop by the market to pick up some sausages for dinner."

At the "s" word, Havoc's ears perked up. Sausage might be the only thing he loved nearly as much as Isobel.

"There's a good lad. C'mon."

He came to his feet and walked straight into the harness I held for him. I clipped the buckles and snapped on his leash, and we trotted down the stairs and around to the high street.

The weather was gorgeous, and as it was one of my days off, I had hours to spend on anything I wanted. We'd start with the walk and a few errands, then maybe I'd think about taking Havoc out to Lochmara for a hike around the loch. Maybe he could have a playdate with Dugal, Kyla and Raleigh's pup. Tall enough to reach my ribs, Havoc dwarfed him, but what Dugal lacked in size, he made up for with enthusiasm.

Rather than continue on past the pub, I kept going on the cross street, following the pavement toward a residential area.

Of course, that took me straight past Hamish's office and, thus, Alex's flat. I didn't let myself glance up at his windows, but that didn't stop me from thinking of him.

It had been two days since Kissageddon.

Forty-eight hours since he'd turned my world upside down —again—and left me wound tighter than a bowstring. The whole thing had been enough to make me almost forget entirely about Afton's recent pregnancy announcement, which had been the whole reason I'd been going to the market on an event day to begin with. There'd been an unfortunate morning sickness incident that meant a last-minute change to the menu.

I hadn't thought through the ramifications of calling on Alex for help. I'd been so caught up in the surprise of having transitioned from merely awkward with Brodie into truly uncomfortable, edging toward feeling legitimately unsafe, that seeing Alex had been a relief. Regardless of the fact that my heart wasn't safe with him, I'd known he'd step in to rescue me without hesitation, and I'd used the only shorthand I could think of to ask without making a scene.

I should've known better. I should have understood that he'd take that to mean I wanted a repeat performance of exactly what he'd done in Edinburgh, with another man who hadn't taken no for an answer. Playing my boyfriend was not, in and of itself, a problem. But then he'd kissed me.

I'd spent years telling myself that I'd romanticized and inflated the whole thing. But the reality was so much better than I remembered. The moment his mouth touched mine, every ounce of resolve I'd had simply melted away, and I'd all but climbed him like a tree. Heat warmed my cheeks at the memory. The echoes of that kiss had been rattling through me ever since, eroding all the walls I'd thrown up against him.

The truth was, my anger at him was waning. My hurt over what he'd done hadn't dimmed in the least, but maintaining that degree of fury for any length of time was so bloody hard to do. I just... didn't have the energy to stay actively mad. That was part of why I'd wanted to avoid him. Because psyching myself up to get angry all over again simply left me knackered.

And then the damned kiss reminded me of everything I was missing. Everything I wanted and gave up on because I'd convinced myself I'd dreamed that kind of chemistry and connection. With the irrefutable proof of it replaying in high definition in my brain, I didn't think I could delude myself again.

Which left me where, exactly?

"Ciara!"

The female voice jerked me out of my musings to find Flora McGowan stepping out of the chemist's. Holy crap, in all my woolgathering, I'd circled all the way back to the high street.

"Mrs. McGowan, hello. How are you today?"

"Fine and well, and you?" She shifted her bag up to the crook of her arm to free her hands and bent to give Havoc a good scratch behind the ears. He groaned and leaned into her touch.

"I'm well. Just doing a spot of dog sitting for Ewan and Isobel, while they're out of town."

"I heard about their engagement. I'm so pleased for them both. They make such a lovely couple."

I smiled. "They do. They've been good for each other."

"Have they set a date for the wedding yet?"

"Oh, not yet. I'm sure that'll depend on album releases and tour schedules, and whatnot. But no doubt word will get around when they do."

Mrs. McGowan's lively green eyes sparked as she smiled at me. "And perhaps you'll be following along next?"

My fingers flexed on the leash. "Pardon?"

"I heard tell you've been stepping out with one of Ewan's

friends. The black-haired one. Hettie Fraser said you had quite the lip-lock outside the market the other day." The pink in the old woman's cheeks said she was delighted by this news.

I should have known that he couldn't have kissed the bejeezus out of me and not have tongues start wagging. I realized I had to decide whether to correct people's assumption that Alex and I were seeing each other. It was exactly the impression I'd intended, insofar as it came to Brodie. So long as he considered me available, he'd keep coming round. But he hadn't been the only one to see, and these were more of those consequences I hadn't foreseen.

This was going to get back to Ewan. Hell, it was probably going to make it to my parents, if not before, then certainly by the time they returned from their cruise. Bollocks. I didn't want to make explanations to any of them. Either I was forced to admit the truth, that the situation with Brodie had gotten out of hand, which would lead to it getting even more out of hand when the men in my life elected to go take care of the situation themselves. Or I had to consider an alternative that was unarguably crazy and one thousand percent ill advised.

I was damned if I did and damned if I didn't.

Forcing what I hoped appeared to be an easy smile, I shrugged. "Oh, I'm in no hurry to walk down the aisle myself."

There. That was neither confirmation nor denial. I needed to get out of here before she asked more questions.

"If you'll excuse me, I need to be getting on. My best to Mr. McGowan." With a little wave, I left her on the pavement, heading for the far end of the high street.

Maybe by the time I made it to my destination, I'd have talked myself out of the lunacy I was contemplating.

ELEVEN

ALEX

Since the good weather had held, I'd finally gotten my way, and we'd opened up the west wall to prepare for installing the rolling garage door. As I took measurements for the framing, Finn and Callum discussed some of the sites they'd scouted on their weekend trip.

"That cliff face would be perfect for abseiling," Finn insisted.

"It would, but I think we need to stick with easier fare to start. The liability insurance for that sort of excursion is bound to be through the roof." That was Callum, always thinking about the practical and the consequences. It was part of what made him a good leader. "We have to consider the level of expertise—or lack thereof—of the clientele we're likely to attract."

As he went off on a tangent about what he considered more appropriate starter offerings, I let my mind drift. Of course, it ended up back on Ciara. She was never far from my thoughts to start, and after that kiss, she'd taken over. I kept replaying that blissed look on her face before her brain kicked back on. She still wanted me as much as I wanted her. But maybe that was simple biology. Maybe what her body wanted didn't matter if her heart was still bruised. If I'd known I'd had such power, I'd have been more careful with it.

"Hello, lads."

I was hallucinating. I would've sworn I just heard—

"Ciara. What are you doing here?"

At Finn's voice, I turned to see the woman herself standing in the doorway to the lobby, Havoc on a leash beside her.

"Sorry, I let myself in. I wanted to pop by and see what all you'd done to the place." She glanced around, taking in the demolition. "Looks like you've made a lot of progress."

"We're in the 'it's worse before it's better' phase," Finn explained.

Her gaze fell on me where I stood in the gaping maw that would eventually be a door. Could it be *we* were in the 'worse before it's better' phase?

"You seem to have a hole in your wall."

Finn, who'd apparently appointed himself official speaker for the group, moved toward her. "Aye, well, we're going to be installing a rolling door."

He and Callum had been gone all weekend, and it was only Monday. Clearly, neither of them had heard any gossip about my having kissed Ciara. But there'd been other people out on the street that day, so I figured it was only a matter of time. In between creating scenarios for winning her back, I'd been considering damage control and what the bloody hell I was going to say when Ewan, or God forbid, their parents, said something about it.

Was that why she was here? She was faking casual really well, but I recognized nerves in the way her fingers tightened around the leash.

"We'd offer you a tour, but, well, you've already more or

less seen it now." I tried to think of an excuse to speak with her alone. Since we'd been avoiding each other like the plague, nothing came to mind. We weren't supposed to actually know each other.

"Right." She squared her shoulders. "Can I speak to you for a moment?"

Straight to the point, then.

"Sure."

I felt my friends' eyes follow me as I crossed the room. They'd be asking me all the questions when I got back, and I needed to be prepared to deflect.

We walked back through the lobby and out front. The building was set far enough back from the road that we shouldn't be overheard by any foot traffic going by.

The moment we were out of earshot, I asked the question that had been niggling. "Are you okay? Is that guy hassling you again?"

Ciara's shoulders lifted and fell in a huge sigh. "No. But he will be." She finally met my gaze. "We have a problem. Rumors are already circulating about you and me. If I correct people's perceptions, it'll inevitably get back to Brodie, and everything will just start back up again."

I didn't like the sound of any of this. "What do you mean, everything will start back up again? What exactly has been going on?"

She fidgeted, her hand reaching to stroke Havoc's ears. "Brodie is my ex. I broke up with him about four months ago, and he's been having some trouble accepting that. In the beginning, it started with small things. Him sending gifts or messages about how much he missed me. He made it very clear he wanted me back. But it just kept... happening. He showed up everywhere. So I got firmer, making it very clear that we aren't getting back together. But I dinna think it's sinking in. He's not accepting the truth of it, and that's why I made the play I did over the weekend. He's the sort who won't leave it alone unless he knows I'm off the market, as it were. But now I'm stuck in this situation where, if I tell the truth about us, it'll either get back to Brodie and start things up again, or all the men in my life are going to try to take care of this for me, which I dinna want."

She wasn't wrong about that. I'd already thought of a multitude of ways to get the point across that it wasn't ever appropriate to harass a woman. If she said no, it meant no. But clearly that wasn't what Ciara wanted. I forced my fists to relax and pointed out the next most logical option.

"Then don't correct everybody."

Her eyes snapped back to mine. "I dinna want to date you, Alex. I just want to make that clear."

Her hesitation left a massive gap for interpretation.

"But?" I prompted.

"But, if you truly want to help make up to me some of what you did three years ago, then yes, I would appreciate if you would pose as my fake boyfriend for just a little while, so I can get him off my back."

Somewhere, for some reason, the universe was smiling on me. I couldn't have orchestrated this better if I'd tried. I wanted another chance with this woman. What better way to show her how good we could be for each other than acting as her real boyfriend?

"Done."

"Hopefully, this will be resolved before Isobel and Ewan get back, and they'll never know. And if they do find out, then we'll just explain that it's all for show, for purposes of getting rid of Brodie without my brother going to prison for murder."

"Oh, if Ewan murdered anybody, we'd all help him dispose

of the body. No one would ever find it to even bring charges, let alone convict him."

The look of utter horror on her face made me remember that she'd never really thought about what the hell any of us had actually done for the Royal Marines.

"Kidding." I wasn't, but she didn't need to know that.

"Right, well, I know you need to get back to work, and so do I. We'll sort out the details later. I—do you need my phone number?"

"Has it changed?"

"No."

The silence spun out as the implication that I'd had her number all these years and hadn't used it settled over us. She was already looking as if maybe she was going to regret this. But this wasn't just about me. She'd never have asked this if she wasn't legitimately worried about what this guy would do.

I reached out but stopped just short of touching her. "Everything's going to be okay."

"I really hope you're right."

TWELVE

CIARA

"I've got what should be the final guest list for the Dowling-Gilbert wedding in December," Kyla announced. "We'll need to coordinate with Charlotte to make absolutely certain we can accommodate everyone in the cottages."

"I'll do that." I made a note on my tablet. Charlotte Vasquez was Raleigh's second mum, who'd followed him to Scotland from Texas when he'd come to claim Lochmara. She'd ended up falling for the grumptastic estate manager, Malcolm Niall, and stayed. Now she managed the array of guest cottages that were a significant source of income for both Lochmara and Ardinmuir. I adored her, as did we all. If I played my cards right, maybe I could wrangle that meeting over a pitcher of her famous margaritas.

"Great. That leaves us with the preliminary menus. Where are we on that, Afton?"

"Working with the original list of food sensitivities and preferences, I've put together a half-dozen options at three different price points, all of which feature locally sourced, seasonal produce."

As she went deeper into those menu options, I struggled to maintain my focus. I was exhausted, having spent the day braced for questions from my coworkers about Alex—either the kiss or the rumors about us dating. I didn't know what I was going to tell them. The truth still carried with it the same problem it always had in terms of they or their men wanting to go handle Brodie. But I also didn't know how they'd respond to the idea of me dating Alex. I mean, I had my suspicions about how my brother would react, but I wasn't sure about the rest of them.

I had to figure out something. For this ruse to work, I was going to have to be seen in public with him. God, that was going to be hard. Not because it was a burden to spend time with him—because I still liked him, damn it. Even the handful of exchanges we'd had—the ones where I hadn't been jumping down his throat—had been a reminder of how and why I'd been so drawn to him from the moment we'd met. The hard part would be remembering why we were doing this and not giving in to the undeniable attraction I still felt for him.

"Ciara, are you okay?"

At the concern in Sophie's voice, I dragged my attention back to the meeting to find everyone staring at me. "What?"

"You just seem really distracted."

"I'm sorry. I'm just tired. Need a bit more time to recharge. Havoc is a total bed hog."

From where he lay on the rug across the room, the dog cracked one eye and looked at me with accusation. How dare I throw him under the bus?

"Maybe come in an hour or two later tomorrow," Kyla suggested. "We've got the time. Get some extra sleep."

"Thanks for that."

As the meeting wrapped up, a quiet knock sounded on the door. "Oh good. I caught you all before you finished." The tall, slim man with a shock of white hair and impish blue eyes who stepped into the room had us all smiling. Great uncle to Kyla and Connor, Angus MacKean, was another of my favorite people. He lived here at Ardinmuir with his husband, Munro, in a different section of the castle from Sophie and Connor. "I made a huge batch of stew and fresh baked rosemary bread if any of you want to stay."

Afton began to pack up her notes. "That sounds incredible, but Hamish and Freya are waiting for me at the pub."

"I'm in for sure. I'll text Raleigh." Kyla pulled out her phone to send the invite.

Angus's attention turned to me. "Ciara?"

Of the entire household, Angus was the one most likely to have heard something. Even his cooking wasn't enough to sway me into a potential interrogation under the guise of family dinner.

"I appreciate the offer, but I think I'm going to head on home. Himself over here will want dinner, and I'm hoping to go to bed early."

"Fair enough. But take some of these fresh Jaffa cakes home with you." He produced a care package of one of my favorite treats from I had no idea where. Really, having a former semi-finalist from *The Great British Bake Off* in my world was tough to beat.

I pressed a smacking kiss to his wrinkled cheek. "You are a god among men. Thank you, Angus."

I gathered up my care package and the dog and headed home. I had no idea what I had in my flat for dinner. If I ended up just having Jaffa cakes, well, I was an adult. That was my prerogative, and there was no one around to judge but the dog. He could be bribed.

"Let's get some food, and then we'll go for a walk, aye?" It wouldn't be a long one, but he'd been such a good boy, hanging out with me at work all day. He needed to stretch his legs.

I pushed open the door to my flat and switched on the light.

The white rectangle on the floor had me immediately on alert.

Not again.

I let Havoc off-leash. If anyone were actually here, he'd be losing his mind. It was fine.

But I picked up the envelope as if it contained a bomb. I recognized my name scrawled in Brodie's familiar hand on the front. This wasn't the first letter he'd left, begging me to take him back. But after our encounter over the weekend, what had felt pitiable before now held a creepy overtone. Sliding the single page out, I skimmed the contents. More of the same he'd been spouting for months. He loved me. He missed me. Please reconsider.

Annoyed, I balled the letter up and took it to the bin just as a knock sounded on my door. Startled, the paper fell from my hand onto the floor.

Christ, had he been waiting to see when I got home to try to talk to me about all this again? That wasn't happening, but neither would I hide in my own place.

"Havoc."

At the sharp tone, he immediately crossed to my side. At this point, I absolutely wasn't above using the dog as a scare tactic.

Braced for confrontation, I opened the door a crack, leaving the security chain on. When I spotted Alex at the top of the stairs, I almost wilted in relief.

"Hold on."

I shut the door and unlatched the chain before opening it wide.

He took one look at my face and his own hardened.

"What's wrong?" There was an unmistakable air of protectiveness in his tone that I liked far too much.

"Nothing."

"It doesn't look like nothing. You look uncomfortable in your own space. Do I need to have a look around?"

He'd do it. I knew if I said the word, he'd sweep my entire place looking for threats. Why did that feel so comforting?

"No, that's not necessary. I have a four-legged guard at the moment, but come on in. We should probably discuss the specifics around us."

"I thought so, too. I brought dinner, in case you haven't eaten yet." He lifted a bag from Village Chippy.

Surprised by his thoughtfulness, I stepped back to let him in. "Not gonna lie. You're saving me from eating nothing but dessert."

"I'll share mine, if you'll share yours."

I had to fight not to smile. "Deal."

While I grabbed plates and silverware, he pulled out portions of crispy golden fish and chips. The smell instantly had me salivating.

"Beer?"

He took a seat, looking far too large at my little round dining table. "Sure."

I popped the tops and came back to the table.

Alex took his bottle and leaned back in his chair. "Okay, this is your show. You set the parameters."

I appreciated his ceding control. I had a feeling that wasn't his default state. Whether by training or inclination, I couldn't say.

"Right. So, obviously, if this is to work, we have to go out, be seen. But it's public-facing only. I'm fine with you touching me." My brain instantly flashed to a memory of his hands exploring my most intimate places, and my face flamed. "Um, necessary PDA only."

My inner hussy wailed in protest because all I'd been able to think about since he'd kissed me was kissing him again. I desperately needed to put some walls back up between us or he'd manage to undo all of my anger and frustration, and I'd turn back into that naïve, hopeful young thing again, dreaming dreams that couldn't be a reality.

"Understood. I want you to be comfortable, so I'll do this however you want."

"Thank you. I appreciate that. And I appreciate you doing this at all. I haven't exactly been nice to you since you moved to Glenlaig."

His big shoulders twitched. "You had good reasons. I handled everything like the world's biggest bawbag. I'm happy to do whatever I can to get you out of a shite situation."

I didn't quite know what to do with that, so I forked up a bite of fish.

Alex did the same, chewing thoughtfully. "It's good, but not as good as Maury's."

I stared at him. "I can't believe you remember him." Maury was the Moroccan man who ran my neighborhood chippy back in Edinburgh. I'd taken Alex there as part of the tour of my city.

His deep brown eyes stayed level on mine. "I remember every moment of our time together."

There it was again. That weighted pull I remembered from the very first moment we'd met. As if some gravitational force existed just between us. But alongside it was the burden of all the things he wouldn't tell me. That was the reason all those dreams were impossible. Because until I had the truth, how could I decide whether he truly deserved forgiveness?

At the thought, the walls around my heart slammed back into place. That was how this had to be.

THIRTEEN

ALEX

"Here we are. One cottage pie and one order of stovies with oatcakes." Laura Craig, the manager and part owner of the pub, who ran everything like clockwork in Ewan's absence, handed over a takeaway bag. "Are you one short on workers today?"

"Pardon?"

"Only food for two."

"Ah. No. This isn't for Finn or Callum. I'm taking lunch out to Ciara at the castle."

Laura's eyes sharpened with interest. "Are you, now?"

I didn't rise to the bait, just left that little detail hanging between us as I lifted the bag in salute. "Cheers."

Picking up lunch had been a calculated move. She wanted a public-facing relationship to back up the fiction we were presenting, so the best way to accomplish that was to be seen as the dutiful boyfriend. If word got back to Ewan—and I was banking on him and Isobel being left in peace at the exclusive studio in the Outer Hebrides—he'd either think Laura was mistaken, or he'd call me directly to ask what was going on. If he did, I'd be honest that this was merely a favor to scare off her ex.

If it turned into something else... Well, I'd cross that bridge if I came to it. I wouldn't make assumptions where Ciara was concerned.

I followed my GPS out to Ardinmuir Castle. Fifteen or twenty minutes out from the village, it rose out of the trees like the fortress it had once been. I knew from conversations with Ewan that Kyla and Connor had been working for years to restore the place. To my eye, they'd come a long way. I didn't know what condition the castle had been in before, but now it looked like what it was... a blend of centuries that represented some of the best of Scotland. No wonder they'd had such success turning it into an event venue.

I had no idea where in the castle Ciara worked, so I parked on the gravel drive in front of the stairs that led to the massive front doors. Surely someone would answer my knock. Grabbing the food, I trotted up the steps. The heavy iron knocker vibrated the door like a battering ram. The wind kicked up as I waited, and I hunched deeper into my tweed walking jacket. I didn't know how far the sound would carry. I was still searching around the doorframe for a bell when the massive door swung open.

"Can I help you?" The man was older, with dark silver hair and an olive complexion. His dark eyes were curious as they took me in.

"Ah, I'm looking for Ciara." I held up the bag. "I brought her food."

Too late, I realized that probably made it sound like I was a delivery boy. But rather than offer to pay me and taking the food, the man opened the door wider.

"I'll take you to her."

"Cheers."

I followed my impromptu guide through labyrinthine halls, trying to look everywhere at once. I wondered if I could talk Ciara into a proper tour of the place. She was cousin to the MacKeans, but on their mother's side, so this wasn't part of her heritage. Still, she'd have an in with the people who could give me a tour. I was immensely curious about the history of the place.

We exited the castle proper and went into a newer part of the structure. Though new was relative. Maybe a couple hundred years versus six hundred. At last, we stopped in front of a paneled door, and my guide knocked once before opening it.

"Ciara, you've a visitor."

"Thanks, Munro. Who is—" Ciara trailed off as I stepped into the room, her eyes going wide. "Alex?"

She stood beside a massive whiteboard covered in a diagram as complex as some of the missions I'd planned. Kyla, Sophie, and Afton sat scattered around the room, surrounded by what appeared to be an explosion of office supplies. They stared at me with undisguised interest. Havoc rose from where he'd been curled up on a dog bed and crossed to sniff at the food.

Suddenly ill at ease with my improvised plan, I lifted the bag in explanation. "I knew you were going to be slammed today, so I brought you lunch." I'd known no such thing, but I'd surmised that she worked hard and long, so I'd taken a shot in the dark.

"Oh, I... Thanks." She seemed flustered by my being here. Maybe work hadn't been included in that public-facing part of the plan. "I'm sorry. I don't really have time to stop and eat with you just now."

Kyla set her tablet aside. "We can take a break." Beneath her casual, breezy tone was a heavy implication that as soon as that break was over, Ciara was expected to tell them absolutely everything about what was going on here.

"A short one," Ciara conceded. "Give me just a minute."

I gave Havoc a scratch behind the ears. "Take your time."

As she finished up whatever she was doing, my attention went back to the board. It was some kind of big flow chart of the logistics of an event.

Ciara capped her marker and set it aside. "C'mon."

"Ladies." I nodded to the others and followed her out of the room, trailed by the dog.

We wound through even more hallways until she led me into a room and shut the door behind us. It was a library. Lots of dark wood and leather and endless shelves of books. Before I could give in to temptation and start perusing titles, Ciara turned. "What are you doing here?"

Taking in the tense expression on her face, I rocked back on my heels. "Overstepping, apparently." I explained my logic. "But I can see now I should have cleared it with you first. I'm sorry."

Her shoulders relaxed fractionally. "No, it's... fine. I just wasn't expecting to see you here. It's an adjustment. All of this is an adjustment." Circling around the massive desk I didn't need anyone to tell me was an antique, she dropped into the chair. Havoc lay down beside her. "Didn't you have to work today?"

I shook off the mental image of spreading her out on that desk in nothing at all. "I did. Do. But they can get on well enough without me for an hour or so."

"So, what did you bring me?"

I stepped up to the desk. "Stovies with oatcakes or cottage pie."

"I will never ever say no to Dom's cottage pie. Hand it over."

As she settled back with her lunch and a disposable fork, I took a seat. "I see you did it."

"Did what?"

"You found a way to make a lateral move with your training in large-scale festival planning into something more to your taste." That had been my advice to her three years ago. She, too, had been in transition, not happy in the field in which she'd earned her degree.

"Ah. Well, I suppose I have."

"It's impressive. And the fact that you've done it by twenty-five speaks to your drive and determination."

"Thank you." She chewed thoughtfully, her brows knit as if she were trying to make up her mind to say something. "Is there anything you can tell me about where you've been the past few years?"

"Home. Largely working in my brother's construction firm in Dumbarton."

"Construction? Somehow, that's not what I imagined you doing." Her cheeks colored.

Because she'd imagined me? Or because she thought she'd said something rude?

"Not that there's anything at all wrong with construction. It's a vital trade and perfectly honest work."

"No offense taken. It wasn't what I expected to be doing either." But after everything had gone sideways, it was the only thing that felt safe. "I needed to be close to home. We lost our dad, and Mum took it hard."

Every drop of antipathy bled out of Ciara's expression. "Oh, Alex. I'm so sorry. What happened?"

I stabbed at my food. "Car accident." That had been the official report, anyway. I'd had my suspicions, but I hadn't been able to prove anything nefarious. Seeming to sense my mood,

Havoc came around the desk and put his head on my knee, wagging his thick tail.

Clearly understanding I didn't want to continue along this path, she changed the subject. "Are you and your brother close?"

Grateful for the diversion, I stroked the dog's ears. "Aye. He and his husband were lifesavers. They just adopted a little girl last year. Niamh's five."

A smile flickered at the edge of Ciara's lips. "And does she have her Uncle Alex wrapped around her little finger?"

I smirked. "Know something about that, do you?"

"Are you saying I'm spoiled?"

"I'm saying you're clearly the apple of your parents' eye and your brother adores you. It was obvious in every picture scattered all over their house."

She hesitated again. "He was who you were coming to meet in Inverness, wasn't he?"

"Aye. It was... a shock when I got to your parents' house and saw photos of you everywhere." I'd half expected the ground to open up and swallow me whole because I'd shagged my best mate's little sister.

"I expect it was." Her tone had gone neutral again. But she didn't pursue the topic.

We lapsed into a silence that wasn't quite comfortable but wasn't entirely contentious either. Havoc stayed beside me, staring hard until I gave in and tossed him one of the oatcakes. He snapped it out of the air, chomping it down in three bites. Once lunch was finished, Ciara gathered up the rubbish and led me out of the castle, through the kitchen.

"I parked round front."

"I'll walk you to your car."

I supposed it was progress that she didn't just boot me out

and send me on my way. Or maybe she was just keeping up appearances.

We passed her little blue Peugeot on the way. I paused at the side, angling my head for a better look.

"Did you always have this scratch?"

"What scratch?" She came around to see what I was looking at. "Bloody hell. Brodie. It had to be Brodie. Some kind of backlash from Saturday. Not that I'll be able to prove it."

"Aren't there security cameras?"

She just looked at me, as if wondering what sort of world I came from. "No. There are no security cameras. It's not a big deal. He's just throwing a tantrum because I've moved on."

I didn't like it. I didn't like it at all. "Was he in the habit of throwing tantrums when you were together?"

"No. Never."

That was something. But still. "What is Brodie's full name?"

Ciara immediately shut down, crossing her arms. "I don't want you doing anything. You're just meant to be a shield."

"I promise I'm not going to go rough him up or anything. I just want to know who I should be listening to references for." And I wanted to know who to dig deeper into. But she didn't need to know that.

After a long hesitation, she finally admitted, "His name is Brodie Drummond. He's from Braemore." She was putting on a tough face, but I could tell that this prolonged lack of resolution was wearing on her.

I took a chance then and gripped her shoulders, pulling her in for a hug. "It's going to be okay."

With a soul-deep sigh, she relaxed into me, not exactly returning the hug, but more just... leaning. I could handle that.

She was the one who stepped back, shaking her head as if

she had to remind herself how she was supposed to feel about me. That she was still angry. I filed that away to mull over later.

"I know you need to get back to work. So do I."

She walked with me around to the front, where I'd left my truck, but she didn't touch me again. "Thanks for lunch."

"Anytime. See you later, Ciara."

Another sigh I didn't know how to read. "See you later, Alex."

FOURTEEN

CIARA

Alex had brought me lunch. All the way out here. That hadn't been part of what we'd discussed last night. I'd been so concerned with making it clear what I didn't want him to do, I guess I hadn't spent much time or effort on what I did. I'd expected a handful of public dates. Some PDA. I guess I hadn't thought beyond that.

He had.

Somehow, it didn't surprise me that he was thorough. It went along with that sense of incredible capability he projected. Royal Marines took care of business. If he was tackling this project with the same level of preparation, I'd be in excellent hands.

I had a flash of those broad palms and rough fingers in the dark.

Stop thinking about his hands!

Today hadn't been about seduction. It had been establishing cover. Clever. Necessary. And maybe it had, to some extent, been about establishing a detente with me. He'd been nothing but respectful and courteous since he'd come back into my life. He'd been nothing but respectful and courteous when we'd met. It was only those lost years. That lack of contact and a why for it all.

He'd lost his father. I thought of what Isobel had said. She probably knew about his loss. Maybe that had been what she meant when she'd said he'd been through a lot.

I knew nothing of his relationship with his family. We hadn't really spoken of those details when we met before. I knew how close I was to my own parents. Losing my da would devastate me. But I didn't think that was why Alex hadn't contacted me. There was no good reason not to tell me about the loss, even if only to say he needed to be home and our one night was one night. Either way, my heart broke for him.

I didn't like this softening I felt toward him. It was dangerous. Softening led to excruciating things like hope. Better to shore up my defenses and get back to work.

I'd meant what I told Alex on his arrival. I really *didn't* have the time to eat with him today. We were up to our eyeballs in planning because one of our upcoming brides had expanded the guestlist by twenty-five percent, and we were trying to figure out how we were going to accommodate all the extra people in only a few short weeks' time. Even so, I dragged my feet going back to work because I knew there'd be questions. On some level, I'd been preparing for that. The whole point of this plan was for people to know that Alex and I were "dating." But bracing for the theoretical was a whole lot different from knowing I was about to walk into an inquisition.

Everybody looked up when I stepped into the room.

"Sorry. Himself needed a walk."

Havoc looked at me, and I'd swear he cocked a canine eyebrow. I ignored him. What good was having a dog around if I couldn't use him as an excuse?

I could tell Angus had been by. There was a tray of sandwiches and biscuits, which would've been what I ate had Alex not shown up. Sophie was nibbling on a cookie and already eying more. Her sweet tooth had been on overdrive since she hit her second trimester. Kyla had half a sandwich in one hand, as she took notes on her tablet with the other. And poor Afton was pale as milk, a partly empty sleeve of crackers on her plate. Morning sickness was kicking her arse.

"Where were we?" I moved back to the board to pick up exactly where I'd left off.

"Hold it."

Damn it. Kyla's mom tone had really come in since Lily had turned two.

"What?"

"Dinna act all innocent. When exactly did *that* happen?" She waved the hand with the sandwich in the vague direction of the door, clearly encompassing everything that was Alex.

"And perhaps more to the point, does your brother know?" Sophie asked.

To buy myself some time, I moved over to the tea station we kept in this room and turned the electric kettle on. "First off, nothing has happened."

Partly true. Nothing had happened in three years. Well, except for Kissageddon, which I wasn't going to count right at this moment.

"A man driving all the way from the village to bring you lunch because he knows you'll be busy is not nothing," Afton declared. "That's either boyfriend behavior or he's courting you, either of which is very exciting."

I spread an even look among them before turning back to pluck a tea bag from our stash. "Are your married lives so dull you have to worry about me?"

Sophie grabbed another biscuit. "Not dull. But if we want to see you as happy as we are, you can't blame us for asking."

I definitely couldn't. And because of that, I decided to give them as much truth as I could. When the kettle beeped, I poured boiling water over the tea bag, watching the steam rise. Setting a timer on my smartwatch, I picked up the mug and simply held it. The warmth between my palms grounded me for what I was about to admit.

"I've been having some problems with Brodie, and Alex stepped in to help by pretending to be my boyfriend." I left out the bit where I'd invoked that precise reaction, because the last thing I wanted was to admit to our past. I didn't bring up the kiss either. If they hadn't already heard about it, I wasn't going to bring it up. "It worked in the moment, so he's agreed to fake date me for a bit until Brodie gets the hint and goes away."

Several beats of silence spun out. Clearly, that hadn't been at all what they'd expected.

Kyla dropped her sandwich back onto the plate, dislodging a crisp that Havoc stealthily snatched from the floor. "Why didn't you say you were having problems with your ex?"

"How long has this been going on?" Sophie demanded.

"If he's been bothering you, that's well outside the bounds of what's okay. We can do something about it," Afton insisted.

"That's exactly why I haven't said anything. I didn't want you or Ewan or Connor or Raleigh going off half-cocked, trying to intimidate him or whatever. This is just simpler."

The three of them exchanged a series of raised-brow looks that clearly questioned my logic.

"Okay, but why are you fake dating him as opposed to actually dating him?" Sophie asked. "Or is he simply that good an actor? Because that definitely didn't look like he was faking interest."

My brain chose that moment to helpfully play a highlight reel of every kiss, every touch that proved Alex wasn't acting at all. No matter what had happened since Edinburgh, I believed he was sincerely still attracted to me. That was exactly why this would be believable. Thankfully, my timer went off, and I turned to remove the tea bag. "This from the woman who was fake engaged to Connor for how long?"

"Aye, it was ridiculous. But here we are, married and happy, with a baby on the way. The question stands."

I didn't have a good answer for it without admitting to things I didn't want to talk about. I added a spoonful of sugar to my tea. "For one, I have no idea how my brother would react." Truth. "For another, I'm not looking for anything with anybody right now. The whole situation with Brodie has rather soured me on relationships at the moment. I'd like some time just on my own where I don't have to worry about someone else."

I turned around in time to catch them having more silent conversations with their eyes. They all definitely had more to say but were holding back. Before they elected someone to tell me I was making a huge mistake, I leaned back against the tea station. "Look, I know this is an imposition, but I would appreciate it if you'd keep the secret that this relationship is fake until such a time as it is reasonable to reveal otherwise to the immediate family. I'm trying to minimize the drama around all of this."

After a long, humming silence, Kyla sighed. "Okay. If that's how you want to handle it."

Afton carefully nibbled another cracker. "We just want what's best for you."

"Just... be careful," Sophie warned. "It gets very hard keeping things fake in situations like this." The warning hit that much harder because she would absolutely know.

"I appreciate your concern. Truly. But I know what I'm doing."

At least, I hoped I did.

"Now, can we get back to work?"

FIFTEEN

ALEX

At the end of the day, I sat down at my desk in front of the trio of monitors my brother affectionately referred to as The Cockpit. This setup was one of the few things I'd brought with me from home. I could do most of what I needed with less, but after years of being responsible for gathering digital intelligence, I preferred having all my tools at my disposal. It had been a while since I'd flexed these intellectual muscles. The last time had been on Isobel's behalf, digging into her manager to get some of the information needed to free her from a shit situation. I considered this thing with Ciara's ex to be in the same category.

Finished with her dinner, Saffron pawed at my leg. With one hand, I scooped her up and set her in my lap. She'd already begun to put on weight, and her fur was soft and healthy. Amazing what a couple weeks of consistent food and good care would accomplish. Her little body arched into my touch as I stroked along her back while my multitude of programs booted up.

I'd start on the surface, scraping the data publicly available

about this twat. People were always revealing more about themselves than they realized on social media. Even deleting posts
and emails wasn't enough. The internet was forever—especially
for someone with my skill set.

I opened a browser, and Saffron climbed onto the desk. She
angled her little head at the screen, then looked at me as if to
ask what the hell I thought I was doing.

"Look, I promised Ciara I wouldn't rough the bawbag up,
and that I only wanted to know who I should be listening for
references to. She doesn't need to know that I can 'listen' in a
multitude of places the average person has no access to."

The kitten slowly blinked at me in a tone that felt unmis-
takably judgmental. Or maybe that was my own conscience
poking at me.

"Don't look at me like that. I'm doing this to protect her.
She makes out like what this guy is doing is no big deal, but I
can tell it bothers her more than she's letting on, or we wouldn't
be in this fake relationship to begin with."

The kitten's tail swished, and she leapt. Startled, I jerked
my head back, but she landed on my chest. Her claws made
little pinpricks as she climbed up to perch on my shoulder like a
wee gargoyle.

"Am I to take that as you're okay with what I'm doing?"

She rubbed her head against mine.

Taking that as her blessing, I opened a browser.

Ciara wanted to see the best in people, myself excluded. If
she was with this guy for a while, she might not want to believe
he was anything but a good person. But there was a significant
line between "I miss you and want you back," and the kind of
harassment he'd been pulling for this amount of time. She
hadn't spelled it out, but I had a feeling that there was more she
hadn't told me. I hadn't pressed because I didn't think she'd
open up more if I did. So I'd do my own research.

A quick Google search for 'Brodie Drummond Braemore' told me he was an independent agent for an insurance company. It might be the sort of job with a set schedule, or it might give him some flexibility in the middle of the day. I wasn't sure. Filing that away, I headed over to social media. His posts were full of photos of him and Ciara. All old. There was nothing more recent than five months ago, which lined up with the breakup.

Out of curiosity, I toggled over to look at Ciara's profiles. She had a better sense of security, as most of her profiles were private, but nothing from her public feeds showed Brodie at all, even before the breakup. I wondered if she'd always done that or if she'd scrubbed him from her social media. I could've hacked in to find out, but I wouldn't invade her privacy like that. Instead, I switched back to Brodie and worked my way backward, trying to get some idea of how long they'd been together.

The earliest posts went back about a year before the breakup. In the beginning, she'd looked happy. I wanted to tell myself she didn't look as happy as she had the last day I'd seen her in Edinburgh, when we'd both been looking toward the future and seeing each other again, but maybe I was lying to myself about that because part of me saw this guy as a rival. Still, over the course of the year, I could see the smile start to become more forced, the body language less close. She'd known for months before she'd broken things off that it wasn't a good fit.

I worked my way backward, digging into Brodie's browser history. The man spent an inordinate amount of time visiting Ciara's social media pages. Multiple times a day. Lots of time on old photos of the two of them. Even visits to the Ardinmuir Event Planning website. I didn't like the additional signs of unhealthy fixation. There were also visits to dating apps.

Was he looking for someone else? That would be a positive step.

But when I dug deeper into those, I found multiple profiles with fake names and details that were clearly designed to match with Ciara. None of the profiles had photos, but I was able to match them all as coming from the same IP address.

What did Brodie think would happen if one of the fake profiles did match with her? That she'd suddenly see the error of her ways and change her mind? Not bloody likely. As I knew from first-hand experience, she wasn't a woman who tolerated lying. Not that I'd lied overtly, but lying by omission was still a thing.

I was just about to hack my way into Brodie's email when someone knocked on the door of my flat. Toggling the screen to go dark, I set Saffron down and went to answer the door.

Callum and Finn were on the other side.

"What's up?"

"We need to talk," Callum announced.

Everything in me tensed. "What's this about? Is something wrong with the business?" We'd poured so much into this already. If we were running into financial difficulties—

Finn strode inside. "Oh no, this isn't about the business. This is about you and Ewan's baby sister."

Well, shite.

Callum shouldered his way past me, too. "When were you planning on telling us you were dating?"

I'd known I'd have to tell them something, but I'd hoped to have more time. "Where did you hear that?"

"Down the pub. Someone mentioned they saw you snogging her right there on the high street." Callum said this as if I clearly ought to have used better sense.

It seemed my plan for getting the gossip mill going had backfired on me. Making a judgment call in the moment, I shut the door. "It's fake. Ciara's ex isn't taking no for an answer, so we're faking a relationship to get him off her back."

Both of them sobered immediately.

"Is it that bad?" Finn demanded.

"Do we need to take care of things?"

I well knew what Callum's version of taking care of things would entail.

"No. She's been very, very clear she doesn't want that."

Finn's gaze tracked behind me. "Is that why you're doing a deep dive on him?"

I turned to find Saffron walking across the keyboard. The screen had lit back up, showing all the windows of my search. Swearing, I scooped the wee monster back up and cuddled her against my chest, where she couldn't do any more damage.

"I have a bad feeling about the situation. I think it's probably worse than she's letting on and that it has the potential to get worse. A couple of days after he found out we were dating, her car was keyed. The timing feels very reactive."

"How long until he jumps from going after her possessions to going after her?" Finn mused.

"He was already invading her personal space and trapping her against her car the day I came up on them and intervened."

"Is that why she asked you? Because you were there?" Callum arched an expectant brow.

"Probably." No reason to share the details of our previous connection. "I stepped in, pretending to be her boyfriend. This keeps the story consistent when it gets back to him."

"Makes sense," Finn agreed. "What does Ewan think of all this? Have you talked to him?"

I worked to school my features, because what Ewan would think was something I'd been concerned about for years. "No."

"This is his sister, mate. Do you think it's wise to keep it from him?"

"I'm following Ciara's lead on this. She doesn't want him to know. I'm hoping when he does find out—because I'm under no delusion that he won't—that he'll understand that I'm looking out for her."

My friends exchanged a look that clearly questioned my general intelligence, but they didn't call me on it.

"Look, can I count on the two of you for your help in this? As extra pairs of eyes?"

"Of course. He's our brother. That makes her family, too." For Callum, it would always be that simple.

Relieved to have my team on board so far as they could be, I relaxed. "Thanks. Do you lot want a beer? We could do some more brainstorming about potential business names."

"Och, that sounds perfect," Finn announced. "I was thinking Tartan Trekking Company."

I went to the fridge. "Did you come up with that with or without alcohol?"

Finn dropped onto the sofa. "Fuck off, Echo."

Grinning, I grabbed three beers and settled in for some friendly ball busting with my best mates.

SIXTEEN

CIARA

My phone vibrated in my pocket, derailing my train of thought yet again. From his spot on the floor, Havoc blew out a breath that echoed my own annoyance. Not checking it wasn't a choice, since this number was the same one I gave to vendors and clients. But when I pulled it out and checked the caller ID, I saw it was Brodie. This was the ninth time he'd called today. I hadn't answered any time. Just kept sending the calls to voice-mail, where he didn't leave a message. I did the same this time and laid the phone on my desk, dropping my head into my hands to rub at the ache blooming in my temples.

I didn't have time for any more of his bullshit.

I'd thought that seeing me move on with someone else would be enough to get the point across that we were truly over. So far, it had resulted in minor vandalism to my car and a renewed vigor around winning me back. I was terrified I'd have to actually let Alex or Ewan or the rest of the men in my life—blood-related and otherwise—scare some sense into him. I didn't want to resort to that, but if he kept this up, I might not be left with any other choice.

Blowing out a breath, I focused again on the seating chart I was trying to make work. Two sets of divorced parents who'd all remarried were a serious challenge to organize in a way where none of them felt slighted. Why they all couldn't get along for the sake of their children's big day, I had no idea. If my family had that kind of contention, I'd straight-up elope. The fact that my parents still adored each other more than thirty years on was a real blessing.

My phone vibrated again, this time with a text. Growling, I snatched it up. Really, I should just block him on every front.

But it wasn't Brodie this time. It was the group text with my girlfriends.

> Skye: :GIF of Ricky from I Love Lucy saying "Lucy, you got some 'splainin' to do.":

> Saoirse: You tried to pawn him off on me when you were interested yourself! What gives?

> Pippa: Spill all the details. I'm living vicariously through you.

Well, obviously they'd heard about me and Alex.

> Skye: Seriously. I heard he laid a big one on you right there on High Street!

I'd seriously underestimated how many times I'd have to tell this story. Opening the messaging app, I tapped a reply.

> Me: He came to my rescue with Brodie, and one thing led to another.

Which was true. I was trying to stick to the truth as much as possible.

> Pippa: :GIF of black and white movie heroine swooning:

> Skye: :GIF of excited My Little Pony vibrating with a squee:

> Saoirse: :GIF of Santana from Glee fanning herself:

> Saoirse: Seriously, is he as good a kisser as I imagine?

> Me: ... Yes?

No sense in lying about that.

There followed another explosion of GIF reactions. Seriously, what did we do before GIFs were a thing?

> Skye: I demand a group hangout! We want to get to know him.

> Saoirse: We want to inspect him.

And there it was. I'd known this would come up, eventually. I'd been bracing for it. Alex and I still hadn't gone out together in public yet. But I'd known we'd have to. Maybe I'd been holding off on that because public meant PDA, and I was seriously on the struggle bus fighting my very real attraction to my fake boyfriend. I thought of the warning Sophie had given about how hard it was to keep things fake under these circumstances. She wasn't wrong. But it had to be done. Alex getting the stamp of approval from my friends would be a necessary phase if we were actually dating.

> Me: I'll see what I can do.

Before I could lose my nerve, I toggled over to his contact and typed out a message.

> Me: Are you free over the weekend?

His answer came back almost immediately.

> Alex: For you, always. What do you have in mind?

Seeing his ready agreement felt weird. Was this still cover, in case someone saw our texts? Or did he mean it? Before I could go down that rabbit hole again, I replied.

> Me: My friends want to get together.

> Alex: They want to check me out, huh?

> Me: Basically.

> Alex: I'm in. Give me the details of where and when.

> Me: I'll let you know when we figure it out.

It felt weirdly coupley to be making these arrangements. Which was the point.

I went back to the group text.

> Me: He's in.

The storm of excited GIFs left me smiling for the first time all day.

> Me: Okay, okay. Slow your roll. What are we going to do?

> Saoirse: I have some ideas.

SEVENTEEN

ALEX

When I agreed to this group date thing, I'd been expecting a
night out at the pub or something else equally low-key. The
whole point was for them to get to know me and decide
whether I was good enough for Ciara, right? I knew better than
to say yes to a mission with insufficient intel, and I was having
deep regrets about not asking more questions.

It wasn't that The Tartan Terrors were bad—though punk
rock wouldn't have been my choice. It was that I was trapped
amid throngs of writhing bodies at an outdoor venue near
Inverness with no clear route of egress and no means of
performing an accurate threat assessment. I wasn't as bad as I'd
been when I first separated from the Royal Marines, but the
uncontrolled crowd was loud and rowdy, and my entire system
was on hyper alert. Despite the cool evening air, sweat beaded
along my back. It was taking every bit of my control to keep
from gluing Ciara to my side and spiriting her away. I hadn't
taken my hand off her since we got here.

For her part, she'd stayed close, hooking a finger in my belt
loop, keeping her arm wrapped around me. It didn't escape me

that she was grounding me now, much as she had that day on the train from London.

Did she know I needed it? Or was this simply performative, to keep up the ruse that we were together?

I was glad we'd at least stopped off for an early dinner at a pub on the drive up, so there'd been an opportunity for conversation. I liked Ciara's friends. They were a disparate group who'd come together intending to start a book club, but they'd been mostly too busy to do the reading and had decided they didn't need the excuse of books to start hanging out. From what I gathered, Skye had moved to Glenlaig to be with Jason McKinnon, who'd been her years-long penpal. He was The Tartan Terrors fan, and I'd heard tell that he was front man himself for The Kilt Lifters, a band that performed bagpipe covers of boy band songs. I couldn't imagine, but the women had assured me they were very popular locally. As a whole, I'd gotten the general impression that they approved of me, which had been the whole point of this excursion. Of course, I'd been on my best behavior, and I was positive Ciara hadn't told them about our past. If she had, they'd have set a much higher bar. Or possibly hit me with it.

On stage, the band reached a fever pitch that had the crowd chanting en masse. As the decibel level rose, I tensed, thinking how easy it would be to use this racket to cover up an attack. Not that there was any reason whatsoever to expect an attack, but this was the legacy of my training. I always expected danger. I wished the concert was closer to over. It was too dark for me to really see much, but that didn't stop me from scanning, searching for trouble.

Ciara turned into me, lifting her arms to my neck as she rose to her toes. For just a moment, the feel of her body flush against mine blotted out every other source of input, and I wanted to hold her here, just like this. She tipped her mouth close to my ear. "Are you okay?" Her fingers kneaded my shoulders as she searched my face for an answer.

"Aye. Why?"

"Let's step away for a bit. Get some air and something to drink."

I didn't know if the request was for herself or for me, and I didn't care. I'd take the opportunity.

She stepped away just long enough to tell the others where we were going, then tucked herself close again as we navigated through the chaos toward the refreshment vendors on the outskirts. Once we reached them, she kept walking another few dozen yards, until no one was within earshot. Then she paused and laid a hand on my chest. "I'm sorry."

I frowned at her. "For what?"

"You've been taut as a bowstring since we got here. I didn't think about how this might be hard for you. All the people. The crowds."

Even in the dim light, compassion shone on her face. Of course she'd understand, at least a little, because of her brother. She'd seen him during his adjustment to civilian life. And she'd been close enough that she'd have felt my body language.

"We can go. We've done what we set out to do. The others would understand."

It meant something to me that she'd look out for me. I hoped it was a sign she was edging toward actually forgiving me.

Resisting the urge to pull her close, I simply laid my hand over hers on my chest. "I appreciate that, but I'm okay. Let's just get something to drink, aye?"

"If you're sure."

"I am. If that changes, I'll let you know."

We moved back to the line for one of the burger vans. Ciara

still had her arm around my waist, and I tried to keep my focus on the feel of her against me instead of the low-level anxiety over the crowd. But I couldn't stop myself from scanning my surroundings.

That was when I saw him.

"What?" Ciara asked. "What is it?"

I swung her around into an embrace, pulling her close so I could both look over her shoulder and murmur into her ear. "Brodie's here."

"What?"

When she would've turned, I tightened my hold. "Don't turn around. He doesn't know he's been spotted."

As I watched him in my periphery, he ducked behind a row of porta-loos.

I nuzzled her ear and almost got distracted by the coconut and lime scent of her hair. She hadn't changed shampoos since Edinburgh. "Does he like this kind of music?"

"I... don't think so. I don't actually like this kind of music. This was all Jason's doing."

"Did you post online somewhere that you were coming tonight?"

"No."

I growled low in my throat. "The idea that Brodie just happens to be here is far too convenient for my taste. I think I'll have a wee word with him."

When I started to let Ciara go, she held tighter. "No. Just leave it. I don't want to make a scene. You're with me. I'm safe. It's fine."

It wasn't fine. Particularly in light of what I'd uncovered in my first wave of snooping. Brodie Drummond was obsessed with her. He was a threat. I felt it in my bones. But I didn't yet have enough intel to go against a direct order.

I pulled my focus back to Ciara, stroking the hair back from her face. "Fine. But you have to promise to let me know if he says or does anything else. I'm serious. Anything else."

Distress flickered in those big blue eyes, but she nodded. "I promise."

We needed to have a more detailed discussion because I suspected there were other things that had happened over the past few months—things she'd dismissed as nothing—that actually showed a pattern of escalation. But that could wait until we got home. Tonight was for friends. As she'd said, I was with her, so she was safe.

I'd make sure she stayed that way.

EIGHTEEN

CIARA

Monday found me clutching my extra-large mug of coffee like Gollum his precious. It was definitely going to be a two-cup morning. We'd gotten back from the concert late Saturday night, and I'd been up early the next morning to catch up on the work I'd blown off to go out. It would be my last weekend outing for several weeks, as we had a whole string of weddings coming up at the castle, including our biggest event to date in a little over a month. My work schedule was one of the things Brodie and I had fought about regularly, but Alex seemed unconcerned. As he pointed out, he worked for himself, and once their adventure company officially opened its doors, he would be working a lot of weekends as well. It had been an oddly coupley sort of conversation, considering we weren't really dating, but I found I appreciated his attitude, nonetheless.

"Ciara."

The sound of my name jerked me out of my own head. "Huh?"

From the look on Sophie's face, it wasn't the first time she'd tried to get my attention. "I asked how the weekend went. Was the concert good?"

"Sorry." My apology was interrupted by a jaw-splitting yawn. "It was fine. Not really my kind of music, but it was still a good time. It was nice to get out of town for a change of scenery."

The excursion had been fun. Hanging out with my friends and with Alex. Despite coming from a wildly different background, he'd seemed to get on with them well. I'd been tense about it at first, but once I got over myself and accepted that I had to act appropriately in front of them, I'd relaxed. It had been easier than I wanted it to be. The truth was, I enjoyed Alex's company. I'd enjoyed him when we'd met on the train. He was easy to be with. And I was trying not to think about how instinctive it had been to stay cuddled close to his side. It made me remember far too clearly what it had been like to be even closer.

Not. Happening. Again.

But God, it was hard not to think about it. Especially when he was in that super alpha protective mode. I knew part of it was his training, and that he struggled as Ewan had with being in crowds in public. But he was taking the situation with Brodie as a serious threat, which was more than I'd expected and more than I'd thought was needed.

But my ex had been at the concert, and I could think of no good reason why that would be. Especially as he'd clearly been skulking around instead of attending like everyone else. While Alex had leapt to some problematic conclusions that I wasn't ready to accept, his attention to my safety made me feel cared for and protected in a way that was, frankly, a problem.

It was becoming harder and harder to hold on to my antipathy. If I forgave him, what did that mean for us? A second chance? Would he want that? Or would it simply open me up to a fresh heartbreak that I still didn't know how to handle?

"Somebody is mooning over her fake boyfriend," Kyla sing-songed.

"I am not mooning. That would require being more than semi-conscious, and I'm not at all certain I qualify just now." Another massive yawn interrupted my self-defense. "I did manage to finish the timeline for the Burton-Sullivan wedding and sent off quote requests to our vendors for the extra tables and chairs for the Dooley-Kelso engagement party."

"Good. That should be most of the time-sensitive stuff that needed dealing with before this weekend's event. The bride and groom are scheduled to arrive on the premises Wednesday. Charlotte's already gathering components for the welcome baskets."

"Oh, Pippa told me this weekend that the next batch of her cheese should be ready tomorrow." I scribbled a note. "I'll head out to her croft to pick that up myself."

"Perfect." Kyla checked something off on her tablet.

Afton turned away from the tea station, a mug of steaming peppermint tea in her hands. "See if she's got any extra we can buy to keep on hand. I've got a few recipes I'd like to try, but we'd need a stockpile to actually offer it as a menu option."

Someone knocked on the doorjamb.

"Come in," Kyla called.

Angus stuck his head into the room. "We're back from our walk, and I've got a delivery here for Ciara."

Havoc pushed past him and made for his bed in the corner.

I frowned. "I wasn't expecting anything."

He stepped inside, a long, narrow box clutched under his arm.

Sophie clapped her hands. "Oh! That's the sort of box my deliveries usually come in. Maybe Alex is sending you flowers!"

I felt a foolish, girly little flutter at the idea of that. Because sending flowers here meant no one but people who were in on the true status of our relationship would know. And that meant... what? That he just wanted to be sweet?

Taking the box from Angus, I slit the tape on either side and carefully worked it open. At the sight of what was nestled inside, I froze.

The flowers inside were dead. Not as if something had gone horribly wrong in shipping, but as if they'd been deliberately gathered that way. The yellow petals were wilted and curled in on themselves, and the leaves and stems were brown and brittle.

Havoc was suddenly beside me, leaning against my legs with a whine.

"What on earth?" Sophie's hand settled on my shoulder as she peered past me into the box. "Those were... yellow carnations, I think. But why would anyone send you this?"

"Sophie, what do yellow carnations mean?" My voice sounded far away to my own ears.

"Um... well, traditionally disappointment or rejection."

Numb, I carefully poked through the box, but there was no card and no return address. Just my name and Ardinmuir Event Planning listed on the label. But I knew. They had to be from Brodie. His latest form of lashing out at me. I could no longer pretend that this was normal or even peripherally acceptable. I was officially in over my head.

Aware of everyone staring, I pulled out my phone and took a picture of the box to text to Alex.

Me: I just got this.

Three seconds later, my phone rang.

"Hey."

"Where are you?" Alex's voice was calm but deadly serious.

"At work. Up at Ardinmuir."

"I'm on my way. Don't touch anything else."

"Okay." I backed away from the box and sank down onto the sofa. Havoc dropped to his haunches beside me, sticking close.

We were still there when Alex strode in twenty minutes later.

He came straight to me, crouching down and taking my hands in his. Only then did Havoc ease back.

"You okay?"

"Not really."

"Can you give us the room?" Alex didn't look at my coworkers as he asked it. He didn't take his eyes off mine.

I expected them to argue, but they quietly cleared out, shutting the door softly behind them.

Alex shifted to sit beside me and pulled me into his arms. I burrowed in, letting myself lean, because he was big and solid, and I knew he had my back.

"I think I made a mistake."

His arms tightened around me. "You did nothing wrong. Seeing the best in people isn't a flaw. Trying to be kind isn't a flaw. It just... doesn't always work."

"Clearly."

He brushed a kiss over my temple. "It's going to be okay. Where's the box?"

I nodded to where it still sat on the table.

Letting me go, he crossed the room and examined the package as carefully as if he were diffusing a bomb. "No note. No return address. Nothing handwritten."

I dug my fingers into Havoc's ruff. The feel of the big dog was grounding, and I could see how he helped with Isobel's anxiety. "There's nothing to tie it to Brodie or anyone else.

There's nothing we can take to the police. What are we supposed to do?"

"We collect evidence. We keep and document all the details because it establishes a pattern. Combined with the damage to your car, I think we can argue escalation."

I thought of the note he'd left under my door that I'd just tossed in the bin. Something must've shown on my face.

"There's been something else. What haven't you told me?"

"I didn't think it was a big deal."

"Ciara..."

"He's been sending me notes, gifts and the like, since I broke up with him."

"What did they say?"

"They were all the same theme. He misses me. Wants me back. Please give him another chance. The last one was the night you came over to discuss the details of this whole thing."

Realization brightened his face. "That's why you were uneasy that night."

"Yeah."

"Did you keep them?"

"No. None of them. I just thought he was being a nuisance and that he'd eventually take the hint."

Alex scrubbed a hand down his face. "Okay. Anything else? Any other personal encounters where you felt uncomfortable?"

I told him about the run-in we'd had at the butcher shop in Braemore.

Hearing it all laid out like this, I could see what I'd refused to consider before: Brodie was being obsessive, and he'd long since crossed the line. Which meant he wasn't the man I'd believed him to be. How the hell had I been such a poor judge of character?

"All right. Probably none of this on its own is enough to

justify a non-harassment order. But you're going to report it either way, so it's documented."

I hoped it didn't come to true legal action, but I didn't argue. At this point, I was afraid of what Brodie might do next.

"Meanwhile, you're getting some extra security. I need to order some things."

As Alex began making a list, I watched him, wondering if I could be wrong about him, too. Because right now, he was acting like the man I'd believed him to be when we met before, not the guy he was after he ghosted me. Which one was the real him? And how could I trust my judgment either way?

NINETEEN

ALEX

Because I'd promised Ciara, I didn't go immediately from Ardinmuir to Braemore to beat the ever-loving shite out of Brodie Drummond. But God, I wanted to. He'd made her afraid and uncertain, which had no doubt been the entire point of that wee stunt with the dead flowers.

I never wanted to see her with less than the ball-busting confidence she'd had from the moment we met. Not because of some entitled gobshite who couldn't take "no" for an answer.

Whether there'd been words attached or not, the flowers were an implied threat. One the local police were taking seriously now that they were aware of the situation. As we'd expected, they couldn't take any actual action without verifiable proof that the package had come from him. Even I, with all my less-than-legal skills, hadn't been able to backtrack and prove that he'd been behind it. But there was zero reason to believe they'd come from anyone else. Who else had motive to harass her?

I had an array of security components on order. I could've gotten them quicker if I'd gone to Glasgow or Edinburgh in person, but I didn't want to leave her alone, and I wasn't ready to ask such a thing of Finn or Callum. For her part, Ciara was sticking close to home and close to work, unless she was with someone else. She didn't like it, but the precaution felt necessary to me. At least until I could do more to ensure Drummond wouldn't come at her again.

That was the whole reason I was here today. I'd be having a word with him about what was and was not acceptable behavior from this point forward. Without using my fists, sadly.

I'd hacked into Drummond's work calendar, finding a time he'd be in the office at the insurance agency. I'd spent the past hour exploring this area of the village, noting any security cameras and the line of sight from each business in the vicinity. I knew from my prior research that there were two other employees who worked for the same agency. They were what kept me from simply walking right in as if I were a prospective client. But I wasn't here to make a scene. I was here to make a point.

As the lunch hour drew near, Drummond stepped out of the office, headed up the street toward one of the local pubs, precisely in the direction I'd expected. No one else was paying attention. Even Drummond himself was buried in his phone as he walked. Easy pickings.

The moment he passed my location, I reached out to snag him, dragging him into the alley and behind a dumpster. I released him with more force than necessary, so he stumbled back up against the wall of the building. No matter how much I itched to, I wouldn't touch him again. Not unless he made a move first.

Surprise and a momentary flash of fear gave way to rage. Red flushed his cheeks, and his hands curled into fists. "What the fuck are you on about?"

I kept my hands open, my stance loose, unconcerned. My

calm would aggravate him even more. "We're having a conversation, you and I."

"I have no interest in talking to you." He made to move by me, but I shifted position, proving that I had him neatly boxed in. The color in his cheeks darkened.

"That's fine. You just have to listen. You're to cease all contact with Ciara. No more notes. No more gifts. No more dead flowers."

Something flickered over his face at that. There and gone again in a flash, but it was enough to confirm for me that he was our culprit.

"You can't tell me what to do. It's a free country. And you have no proof that I've done anything."

"What I have is a record of increased, unwanted contact with Ciara. She's repeatedly told you that your relationship is over. But you persist in continually showing up where she is, even when you shouldn't be there."

"I had every right to be at that concert."

"Sure you did. But skulking around, hiding because you're stalking your ex-girlfriend? It's not a good look."

He bowed up again. "I'm not stalking her! I'm not some kind of creep. I love her."

Love.

I nearly plowed my fist into his face then and there. "That's not love. That's obsession. She's not a thing you can own. Not a prize to be won. She's a person who can make her own choice, and you weren't it. Sorry, mate. But you're not. And she made that decision long before I came along. Just admit that you've lost and accept your defeat gracefully."

"There's no law against trying to win her back."

My smile was cold and deadly. "There's the law of me. You don't want to cross me, Drummond. I have a certain set of skills, and I can assure you that you do not want me to turn them in your direction. Because I can and will make your life a living hell without ever laying a hand on you if you don't leave her alone. It's over. You lost her. And that's the end of it."

"You can't threaten me. I'll go to the police."

"Feel free. We'd love to have you go to the police to counter all the reports we've made about your activities. That won't be a good look for you, either. If there's evidence somewhere linking you to all the harassment she's been enduring, I'll find it. There's no backtracking or cleanup you can do that can hide you from me. So go on with your sad, lonely wee life. I don't give a fuck. But stay away from Ciara."

He'd lost several shades of color by the end.

I didn't wait around for a verbal confirmation that he understood the terms. It wouldn't have been worth the breath used to utter it. Only time would tell if a more direct approach would solve the problem.

In the meantime, I'd be standing between him and Ciara.

TWENTY

CIARA

Despite the chill wind that told me winter was well on the way, I leaned over the fence rail to scratch the nearest shaggy head of one of Pippa's herd of Heiland coos. They provided the milk she turned into the artisan cheese that was her passion. It hadn't yet outstripped her remote computer coding gig as a job, but all the progress she'd made in the past few years meant she was well on her way to being able to call herself the Cheese Queen of the Highlands. Not that she'd ever call herself such a thing. She was far too shy to make such an assertion. But I absolutely would on her behalf. That was what friends did.

The cow leaned into my touch with a groan.

"Betsy likes that, she does. She'll take all the cuddles."

"Do you ever want to bring them in, like Raleigh and Kyla did Mabel when she was a baby?"

My cousin and her husband had found an orphaned calf in the wild and brought her back home. In the early days, she'd been kept inside like a big dog, and even now that she'd moved fully outside, she raced around with their pup, Dugal, as if he were her very tiny brother.

"I have my moments, but sanity usually prevails. I do keep a cot out in the barn, though, just in case my ladies need anything." Pippa reached over the rail to love on one of the other cows that had sidled up for some attention. "How are you? How are... things?"

That was as good a way as any to describe the situation with Brodie. I jerked my shoulders in a restless shrug. "It's been almost two weeks. There've been no weird deliveries or messages. No hang up phone calls. It's been quiet, which has me a bit paranoid, I guess. I want to believe it's over, but I don't trust it, you know?"

"Given everything he's pulled, that's not surprising."

After the dead flowers, I'd finally broken down and told my friends and cousins everything. I'd convinced them to keep it from Ewan, as I knew he'd rush back, and I didn't want to do anything to interrupt Isobel's creative focus. As I'd predicted, all the assorted menfolk had been furious I hadn't come to them for help. Alex had intervened there and reassured them he had the situation well in hand. What that meant, I had no idea. I wasn't sure I wanted to. But it put everyone else's mind at ease. I'd also asked everyone to hold off on telling my parents, who'd been out of the country on a three-week river cruise through Europe. They'd gotten home last night, and no doubt, I'd have explanations to make at the next family dinner, but at least I'd bought myself some time.

"Honestly, the only thing keeping my parents from demanding I move home is the fact that Alex installed security on my flat, and he's still escorting me to and from work." I gave an uneasy laugh. "I feel a little like I'm playing hooky right now, coming out here on my own for this pickup." I'd even left Havoc back at the castle. It hadn't seemed fair to stuff him into my car for the long drive both ways when he wouldn't get a good chance for a romp in between.

Pippa's brows drew together. "Should you be on your own?"

"I can't always have a bodyguard. Alex has his own job." And I didn't want to change my whole life because of a threat that might be over.

"How are things going with him?"

I hardly knew what to say. The truth was that things with Alex were feeling all too real, exactly as Sophie had warned me they would. We'd been spending more and more time together because of the situation with Brodie. I actually had to remind myself on the regular that we weren't really together, because he was the first person I contacted when I woke up in the morning and the last one I spoke to at night because we usually shared our evening meal.

If everything with Brodie was truly over, then I needed to put an end to this fake relationship before I got in over my head.

I ignored the voice in the back of my mind that insisted I was already going under for the third time.

Pippa was still studying me with those big, dark eyes behind her glasses.

"Things are fine."

The beads on her braids clacked as she angled her head and arched one dark brow. "When I've seen you two together, it definitely looks more than fine. But I can't blame you for being wary and taking things one day at a time after everything that happened with Brodie. That has to have shaken your confidence."

My confidence had been shaken long before Brodie, when I'd let myself believe that a one-night stand might be the start of forever. But the latest situation certainly didn't help matters in that department.

"True enough." Stepping back from the fence, I shoved my

hands into my pockets. "I should get back. Afton sends her profound thanks for the extra cheese for recipe testing. She's got big plans."

"I hope she'll share some of whatever she makes with it. I'm always interested in trying new applications."

"I'm sure she will. You know there's nothing she loves more than sharing her food."

"Must be nice working with her."

I laughed. "It does not suck."

Bidding my friend farewell, I got into my car and headed back toward Ardinmuir. It was a twenty-five-minute drive from Pippa's croft at Lochmara all the way back to the castle. Good thinking time before I got back to work and immersed myself in the plans for our latest client.

Really, calling things off with Alex was the only sane move. We weren't like Connor and Sophie. This wasn't going to turn into some kind of new romance. We weren't going to get a surprise happily ever after. Despite being surrounded by them, I wasn't at all sure they truly existed. Not for me. Alex hadn't said anything about changing the terms of our arrangement, making things real. If I'd harbored a few fantasies in that direction, well, I was no longer letting that foolish schoolgirl run my life. I was smarter now. More independent. I didn't need a man in my life to be complete.

But God, I wanted one. Or more properly, I wanted him. I'd probably want Alex Conroy as long as my body still drew breath.

But there could be no possibility of a second chance—or even, really, a true first—without trust. A part of me wanted to give more trust because he was so close to Ewan. But that trust only extended so far as believing he truly wanted to protect me and had the skills to do so. I knew my brother had trusted his life to these men and vice versa. That didn't automatically make them all decent relationship prospects for anyone, though. The reality was that Alex didn't trust me enough to tell me the truth of why he'd ghosted me three years ago. And I didn't trust my own judgment when it came to relationships anymore. Which left us right back at square one.

Another vehicle came up fast behind me. My attention automatically shifted to the mirror. Not a 4x4 I recognized, but they were ubiquitous up here. With the glare off the windscreen, I couldn't see who might be driving. Their flashers weren't on, but maybe the driver had some sort of emergency. I tapped the brake, intending to slow down and pull over so they could pass.

But nothing happened. My car didn't slow.

Heart leaping into my throat, I pressed the brake again and again, feeling less resistance each time.

The dark SUV was right on my bumper, but I could hardly focus on that. I had no brakes, and my car was picking up speed. My hands gripped the wheel so hard, my knuckles turned white.

Think, think, think!

I pressed the button on the wheel to activate hands-free calling. "Call Alex!"

"Calling Alex."

The phone rang once, twice. "Ciara?"

"My brakes are out, someone is riding my bumper, and I don't know what to do!"

"Where are you?" His voice was sharp but calm, which cut through a little of my own terror.

"On the forest road headed back from Lochmara. I'm maybe a mile from the bridge over the gorge."

"Take your foot off the gas entirely."

"I did that already. I'm going downhill."

"Pump the brakes. Sometimes it'll build enough pressure to give you a little bit of braking power."

I did as he ordered. "Nothing."

"Okay. It's okay. I want you to downshift your car."

I hit the clutch and did as he said. The car bucked and shuddered, but slowed a little bit. "It's doing something."

"Good. Keep going. All the way down."

I'd made it to second gear when the SUV hit my bumper. My body whipped forward with the impact, and I screamed.

"Ciara!" Alex wasn't calm now. I could hear panic in his tone.

"The other driver just rammed me. Whatever speed I lost, I'm moving fast again."

He swore low and vicious. I could hear noises in the background, like he was getting into a vehicle himself. "Try to pull the emergency brake."

I yanked the lever, but nothing happened. "It didn't work."

"Can you turn at all? Are there any other hills on either side of the road? Any brush?"

"No. No, there's the river to one side and trees to the other."

"Any guardrails you can brush?"

"Not until the bridge itself, and I don't think I can make the curve at this speed."

"Are you wearing your safety belt?"

"Aye."

"Okay, I want you to take it off."

"What?"

"You're going to steer toward the river."

"Are you crazy?"

"It gives the best odds for survival. Angle toward it rather than straight on. Make sure the windows are down. Use your hands and feet to protect your head and neck on impact, and get clear of the car as soon as it's submerged. The current may carry you downstream, but if you just float along, it'll help prevent injury. It's going to be okay. I'm coming for you."

Tears streamed down my cheeks because I knew there was no possible way he'd make it in time. "Alex, I'm scared."

"I know. So am I. But it's going to be okay. Aim for the river, Hellcat."

I stabbed the buttons to lower the windows. Wind immediately whipped into the car, yanking at my hair.

"I'm almost to the bridge!" I shouted. "I'm going for it!"

But just as I was reaching for the button to release my safety belt, the SUV rammed into me again, this time sending me into a spin. I screamed as I felt my tires leave the road, and the car began to roll.

TWENTY-ONE

ALEX

As part of my training, I'd been taught to control and master my own fear, overriding physiological responses to do what needed to be done. But absolutely nothing could have prepared me for the bone-deep terror of hearing Ciara's scream. The sound of tearing metal wrenched my chest straight open, exposing the heart I'd tried so desperately to guard, and I shouted into the phone, as if by will alone I could reach out to catch her. But my terror was met with only silence.

Shut it down, Conroy. Just get to her.

Viciously, I shifted gears, pushing my 4x4 to its absolute limit of speed. It groaned as I took curves too fast, and tires barked as I drifted into turns. It didn't matter. Nothing mattered now but getting to her.

I knew Callum and Finn would be right behind me. I hadn't stopped to explain a damned thing as I'd raced out of the office like the hounds of hell were on my heels. They wouldn't need an explanation. They'd heard enough to understand the instructions I'd been giving her. They knew something was desperately wrong, and they'd come.

Someone had run her off the bleeding road, and that changed everything. Drummond was an entitled son of a bitch, but he wasn't a killer. Which meant I'd been wrong. I'd miscalculated. It was happening all over again. And this time—this time, I wouldn't survive it.

It took an absolute eternity to reach the bridge over the gorge. A thin trail of smoke curled up from somewhere out of sight, down by the river. I couldn't think about what that smoke meant. Not now. Not yet.

On the far side, I spotted a farm truck pulled to the side of the road. A man stood at the side of it, just inside the open door. Friend or foe? He lifted both arms to wave me down. Probably friend, then. A bystander who'd happened by just after the crash. The perpetrator wouldn't have stuck around.

I screeched to a halt on the opposite side of the road and hurled myself out of the driver's seat. My legs didn't want to hold me, and it felt as if every cell in my body was vibrating with fear and desperate hope.

The man moved out of the way to reveal another pale figure on the seat. An impossible figure with long, dark hair and blood streaking down her face. She was wrapped in a coat that was many sizes too big, and those big, beautiful blue eyes fixed on me. Alive.

"Ciara." Her name ripped from my throat on something that was halfway to a sob as relief and gratitude all but took me to my knees.

I closed the distance between us, only stopping myself at the very last moment from hauling her into my arms and crushing her to me. That might hurt her further. I had no idea what other injuries she'd sustained in the accident.

But I needed to touch her. Needed to reassure myself that she was here and not some desperate hallucination. With one trembling hand, I gently brushed her cheek. The one thing I could be reasonably sure wasn't damaged.

It was as if that touch unfroze her.

She tumbled off the seat, straight into my arms, wrapping her own around me tight enough that I was assured she definitely wasn't paralyzed. Very, very carefully, I held her close, burying my face in her hair and sending up prayers of thanks to every deity I could think of. She was alive. She'd survived.

Swallowing down the emotion that wanted to fell me, I choked out, "Where are you hurt?"

"I don't know. My head? Mostly I'm fine. I'm just shaken up."

She trembled so hard it shook us both. Adrenaline was probably masking other injuries, and no doubt she'd have a multitude of bruises and other aches that would make themselves known later. But it could have been so much worse.

I finally managed to look past the truck to where she'd gone over. The car had clearly rolled a few times before finally coming to rest semi-upright against a cluster of boulders that had been the only thing that stopped her from tumbling straight into the gorge.

My blood turned to ice.

She'd come so close to dying. And it was all my fault.

Lock it down. She needs you to stay calm.

My control was tenuous at best, but I'd do what had to be done for Ciara.

Finn and Callum were down by the car. I hadn't even known they'd arrived. Even if they didn't know the why, I knew they'd check for the things I'd want to check. The things I wouldn't have a chance to check, once emergency services came and removed the car. There was a remote possibility the brakes could have gone out on their own. But that combined with someone deliberately running her off the road? That was something else. Something I'd have to deal with.

Shoving that aside, I pulled back only far enough to look down into Ciara's face, automatically checking her eyes. Both dilated with shock, but responding to light stimuli. That was good.

"You need to see a doctor."

"Emergency services are on the way. I called them from my mobile."

I turned toward the man who'd stopped, taking him in for the first time. He was older, with a shock of gray hair and a weathered face that likely hid his true age.

I extended a hand. "I'm indebted to you, sir."

"Och, I didnae do anything but help the lass up the hill. She was already halfway out of the car by the time I got here."

"Still. Thank you, Hugh. My mum will certainly be sending loads of baked goods to you and Flora."

Of course, Ciara knew him. She knew practically everyone. Even in her Edinburgh neighborhood back in university. It had been one of the things that had intrigued me about her. That easy networking she seemed to do everywhere she went.

"Not necessary, but appreciated all the same."

The wail of sirens sounded in the distance, and with them time snapped back into focus.

There'd be questions from the police. Hopefully, a medical evaluation by paramedics here on the scene before she got taken to the hospital for a more thorough series of scans to ensure there was no internal bleeding or other damage we couldn't see.

And then... then I'd have to reassess the situation through this new lens. Backtrack and figure out what else I'd missed before anyone else became a casualty in this war no one knew I was the target of.

TWENTY-TWO

CIARA

Alex stood in the corner of the exam room at the village clinic, glowering like a gargoyle. He'd wanted me to go straight to the hospital in Inverness, but I kept insisting I was fine. I mean, objectively, I wasn't fine. But I didn't think I was get-admitted-to-the-hospital bad. He'd only relented when I agreed that if the doctor here believed I needed further tests, I'd go without complaint.

Teagan Donaldson shone a light in my eyes.

I flinched away with a hiss and sensed rather than heard Alex take a step in our direction before he caught himself.

"Sorry. Necessary evil. But the good news is your pupils are reacting normally."

I knew of Dr. Donaldson, of course. It had been big news when she'd joined Doc Albright's practice a year and a half ago. But I didn't *know* her. She seemed kind and more than capable as she asked me more questions and checked every inch of me over.

"Okay, I need to see what's going on under your shirt now."

She glanced toward Alex. "Do you want your friend to step out?"

He hadn't left my side since he'd made it to the accident site, and I definitely felt steadier with him here. Besides, despite the fact that we weren't sleeping together now, there was nothing he hadn't seen before.

"No. He stays."

"I'll turn my back."

Sweet of him, but unnecessary. I wasn't overly concerned with modesty just now. The doctor helped me off with my jumper and winced at what lay beneath.

"Definite bruising from the safety belt. Some other scrapes. That's all to be expected." She disinfected those scrapes, including several I wondered how I got. "I'm going to check your ribs now. Is that all right?"

"Go ahead."

Very carefully, she felt along each rib, asking if anything hurt.

"I mean, everything hurts, but nothing more than anything else. Other than my head."

She pressed the stethoscope to my back and chest and had me take several deep breaths. "No trouble breathing. That's good. It's possible your ribs on the right might come up bruised from where the belt caught you, but nothing's broken." After a thorough palpation of the rest of my torso, Dr. Donaldson finally stepped back. "Well, you're banged up, to be sure. But all in all, you were very lucky."

Lucky.

I supposed I was. Someone had tried to kill me and failed. At least, I assumed that was the point of running me off the road. That hadn't been a case of overblown road rage. I didn't know what it had been. I didn't know why. And I was trying very hard not to think about any of that. Not yet. But I'd survived. And that was likely only because of Alex and his level head.

When everything had gone to absolute shite, my instinct had been to reach out to him. He'd been there for me. He'd come for me as fast as he possibly could. And in that moment when I'd gone off the road and thought I was going to die, my last thoughts had been that I hadn't given him another chance. A real one. That was something I'd have to think about when my head was no longer ringing.

A scuffle sounded from the hall.

"Where's our daughter?"

A softer-voiced nurse replied, but I didn't understand what she said.

"I think that's my da." It was hard to tell with the yelling. That wasn't his default state. "Mum's probably with him."

"Right, why don't I handle that while you get dressed, and then we'll talk? Do you want them to know what's going on with you?"

"That's fine. I'd be telling them everything, anyway."

"Okay. I'll be back in a little while." Dr. Donaldson slipped out of the room.

Alex was still standing facing the corner.

"You can turn around now. I think I'm going to need a little help."

"Are you sure?"

"It's nothing you haven't seen before."

There was heat in his eyes as he turned. Then his gaze slid down to the rest of me, and he swore.

"Did they offer you all a program in profanity as part of your training as a Royal Marine? You truly do have the most magnificent swears."

Alex didn't laugh as I'd hoped. He started to reach for me, then stopped himself, as if he were afraid I'd break. I knew self-recrimination when I saw it, and blame was written all over his face.

"This is all my fault."

I reached for his hand, pulling him closer. "It would have been a whole lot worse if not for you. You kept me from panicking, and that gave me a chance I wouldn't otherwise have had."

He still looked as if he believed he should be jabbed repeatedly with a flaming hot poker, so I reached up to frame his face, forcing him to look into my eyes instead of at the array of bruises. "Look at me. I'm okay. I'm alive."

With a choked sound, he pressed his brow ever so gently to mine. "You nearly weren't."

I held in the wince because I knew he'd curse himself all over again for thoughtlessness. "A near miss is as good as a mile."

"I suppose the fact that you can still be sarcastic means you're not too bad off."

"Exactly. Now help me on with this jumper."

I was fully dressed by the time someone knocked on the door.

"Come in."

Dr. Donaldson stepped back inside, followed by my parents, who were beside themselves. They rushed me where I sat on the exam table, brought up short when Alex stepped forward.

"Careful. She's bruised."

My mother blinked. "Alex. What are you doing here?"

Before I could decide exactly what to say about that, Alex answered for me.

"We're together."

So much room for interpretation in that statement. I decided that untangling the threads was a problem for Future Ciara. My head hurt far too much, and now that the adrenaline dump had faded, the only thing I wanted was a nap, if I could manage it.

Dr. Donaldson cleared her throat. "Right. We've checked her over. She has some bumps and bruises, scrapes, and that nasty wee gash on her forehead. But nothing's broken, and there's no sign of any internal injuries. She does have a concussion, but it could have absolutely been a great deal worse."

My mother covered her mouth with a gasp. Had someone told her I'd been run off the road? I wasn't prepared for that conversation yet. I'd already gone over it with the police briefly before coming here.

"Now, she's going to be on a concussion protocol. Someone will need to wake her every hour, to make sure she can still answer questions, check her pupil reactivity and the like. And of course, if anything should suddenly start hurting or get a lot worse, you have my number. Call me. But otherwise, you're free to go. I've got a prescription for some painkillers." She plucked a sheet out of a drawer. "Who needs the list of concussion protocols?"

I saw Alex about to volunteer and rushed to speak first. "I'll be staying with my parents tonight."

A flash of hurt crossed his face before he blanked it again. This wasn't about not wanting to be near him. It was, in fact, because I didn't want to be away from him. I laid a hand on his arm. "They're going to need that reassurance."

And I was going to need some distance from him to figure out how I really felt when I wasn't in imminent danger of dying.

TWENTY-THREE

ALEX

"Are you sure you don't need anything else?" I was aware I'd already done everything that needed doing for Ciara, including packing a bag and getting her settled at her parents' house, but I didn't want to leave her. I was too paranoid about what might happen if I wasn't here to stop it.

She blinked at me with eyes that were bruised from fatigue. In the wake of the adrenaline dump, and all that came after, her energy had run out. "Yeah. I'm good. Thanks, Alex."

The quiet tone of dismissal told me I wouldn't have any luck trying to sleep on her floor as the resident bodyguard, and I didn't want to alarm her or her parents any more than they already were. Of course they needed to fuss over her. She was their baby.

"Right." No more putting it off. "I guess I'll go so you can get some rest."

Ewan's dad extended a hand. "Grateful to you, lad, for looking out for our girl."

He had no way of knowing how those words strained the guilt I was barely holding at bay.

I accepted his firm handshake.

"We're a little surprised about you two, but very pleased," Mrs. McBride added.

That just added to the guilt. I'd just blurted out our supposed relationship status in the moment because I'd wanted to justify my right to be there. And because, with everything going on, Ciara felt like mine. Mine to protect. Mine to care for. The walls between us had been eroding since we'd started this ruse, but I knew the reality was something we'd have to discuss later, after she'd had some time to recover.

I ducked my head in a nod and looked back to Ciara, who'd slumped down on the sofa. "If you need anything—any of you —don't hesitate to call."

She sat partway up and winced. "I thought of one thing."

"Name it." Any task would be better than none and would help keep me away from the edge of the spiral threatening to suck me under.

"It's probably stupid, but can you check with the police about my car to see if they found any of Pippa's cheese?"

"You want me to look for... cheese?" Was that a sign of confusion? I checked her pupils again.

"I was bringing a big batch of it back for Afton. It probably flew out of the car, but in case it didn't... It's going to be a while before the next batch is ready."

Work. She was thinking about work. That was probably more of a sign that she was okay than anything else. "I'll check on the cheese."

It meant going back to the car, either at the accident site or wherever it had been impounded, which I'd planned to do, anyway. I wasn't missing the opportunity to examine her brake lines myself this time.

With one last round of goodbyes, I finally pushed myself out the door. I had less than an hour of daylight left. I'd try the accident scene first. In an area this small, I'd be surprised if emergency services had already been able to remove her car. Fifteen minutes later, I crossed the gorge bridge again to find Finn and Callum still at the scene.

"What are you lot still doing here?"

"Car hasnae been moved, so we're guarding it," Callum said easily.

And this was one of the reasons these men were my closest mates.

"How's Ciara?" Finn asked.

"Concussed, but alive. She's at her parents' resting."

Callum jerked a thumb down the hill toward the remains of the car. "There's something you'll want to see."

I followed him down the embankment, holding in a shudder as I realized exactly how close she'd come to ending up in the gorge. Another fifty feet, and she'd be dead.

Shut it down, Conroy.

Half the undercarriage of the car was exposed by how it had landed. I accepted the torch Callum offered and crouched down to inspect it. The brake lines weren't hard to find. I traced the length of each, seeing the oily residue of brake fluid. It took me less than a minute to find what I'd been looking for. Small punctures in the lines, near the edge of the metal coupling. They'd been made in such a way that had there only been one, it might have been attributed to wear and tear or faulty lines. But there were two, damaged in an identical fashion that would bleed fluid slowly, until the brakes simply gave out. No real way to estimate how long it would take or where it would happen. Ciara didn't keep a consistent daily schedule. This sort of tampering, on its own, would've been enough to hurt or kill her. But that someone had helped her along absolutely verified this wasn't any sort of accident.

The situation reminded me far too much of what had

happened with my father. I'd never gotten the opportunity to look over that vehicle to prove what I knew in my gut was true. His car crash had been no accident, either.

"Do you think her ex would go this far?" Finn asked. "An 'If I can't have her, no one can' sort of thing?"

I considered the question. "The man is an entitled twat and totally believes Ciara should be his, but I don't see him as a killer. At least not like this. This shows premeditation and at least a modicum of mechanical skill. I could see Drummond losing his shite in a crime of passion sort of way, but not doing something this cold and calculated."

"Can't hurt to call the police and ask about him, now can it?" Finn prompted.

"True enough. Did you get photos of the tampering here?"

"Aye," Callum confirmed.

"Good." Pulling out my mobile, I dialed the number for the constable we'd spoken to when Ciara had reported Brodie's harassment.

Constable Darci Williamson answered on the first ring. "Mr. Conroy, I expected to hear from you. How is Miss McBride?"

"Alive. Thank God. You ken what I'm calling about, aye?"

"You want to know whether Brodie Drummond could be behind today's accident."

"I do."

"As soon as the report came in, I went personally to check on him. He has an airtight alibi for the time in question. Was in the middle of a meeting with multiple coworkers at the time. Whoever did this, it wasn't him. But we'll keep looking. We won't let reckless endangerment like this stand."

"It's quite a bit more than reckless endangerment. The brake lines were sabotaged. I've got photos to send you of the damage."

There was a beat of silence. "You do that. I'll see that we bring in an expert to go over the car with a fine-toothed comb."

"I appreciate that." I rang off. "Alibied. Which I expected."

"He could've paid someone," Callum suggested.

"He could've."

"But you don't think he did," Finn finished.

"No." I thought this went beyond Brodie Drummond in ways I hadn't yet had a chance to fully process.

"You have other ideas about who might have done this?" Callum prompted.

They hadn't been read in. Hadn't been part of the mission I'd run that had started all of this.

"Maybe. But none I'm ready to discuss yet. Need to do some digging."

"Okay." Finn squeezed my shoulder. "You know we're here when you're ready."

"And we've got your back in the meantime."

This was why these men were my brothers in ways that blood family could never understand.

"Thanks." I took the torch and moved around to look at the inside of the car.

Callum peered in the other side. "What are you looking for?"

"Cheese. Ciara was on her way to deliver some to Afton when all of this happened. She asked me to see if it survived the crash." I panned the light around the interior.

I didn't have to look to know my friends were staring at me.

"This thing you're doing with her, it started out fake, but you feel something for her," Finn said. "When she called in trouble, you tore out of the office as if the Cù Sith were on your six."

There was no sense in denying it. My behavior had made it clear enough.

"Aye, I feel something for her." Such a pale, weak statement for the reality.

"What are you going to do about it?"

That was the question. Because it wasn't as simple as boy likes girl and boy asks girl on a date for real. Because I wasn't a normal man. I'd moved to Glenlaig because I'd believed that it was safe. But it seemed I'd been too presumptive. My past was catching up to me. Again. And this time it was bleeding over onto Ciara because I'd been deluded enough to think I'd reached a point in my life where I could legitimately start over, free of the shadow that had cast a pall over my life for far too long. Because she'd asked me for help. She was being targeted because she was important to me, and I'd made sure the public at large knew it.

"I don't know. But I'll start with tracking down the fucker who did this and make certain he can't do it again."

TWENTY-FOUR

CIARA

I loved my parents. Truly, I did. But after three days back home, Mum was resembling a smother rather than a mother, and Da was putting off work he needed to do, hanging around the house, staying underfoot, generally driving both of us mad. I couldn't blame them. The police were no closer to answers about who'd run me off the road. They'd come to talk to me further, and I'd found out that my brake lines had been tampered with by someone other than Brodie. I hadn't breathed a word of that to my parents. They were freaked out enough. But if I didn't get out of this house, I was going to lose my bloody mind.

I needed to talk to Alex.

He'd been in contact every day but had otherwise kept his distance, allowing me to rest and recover. I missed him way more than I ought to. I wanted to lean on him. I wanted this thing we'd been doing to be real. Real hadn't been on the table since he moved to Glenlaig. This favor to me was simply repaying a debt. Balancing the scales for him having treated me poorly after our last parting. For my own sake, I needed to break it off because I was losing all objectivity where he was concerned. If I'd ever really had any at all.

I finally texted him around two in the afternoon.

> **Me:** I need a non-life-threatened rescue. My person is safe, but my sanity is iffy.

The dots indicating he was typing a reply began to bounce almost immediately.

> **Alex:** Ready to go back home?

> **Me:** So much.

> **Alex:** Pack your bag. I'll be by in an hour.

> **Me:** You're a godsend.

I took my time packing, mostly to give myself the privacy to psych myself up for the conversation I didn't actually want to have. I was still stiff, and the bruises from the safety belt were a lovely array of deep purples all the way to yellow. But the headache had mostly faded, and the cut on my temple had begun to heal. Connor and Sophie had kept Havoc at Ardinmuir, as I hadn't been in any shape to walk him the past few days. I missed the big furry lunk, but maybe I'd give it another day or two to see how I was feeling before I added him back to my schedule.

Good as his word, Alex showed up fifty-eight minutes later.

My mum was in the process of offering tea and biscuits when I came out with my bag. The sense of relief I felt at the sight of him almost made me weak.

"Hey."

"Hey. How are you feeling?"

"Better." Especially as I knew he was here to spring me.

"Are you ready to go home?"

"Oh, but—" Mum started to protest.

"Don't worry. I promise to take her straight back to her flat and not allow her to overdo," Alex assured her.

Da came into the kitchen. "What's happening?"

Mum twisted a tea towel in her hands. "Ciara's leaving."

"Is that wise?" Da wanted to know.

"I have to get back to my life sometime. Thank you both for taking care of me." I hugged them both to take the sting out of my departure.

It was obvious my parents had questions and concerns, but they kept them to themselves, probably because I was leaving with Alex.

Once we were in his 4x4, I dropped my head back against the seat and sighed. "Freedom."

"It's hard to go home again, aye?"

I looked toward him in the driver's seat. "Did your mum fuss over you when you retired?"

"So much. For a little while, it was grand. All my favorite meals. Someone else to do my laundry. All of which I realize is sexist but was nice just the same. But it started to chafe pretty fast. I expect that's even worse for you because you're the baby of the family."

"They're mostly good about treating me as an adult, but after all this... I'm ready for my own space again."

We lapsed into silence for the rest of the short drive. I was still working my way up to broaching the subject of our fake relationship when he carried my bag upstairs and unlocked the door. He set the bag aside and disabled the alarm he'd installed. Then he did a quick sweep of the whole place. Evidently satisfied there were no assailants hiding in the closet or under the bed, he pulled a small device out of his pocket and began running it over every surface in the flat.

"What are you doing?"

"Looking for surveillance equipment."

Because he'd said it with utter seriousness, I stared for several moments. "Why would my flat be bugged?"

He made a hand gesture for me to wait until he'd finished.

I wanted to believe that this was an overreaction. But someone had sabotaged the brakes on my car, so clearly, whatever was going on was more in his wheelhouse than mine.

To keep myself busy, I made a cuppa tea for us both. I'd learned how he took it over the past few weeks.

"No evidence of listening devices or cameras."

He probably meant for that to be comforting, but the fact that he'd been looking at all had a fresh bout of anxiety brewing.

"I'll ask again... why would my flat be bugged?"

He put the device away and sighed. "Sit. I need to talk to you."

I'd been planning to say the same thing to him, but the words died in my throat at his serious expression. I took my tea and sat.

He grabbed his. "Thanks." But he didn't drink, instead sitting on the ottoman that served as my coffee table so he was directly across from me.

"I want to tell you the truth. The real truth about why I didn't contact you three years ago. There are still specifics that I can't share because you don't have the security clearance. But you have a right to know, especially as what happened to you is directly my fault."

My heart began to pound. I'd given up on the idea that he'd ever really tell me the why I'd so desperately wanted to know.

"Okay."

Alex set his tea aside and braced his elbows on his knees, clearly trying to gather his thoughts. "I had a successful undercover career in the Royal Marines. I had absolutely no intention of retiring as soon as I did, but a group of anarchist hackers and activists began exposing classified details on undercover military operatives. Due to their leaks, some of my past aliases were compromised, which effectively ended my ability to safely work undercover, thus forcing my early retirement. That's when I met you."

Lacing his fingers, he began absently rubbing circles on his palm with his thumb. "You upended my world, made me question everything I thought I wanted. The morning I left you, I meant what I said with every fiber of my being. I wanted to explore what was between us. And then I got up here and had dinner at your parents' house, saw all your photos, and I kind of freaked out. I needed a little bit of time to process that you were Ewan's sister. I still wasn't planning to ghost you at that point. I just needed to get my head screwed on straight before I contacted you again."

"I can't blame you for that."

"But shortly after that, I was recruited by British intelligence to help dismantle the hacking collective that was behind the information leaks. I saw it as a chance to get payback against the group that cut my career short and a means of protecting others still out there. It was completely off-book, and it was inherently going to bring more turmoil and danger into my world. I didn't want to risk you, so I didn't contact you again. That wasn't fair to you. I should, in retrospect, have come up with something to tell you to at least give you closure rather than let you think what you've thought all these years. Hindsight being 20/20 and all that."

He shrugged. "Anyway, during the middle of all of this, my father died under mysterious circumstances. A one-vehicle car accident."

My head was spinning. If I were to believe what Alex was saying—and knowing him as I did, how could I not?—then his disappearing act really wasn't about me or us. And I was feeling ill because, deep down, I knew where this was going.

"I've always suspected it was connected to the contract work I was doing, but I couldn't prove it without compromising myself or my investigation." He took a deep breath and let it out again, slowly. "The operation took two years. In the end, the parties responsible were caught, and I was finally free to get back to a life. But I didn't want to get close to anybody lest I put them in danger. That was why I stayed away. The reason I never contacted you wasn't about your brother, at least not mostly. It was about your safety."

I sat in stunned silence for a long time. I did not have *Involved in dangerous clandestine government operation* on my bingo card of reasons why he'd disappeared so thoroughly from my life. This was everything I'd wanted to know. This was the piece he hadn't trusted me enough to tell me. But obviously something had changed.

"Why are you telling me all of this now?"

"Because your brake lines were tampered with in a way that suggests a professional. We already know that Brodie has an alibi, and I think it's highly unlikely he'd hire someone to do that. Much of a shite as he is, he's no murderer. I believe that you're being targeted because of me. Because we're involved. At least, everyone thinks we are. Because the mission I thought was over still has someone out there who wants to hurt me. And they're trying to do it through you."

TWENTY-FIVE

ALEX

When Ciara only stared at me in stunned disbelief, I dropped my gaze. Guilt draped over me like a chain mail blanket. I'd brought this to her doorstep. Not deliberately, but what did that matter in the end? I should never have come here. Never have assumed I'd get to move on and have a normal life. I'd made enemies. The choices I'd made would impact the people I cared about for the rest of my life.

Ciara still hadn't spoken. I didn't know what else to say, but I tried anyway.

"I owed you the truth. That's it. Or as much of it as I can give you. I don't know what happens next, but I swear to you, I will do whatever I have to in order to make sure you're safe. No one else will get to you again."

"I know."

At her calm, matter-of-fact statement, I lifted my head.

I saw none of the hostility and anger she'd had when I first came back into her life. There wasn't even really worry, though I was sure that would come later, after she'd had a chance to process. She was looking at me as she had when we met three years ago. With that open acceptance that had been as heady as any drug.

Leaning forward, she cupped my face between her palms and kissed me. Although every instinct I had roared to haul her into me and devour her mouth, glorying in this connection, this moment, I held very still because I didn't deserve this. I didn't deserve anything from her.

Easing back, she skimmed her fingers through my hair. "Alex." Her eyes searched mine. "You were in an impossible situation. And I'm sorry I made it worse."

I jerked in her hold. "You didn't—"

"I did. I'd like to think I would have understood three years ago. My brother was in the Royal Marines for a long time. He never talks about his service. I know some of that is because of security reasons and some because of trauma. We've never pushed him. If I'd realized who you were to begin with, I'd probably have been more forgiving."

Looking into those blue eyes that had haunted my dreams, I gave her the honesty I hadn't been able to offer before. "If I'd realized who you were to begin with, I never would have touched you."

She flinched back. Damn it, that wasn't what I'd meant. "That's nothing against you. Your brother is one of my closest friends and was my commanding officer to boot. It was just a line I wouldn't have knowingly crossed."

Her expression turned fierce, which was somehow both adorable and attractive. "Then I'm glad you didn't know, because I don't regret being with you."

Her words struck me speechless. Ever since I'd gotten to Glenlaig, I'd felt like one big walking regret. As if I were a permanent reminder to her of a mistake she wished she hadn't made. I hadn't blamed her for that at all. Not when I'd handled things with her so poorly.

This was forgiveness I wasn't at all sure I deserved. But I wanted to grab on with both hands. So I admitted the truth, because I didn't want to lie to her anymore about anything, if I could help it. "Neither do I."

How could I regret a moment with this woman? Sure, our connection was awkward and complicated because of my prior relationship with her brother. And I had no idea where we went from here, one way or the other. But I knew exactly how short life could be. If she was willing to give me another chance, who was I to waste it?

Her thumb stroked my stubbled cheek in a slow, back-and-forth rhythm as she stared at me. "Will you be with me now, knowing exactly who I am?"

I went still at the question. She didn't know what she was asking. I wanted her. I always wanted her. But it wasn't that simple. I'd been holding myself back for what felt like so long. I didn't know if I could give her what she needed. "You're hurt."

It was a reminder as much to myself as to her.

Her lips curved, and she skimmed her hands across my shoulders. "I'm fine. A little sore, maybe. But orgasms are excellent painkillers."

I huffed a laugh. "Cheeky minx."

That smile turned feline as she closed the distance. "You like it."

"God, do I."

This time, when she kissed me, I lost the war with myself. Angling my head, I licked along the seam of her lips, groaning as she opened for me. The taste of her was intoxicating. I'd kissed her several times since we'd started this fake dating thing, but she'd always held something back. I could feel the difference of kissing her with no more resistance, no more barriers, no more lies. It was like it had been the first time, but more.

Because she was more. And a part of me had known she would be from the moment we met.

Mindful of her injuries, I carefully pulled her in, needing her close, wanting to dive deeper. But my efforts to drag her into my lap were thwarted by our awkward positions. Without breaking the kiss, I rose, lifting her easily before turning and sinking down where she'd been on the sofa, this time with her straddling my hips.

With a contented purr, Ciara settled more firmly against my erection and began to roll her hips. When I'd been with her before, I'd loved how unapologetically she chased her own pleasure. She was a woman who knew what she wanted and went after it. And I was the luckiest bastard that she wanted me, despite everything.

As I worshiped her mouth, I slid my hands beneath her jumper to find soft, velvety skin. She arched into my touch, reaching back to drag off the jumper. I caught a flash of livid bruising from her shoulder, down her chest, and froze.

Ciara slid her fingers into my hair and tipped my head back. "Eyes up here. Unless you're planning to kiss it all better."

"That might take a while."

"We have time," she insisted and took my mouth again.

And that was my own personal miracle.

We'd only had one night before, and we'd made the most of it. But now I wanted to take my time. To savor and explore every inch. I didn't know how this situation would end, but I'd treat this as a beginning, and I'd give her every part of myself I could for as long as she wanted me.

TWENTY-SIX

CIARA

Alex had been holding back, so terribly concerned about hurting me. But I felt the change in him as he deepened the kiss and stroked those big, broad palms up and down my back. I hummed encouragement as I blindly sought the hem of his shirt. I needed to feel more of him. But then his mouth left mine, and he began to trail soft, reverent kisses down my throat and along the bruises, and I forgot what I was doing. He flicked open the clasp of my bra and drew it off.

The hungry expression on his face at the sight of my breasts had my already budded nipples drawing tighter, begging for his touch, his mouth. He didn't disappoint, bending to take one into his mouth and swirling his tongue around the sensitive tip. I drove my fingers into his hair, holding him close because that felt amazing. Restless, I rocked against him. His hand came up to cup my other breast, his callused fingers rolling my nipple, and my head fell back. God, I'd missed this. I'd never had this intense a reaction to anyone before or since him. Lost to sensation, I continued to rock, chasing that tension coiling in my core. When his teeth scraped lightly along my nipple, I flashed over the edge on a gasping cry.

During the quaking aftermath, he abandoned my breast, kissing his way back up my chest and neck. "You okay?"

When I'd caught my breath enough to speak, I mustered a feline smile. "That was an excellent start. But you're getting behind."

"Can't have that," he rumbled. "Hold on."

When he stood, I wrapped my legs around his waist. Smooth and efficient, he carried me back to the bedroom and gently settled me onto the bed. I'd imagined him here so many times, long before he ever came to Glenlaig. And now here he was. Mine. At least for now.

I tugged at his shirt but couldn't quite get it. "Off," I demanded.

He did that one-handed tug that was so inexplicably sexy and tossed his shirt to the floor. He was every bit as fit as I remembered. I skimmed my fingers over the hard warmth of his skin, noting the scars and tattoos. I wanted to spend some time on those later, exploring what he'd seen fit to permanently etch into his skin. But he kissed me again, distracting me from my goal.

He trailed his lips and hands over every inch of my body, seeming to map every dip and curve in a way that left me somehow both languid with pleasure and wound tight as a spring. I watched him draw off my shoes with infinite care. He'd been a thorough and attentive lover our first time together, but this was a whole new level. His exquisite care made me feel cherished. Maybe that was my inherent romanticism talking, but I made no effort to shut it down. I was done fighting what I felt for him. It hadn't made a damned bit of difference, and I wanted this with him, however long it lasted.

When he had me bare, he paused, his big hands on my calves, and I shuddered in anticipation.

"Are you cold?"

"Not even a little bit." I parted my legs in invitation, remembering how good he'd been at this before.

Those dark eyes heated as he settled between them, using his fingers to part my folds. "So fucking beautiful." Then he dipped his head and took a long, slow lick up my center.

I bowed off the bed with a shout.

"Okay?"

"Don't you dare stop," I gasped.

"As you wish."

He truly went to work then, driving me up with his mouth and tongue until I forgot about any hint of pain and all I could do was beg for more. He slid one finger into the ache, then a second, working me to a fever pitch. When he curled them, I shot over the edge even harder.

I was still vibrating as he moved away to shuck his jeans and roll on a condom. God, he was beautiful. Big and battle-hardened. No wonder I hadn't been truly satisfied with anyone else. I opened my arms for him, but instead of crawling up my body, he stretched out beside me on his back.

"It's been a while, aye? Let's take our time with it." He urged me on top of him.

Patience had never been one of my virtues, and holding back now was even harder because I'd wanted him here ever since he'd walked out of my life. I notched him at my entrance and linked our hands. Keeping my gaze fastened to his, I sank down, down, down, until he filled me completely. And, oh God, yes. This was what I'd been missing. *He* was what I'd been missing. I had no more defenses against what I felt for this man. What I'd felt for him almost from the moment we'd met.

Against all rationality, I loved him. And I was absolutely done punishing us both.

When the words wanted to spill out, I kissed him instead and began to ride, pouring everything I felt into the moment and heat we made together. It was too much too soon. Chances were, it would ruin everything. We had enough challenges already.

Alex matched me beat for slow beat, until our bodies slicked with sweat. When the tide rose again, he rolled me beneath him, driving slower, deeper, until we both slid shuddering over the edge.

TWENTY-SEVEN

ALEX

Moving with the stealth I'd honed to perfection in the Royal Marines, I left Ciara napping soundly in her bed. Between the concussion protocol and her parents' fussing, I suspected she hadn't slept well in days. Gathering up my clothes, I slipped out of the bedroom and dressed.

The plan had always been to eliminate the threat. But now that a second chance with her was a real possibility, I was doubly motivated. I had a lot of work to do, and I'd exhausted what I could manage entirely on my own. It was time to call in my team. But first, I needed to invoke protocol.

Pulling out my laptop, I logged into RealmQuest, a popular, massive multiplayer online role-playing game set in a fantasy realm with lots of clans and quests. There were millions of accounts all over the world, so piggybacking on their player messaging system was an easy and nigh untraceable means of contacting my handler. Especially as I'd managed to hack in and add a custom "shop" location that no other player was likely to find. I portaled my character, Echo—a throwback to my call sign—to The Craggy Coast, a remote, rocky beach area in the far northwest corner of one of the upper-level maps. It was a treacherous landscape, filled with cliffs, tide pools, and sea caves, which were home to a multitude of mythical sea creatures like kelpies, selkies, and other threats that could be friend but were more usually foe.

Carefully checking the map to make sure no actual players were around me, I dropped off the side of a cliff and into the water. I had a narrow window of breath to swim my character through a narrow tunnel to a hidden sea cave with no other access. I was down to my last bar of health by the time Echo surfaced inside the cave. Clambering onto shore, I made my way to the other character on the screen, a solitary orc shopkeeper NPC named Grumlik. Functionally, Grumlik sold obscure magical supplies not available anywhere else. It was through his custom order capability that I left my message for a "special order" that was our signal for a meet.

I had no idea how long it might take my handler to get back to me. It had been more than a year since we'd used this channel for communication, and I could only hope it was still being monitored. I was out of the game, and I needed someone on the inside to tell me what had been happening that I couldn't find out myself. I sincerely hoped I hadn't been cut off and hung out to dry. But, even if I had, I knew I could count on my friends. There were no other men I trusted more to watch my back and Ciara's.

Me: Need you both to pop by Ciara's flat.

Finn: Might there be food involved?

Me: There can be.

Food would probably be a good idea. I'd certainly worked up an appetite, and Ciara would be hungry when she woke.

Finn: I'm in.

Callum: What's this about?

Me: Sitrep.

Callum: Understood.

I knew they'd come when they could. Meanwhile, I had a lot of logistics to work out.

Under the circumstances, I wasn't leaving Ciara alone, which meant either I was moving in here, or she was moving in with me. As she had a lot more stuff, and I'd already made some security upgrades to the flat, it made more sense for me to move. I'd just need to pack up some clothes, my computers, and Saffron. I had no idea how she felt about cats, but we'd cross that bridge when we came to it.

I was still working on my list when my friends arrived.

"Keep your voices down, aye? Ciara's resting."

They both stepped inside the flat, then stared at me. Belatedly, it occurred to me I probably looked like I'd been thoroughly shagged because—well—I had. Making myself presentable hadn't been on my radar of priorities, other than making sure I was dressed. They weren't stupid men, but I wouldn't address the issue unless directly asked.

Moving past them, I dropped into the armchair, leaving the sofa for both of them. "I need to read you in."

Predictably, this shifted them into mission mode. I gave them more or less the same story I'd told Ciara, minus the part where she featured in. "I can't get into any more specifics without violating clearances, but it is my belief that Ciara is in danger because of me. And I'm asking for your help to keep her safe."

"Understood," Callum rumbled. "This is your mission. How do you want to handle it?"

"Right now I'm doing what I do best and gathering intelligence. I've got a line into my handler to see if I can find out anything from that side. I need to know the status of certain parties that were involved in this operation before I can begin drilling down on who might be behind this. I've spent the last several days going over the entire scope of my original mission, racking my brain to figure out what I missed from before. Because so far as my superiors and I were concerned, this situation was resolved and everyone who was behind it was dealt with."

"Except, clearly, it's not," Finn pointed out.

"Aye. So, at the moment, security is my biggest concern. Making sure that Ciara has coverage. I'm sorry to leave you two in the lurch with the renovations, but for now, I'll be functioning as her bodyguard. When I can't, I'd appreciate it if one of you could step in. And otherwise, I'd like to set up additional security measures for monitoring."

"When are you going to tell Ewan?"

I didn't have a good answer for that, especially as I knew perfectly well that Callum meant about Ciara and me as a real thing. But I chose to deliberately misinterpret the question.

"I'd rather wait until I have more information."

The bedroom door opened, and I whipped around to warn Ciara that we weren't alone. But she was more aware than I'd given her credit for. Not only was she dressed, but she'd taken the time to wash her face and tidy her hair, so she didn't look thoroughly mussed.

"Hey. Are we having a summit meeting, then?"

"Aye. Something like that. You're going to be under full-time security. One of the three of us—mostly me—will be with you until all this is sorted."

I braced myself for an argument. Ciara was a woman who prized her independence.

But she only nodded.

"Then I guess you'd better go get your cat."

TWENTY-EIGHT

CIARA

I glanced at Alex in the driver's seat. "Are you sure you're okay with this? I know you have your own business and your own work to do."

He reached over to settle a hand on my thigh. "You're my priority until this is sorted. Period. That means I'm your body-guard whenever and wherever you go. Besides, I've got some stuff I can work on from my laptop.

"Like hacker kind of stuff?" We'd talked late into the night, with him filling me in more on the sort of work that was his specialty. When Isobel had been under threat and Ewan had needed information on her manager, Alex had been his go-to source. I was fascinated and curious.

He laughed. "No. That I would not be doing from just anywhere. I'm on hold in that arena until I hear from my handler."

His handler. Because he'd had one of those. It sounded very James Bond, though he'd assured me that the reality was nothing at all like that.

"No, I'll be working on basic stuff for the business. We're

going to need a website, newsletter, that kind of thing. All that stuff is also in my wheelhouse."

"Oh yeah. That makes sense." Kyla was responsible for those things for Ardinmuir Event Planning.

"Before we get there, we should go over what you're going to tell everyone. The fewer people who are aware that your brakes were tampered with, the better. Not that I think any of your family or coworkers were involved, but the fewer people who know, the less likely that information is to spread."

"Right. Of course. The police said the same. I'll just tell them that since I'm without a car, you're playing chauffeur. Easy enough. For bodyguard purposes, do you need to be in the same room or simply on the premises nearby?"

"Same room is easier, but that's harder to explain. I have no reason to believe you won't be safe at the castle, so long as you stay with others and don't leave on your own. So if you can find me a workspace near where you'll be working, I'll be fine. I just need a decent internet connection."

"We can handle that. Go on and park around back. We'll go in through the kitchen. If we're lucky, Angus has been baking. There might be pastries for breakfast."

"I won't say no."

He parked beside Kyla's car.

Before we got out, I laid a hand over his. "There's just one more thing you should know."

"What's that?"

"Given you're here and you're a physically capable individual, there's a very strong possibility you'll get drafted to lift heavy things. Everyone's significant others help with that when they're around."

The corner of his mouth lifted. "I'm happy to do anything and everything as your significant other, Hellcat." He hooked a hand behind my neck and drew me in for a kiss that addled my brain and made me rethink the wisdom of coming to work instead of staying home, where we'd be in close proximity to privacy and horizontal surfaces.

"Remind me why I thought I should come to work?"

"I seem to recall something along the lines of not wanting to leave everyone hanging with the wedding coming up this weekend."

"Right." I reached out to trace a finger over his lips. "Just... put a pin in this for later?"

He nipped the tip of that finger. "Aye, I can do that."

I was grateful for the stiff wind that cooled my cheeks before we stepped into the kitchen.

Angus and Munro were lingering over their morning cuppas and the paper. As I'd hoped, fresh scones were cooling on racks lining the big center island.

"Ciara, love, what are you doing here?" Angus demanded. "You're supposed to be resting!"

I accepted his warm, vanilla-scented hug. "I've rested until I can't rest anymore. Time to get back to work."

Munro was next. He gave me a gentle squeeze and studied me with dark eyes. "You don't look too bad off. Maybe a little tired around the edges."

"Concussions will do that. But I'm on the mend. Promise."

He glanced behind me to where Alex stood just inside the doorway. "I see you've brought your young man. Welcome back to Ardinmuir."

"Thanks. We weren't formally introduced last time I was here. I'm Alex Conroy."

"Good to meet you. You're one of the lot opening the outdoor adventure company in town?"

"I am. You'll have to come down and check us out when we're open. We aim to have something for everyone."

"We'll have to do that." Angus draped an arm around his husband. "Have to try new things to keep ourselves young."

I leaned in to kiss both their cheeks. "Neither of you will ever be old."

Angus's cheeks pinked. "Oh, go on now."

"Only if I can steal a scone for the road, as it were."

"Take as many as you like, lass."

"You're the best!" I snagged two. When Alex started to move on by, I gave him a pointed look. "If you want one, you'll need to grab your own. These are both for me." To emphasize the point, I took a big bite. "Mmm. Apple cinnamon."

"So it's like that, is it? Fine, fine." Grinning, he picked up a scone for himself and followed me out of the kitchen.

I'd already devoured my first one by the time we made it to the office. Kyla, Afton, and Sophie were in the middle of a meeting when I strode in.

"What are you doing here?" Kyla demanded.

"Last time I checked, I still work here."

"But you were injured," Sophie insisted.

"I'm going stir crazy at home. I can work, and I want to work. So here I am."

They all looked past me to Alex.

"Alex is playing chauffeur for me right now since I'm without a car. I'm waiting for insurance to process my claim, and that might take a while."

He lifted a hand in a wave.

"He's got some work of his own to see to, but he'll be around and available to do any heavy lifting, should we need him."

"Happy to help," he seconded. "Where do you want me to set up?"

"I was thinking he could borrow your office, Sophie? He

needs decent internet, and I know it's spotty in various parts of the castle."

"Of course. That's fine. I'll show you where to go. It's just down the hall."

When Sophie started to rise, I waved her back down. "No, no. I've got it. No reason to make you fight gravity if you don't have to."

"Do you want some tea or coffee to go with your scone before you go?"

"I'll be fine. I can make my way back to the kitchen if I need to."

"Are you sure? Because there are a lot of twists and turns between here and there, and I promise you'll want another of those scones once you taste it."

"I navigated the Amazon jungle in the dark with no gear. I think I can make it back to the kitchen."

I blinked at him. "Why is that so hot?"

His smile spread, slow and wicked. "Competence porn."

"Yeah, we're having a conversation later about why you even know what that is. Come on, Mr. I Don't Need Directions. I'll show you to Sophie's office."

Once I got him settled and set up with the Wi-Fi password, I went back to get to work myself.

"Okay, catch me up. Where are we on this weekend's event?"

All three of them were staring at me in expectation.

"What?"

Sophie just arched a brow. "That didn't look very fake to me."

I thought of what had happened between us yesterday and fought not to blush. "We've gotten close," I admitted.

"How close?" Kyla asked.

The blush was a losing battle. "A girl doesn't kiss and tell."

"I'm betting he's a hell of a kisser," Afton sighed.

"You're pregnant and married," Kyla reminded her.

"Exactly. Pregnant and married. Not dead. You heard him. Competence porn. It's attractive for a reason."

I really needed them to stop talking about Alex and any kind of porn in the same sentence. "Right, well, Ewan still doesn't know, and it's going to stay that way until I can talk to him in person myself. I'm not at all sure how he'll handle the idea of me dating one of his mates. So, can we just table this and get to work?"

TWENTY-NINE

ALEX

By mid-afternoon, I'd set up a decent shell of a website for the adventure company. I'd be able to do more once we settled on an actual name. For the moment, I had it hosted under a private sandbox, so I could build and tweak to my heart's content without worrying about anyone seeing the work in progress.

Because I'd hit a stopping point, I logged into RealmQuest, making my way back to Grumlik's cave to check the message board for a reply from my handler. A scroll icon hovered above Grumlik's head. Thank God.

I opened the message.

Re: Your custom order

I would be honored to take your commission, but the price is not cheap. 1600 rubies. Please return when you have gathered the fee from the usual places, and I shall begin.

So Cardinal would call at 4 PM from a secured line.

I checked my watch. Ten minutes. I needed somewhere more private, where no one was likely to walk in on me. Shutting down the game, I went to check on Ciara. She was buried in a mountain of notes.

"I have a call coming in shortly. I'm going to be out of pocket for a little while. Don't go anywhere."

Her salute was distracted, but I was confident enough that she'd heard me. I wandered my way through the castle, keeping an eye on the signal from my mobile. In a place this size, I wasn't concerned about surveillance. There was no reason to believe that whoever was behind this had gained access, and there was too much ground to cover to properly surveil the place on the off-chance that they'd get information on Ciara. In the end, I ducked into a room in the older part of the castle. This section was built of rough-hewn stone and, according to what Kyla had mentioned at lunch, it dated back to the sixth century. Some other time I'd geek out over the full suits of armor and ancient weapons I found. For now, my focus was on what was coming.

The call came in precisely at 1600.

"Hello?"

The voice on the other end began the official coded exchange. "The falcon can't find purchase."

"When the cliff face crumbles."

"Leaving only the valley below."

"Or the open sky above."

"We still have a lot of ground to cover."

"And a long trail to blaze," I finished.

"This is Cardinal. What is your status, Echo?"

"Echo is secure. Thanks for getting back to me, Cardinal."

"I have to confess, I was surprised to hear from you."

"Aye. I was hoping we'd never have cause to communicate again, but the situation has changed."

"How?"

As succinctly as possible, I explained what had happened. "I need to know if everyone who was documented as involved with the op is still incarcerated."

"Standby, I'll check." The clear clicking of keys sounded over the line as my handler accessed systems I didn't have clearance to check myself.

"All targets are locked up tight. What makes you think this situation has anything to do with us?"

"My father died while I was running this mission."

"That was ruled an accident."

"You and I both know such things are easy to change. I couldn't get access to his vehicle to verify my suspicions. I didn't make that mistake again. Her brakes were sabotaged by a professional. We're talking about a woman who works for an event planning company. She's twenty-five. She hasn't led the kind of life or met the sort of people who do such a thing. I'm the common denominator here."

"What are you suggesting, Echo?"

"I'm wondering if there's any way that any of the primary actors could have connections on the outside who might be willing to exact payback on their behalf. There are bound to be a lot of people who are angry with me for the role I played in taking them and their organization down. I cost them a lot of money. They shouldn't have been aware that it was me behind it, but my original aliases should never have been leaked, either."

"Well, you and I both know that we should never say never in this business. That said, a multitude of efforts have been made to prevent such things. But I'll certainly look into it and let you know what I find out. Replies will come through the usual channels."

"Thanks, Cardinal. I appreciate it."

"You were an asset to your country, Echo. You deserve better than this. Cardinal out."

He was gone before I could say anything else.

I paced a restless circuit of the room, not feeling any better than I had before. If my handler said he'd look into it, I trusted he would. But I couldn't shake the sense that he thought I was simply being paranoid.

Was I?

There was no question someone was out to hurt Ciara. But who? And why? I couldn't fathom that she'd pissed off someone enough to do this. Her being targeted because of me was the only thing that made sense in this scenario.

But maybe I should go back to Brodie. Do a deeper dive into the man. Maybe there was something under the surface that I hadn't found yet and hadn't considered. Maybe Brodie Drummond wasn't who he seemed to be.

No closer to clear answers, I struggled to throw off my frustration as I wound my way through the labyrinthine halls of the castle, back to the area the event planning company used as an office, thus proving that competence I'd teased Ciara about this morning.

"As two of the four of us are pregnant, and one is barely recovered from a concussion, I'm calling us done for the day," Kyla announced.

"I'm for that." Ciara rubbed at her neck.

"I'm at a good stopping place, too. Ready to leave whenever you are. I just need to pack up my laptop." I crossed over and closed my hands over her shoulders and neck, digging my fingers into the knots there.

She made a whimpering noise. "We can leave in a century or two, when you've finished with that."

"I'd say you've earned some of Dom's cottage pie and *Gilmore Girls* reruns."

Ciara cracked an eye, tipping her head back to look up at me. "Are you trying to win points?"

"Trying? No. It's just completely natural."

"I'd be annoyed at that cocky attitude, but this feels too good."

"Speaking of dinner..." Sophie drawled.

"Were we?" Ciara wanted to know.

"Someone's talking food, and as previously mentioned, I'm pregnant. So yes, that means we were talking dinner. Don't argue with the preggo logic."

"Understood. Speaking of dinner?" Ciara prompted.

"Family dinner is tomorrow night. You should bring Alex."

"We're hosting," Kyla added.

My hands stilled. "Family dinner?"

"She means she wants to introduce you to all the husbands in connection to me. Honestly, it's probably a good trial run before we tell my brother."

I'd been trained to survive literal torture. I could handle this just fine. Right?

"I'd be happy to."

THIRTY

CIARA

It took me less than twenty-four hours to have second thoughts about the wisdom of subjecting Alex to friend-family dinner.

"I'm not that far out from injury. I can just text them to say I'm not feeling well, and we can stay home."

Alex skimmed his hands from my shoulders down to lace his fingers with mine. "Is it because we have to go over the gorge bridge to get there? You haven't been back since the accident."

"Well, shite, I hadn't even thought of that." And I didn't plan to start now. "No, I'm trying to protect you."

He slanted me a bemused look. "Don't be such a feartie. I'm a big lad. I can handle myself." The suggestive eyebrow waggle took any sting out of the teasing.

"Aye, I'm well aware of exactly how well you can handle yourself." I was still thinking about the demonstration of... er... competence he'd treated me to when we'd gotten home last night. "But this isn't about your capability. This is about all the men of my extended found family being frustrated that they didn't know about us sooner and taking it out on you. I really don't know how they're going to behave."

His dark eyes searched my face. "Are you having regrets about changing the dynamic between us, Hellcat? It's all right if you have. You've been through a lot the last several days. If you want to change your mind—"

I pressed a finger to his lips. "I'm not changing my mind about you. About us. God knows, it took us long enough to get here. I just... feel weird lying to people. Not only about when and how we met, but about the nature of the threat to me."

"Would you prefer to introduce me as the incredible shag you had three years ago?" His arched brows underscored the absurdity of the notion.

"Sarcasm is not appreciated, sir."

"Who's being sarcastic? It *was* an incredible shag. I believe there were multiple orgasms on your part to prove it."

"Six. So not the point."

"Ah, so you *do* remember," he teased.

"Alex."

"Sorry. I understand your frustration. But explaining that we knew each other before also means explaining why we didn't admit it. and why you were angry with me. It's just... complicated. As to the rest, spreading the word that your brakes were tampered with would likely result in a lot of alarmist behavior that would get you even more on lockdown than you already are with me."

I blew out a breath. "I know. I just... I'm ready for something to be simple."

The mouth that haunted my dreams curled into a smile. "You aren't a simple woman, Ciara McBride. Simple would bore you inside of five minutes. It's one of the things I love about you. Now come on. Get your bag. I'll get the food. You can brief me on who everybody is on the drive."

When he nudged me toward the table where I'd left my purse, I went, but my brain was still stuck on what he'd said.

It's one of the things I love about you.

That wasn't the same thing as loving me. Being *in* love with me. But it didn't stop my heart from leaping into a hopeful gallop. I knew I mattered to him beyond just being Ewan's sister. He wouldn't be going to all these lengths to protect me personally if I didn't. I knew I was more than obligation and guilt over the past.

But I wanted more than that. I wanted that timeless, forever kind of love I saw in my parents. In Ewan and Isobel. Among the rest of my circle of friends who I considered family —those who'd be part of tonight's probable interrogation. It was what I'd always wanted. I'd wasted so much time fooling myself that I could grow into this with Brodie. But that wasn't how it worked. The roots were either there or they weren't.

I'd believed they'd been there when Alex and I had met on that train, and then they'd been brutally ripped out. Initially, I'd told myself that this time with him would be the closure I hadn't gotten before. But those damaged roots had found the lingering cracks in the wall I'd built between us and dug in deep, reaching all the way to the heart he'd bruised and wrapping it tight. I was in over my head with him. Again. Maybe I always had been. But I had to hope that when the threat was over, I wouldn't find myself in this alone.

"Are you ready?" Alex stood by the door, the plasticware container of salad I'd made under one arm.

Not even a little bit.

"Yeah." Grabbing my purse, I watched him set the alarm, then we headed out the door.

As he'd asked, I gave him a quick overview of who everyone was and how they were connected.

"Okay, so you've already met my cousin Kyla. She's married to Raleigh Beaumont, the current Baron of Lochmara."

"Beaumont doesn't sound especially Scottish."

"It's not, though he's got Scots heritage on his mother's side. He's a cowboy from Texas, who won the estate from Afton in a high-stakes poker game in Vegas."

"From Afton?"

"Well, more properly, she threw the game because she'd hand-picked him to be her successor. She was supposed to marry Kyla's brother, Connor, because of a three-hundred-year-old marriage pact; otherwise, both estates would've been forfeit to the Crown. When Afton pulled a runaway bride, which put Kyla in the hot seat with Raleigh, and they had to enter a marriage of convenience to fulfill the terms of the pact. They'd planned to divorce in a year, but ended up falling in love with each other instead. Connor, as it turned out, was actually in love with Kyla's best friend, Sophie, so it all worked out in the end."

"How exactly did Afton end up back here after all that?"

"Oh, she showed back up at Connor and Sophie's wedding. There was a moment when everyone thought she'd come back to object, but it was just poor timing of her arrival, as the ceremony had already started. Turned out *she'd* always been in love with Hamish, who's Connor's best mate."

"You've been on hand for a bloody soap opera."

I grinned. "It hasn't been dull. Of course, you've met Kyla and Connor's great uncle Angus and his husband Munro. Total second chance romance there. Angus is also a former semifinalist on *The Great British Bake Off*."

"That explains the Jaffa cakes."

"Then there's also Charlotte Vasquez, Raleigh's second mum, who followed him over from Texas and ended up married to Malcolm Niall, the estate manager at Lochmara.

They have a foster son, Gavin, who's about to head off to his first year of uni."

He frowned in intense concentration. "Anyone else?"

Watching him listen intently, with a clear ear toward memorizing everything I'd told him, was rather fascinating. It was a good distraction from the fact that we did, indeed, have to cross over the gorge bridge on the way to Lochmara. I white-knuckled it the whole way, but I made it to the other side without giving in to the anxiety that settled in my gut at the sight of it.

Because I'd faffed about, we were the last to arrive at the manor house. Alex parked beside Hamish's car, and I led him to the kitchen entrance. This was family, so I didn't knock, simply opened the door and stepped into the chaos that seemed a bit more pronounced than usual. People were everywhere. Lily, Kyla and Raleigh's daughter, who was now two, was racing around barefoot, in nothing but a nappy, shrieking in glee as her father gave chase.

"We've got a runner!" he announced.

Lily darted behind Hamish and ducked under the kitchen table, followed by Dugal, the family dog, who thought this was a marvelous game.

A harried Kyla wandered in with a wet shirt and some piece of child's clothing in hand. "She's slippery as an eel, that one. Lily, love, you have to put on clothes for dinner."

Connor crouched at the edge of the table. "C'mon, wee one. Uncle Connor will protect you."

Lily crawled out, lifting her arms in the universal gesture for "Up!"

My cousin scooped her into his arms and promptly blew on her belly. His niece erupted in more giggles before he passed her off to Sophie, who pressed smacking kisses to both of Lily's cheeks, before passing her on to Munro. And so it went, from adult to adult, until the squirmy wee tyke landed in my arms.

"Are you having a laugh at your mum and da?" I asked her.

"Yeah!"

I settled her on my hip and peppered her face with kisses, delighting in the little girl's laughter. When she spotted Alex, her giggles faded, and the golden-brown eyes she'd gotten from her father fixed on him.

"Who dat?"

Leave it to the toddler to get straight to the point.

"That's my special friend, Alex."

"Is that what they're calling it these days?" Connor muttered.

I ignored him and pivoted toward Alex. "Can you say hello?"

"'Lo." She reached for him.

To my utter shock, Alex didn't hesitate a moment before plucking her up. "You must be Lily."

She nodded soberly and promptly stuck her fingers in her mouth.

"I have a wee niece a little older than you. Do you know what she loves?"

"Wha?"

"Putting on a fashion show for dinner. She wears something different every night."

Lily's eyes rounded. "Show, dada!"

Raleigh came to collect his offspring with a look of grudging respect. "Well played. Let's go pick out your outfit so we can eat. Grandma Charlotte made your favorite mashed potatoes."

"Tatties!"

They exited the kitchen, and suddenly everyone was staring at us. I immediately wished for my wiggly wee shield again. "Right. Everyone, this is Alex Conroy. Alex, this is most of my extended family. I believe you've met several of them already."

"Your special friend," Connor repeated.

I fixed him with an infinitely patient expression. "Do you want to explain the nuance of 'boyfriend' to a two-year-old?"

"I'm guessing you're Connor MacKean. You're a blacksmith, aye? I've seen the sword you made for Ewan. It's incredible work. Do you take commissions?"

Some of my cousin's belligerence faded. "I do."

"We should talk."

By the time the rest of the formal introductions were made, Raleigh was back, a pajamaed Lily riding his shoulders, with a miniature tiara in her red curls.

"What are we actually having tonight?" I asked.

"Steak," Raleigh announced, with all the satisfaction of a lifelong cattleman.

"Can I do anything?" Alex offered. "Light the barbecue?"

Raleigh, who'd been on his way to the door to step outside to do the honors himself, froze as the rest of us collectively groaned.

"Now you've done it," Connor muttered.

Raleigh turned, hand over his heart, a look of deep pity etched on his face. "My good man, you must be educated. Barbecue is a thing that you cook or method of cooking. The device on which it is done is a grill or a smoker."

"Please don't get him started," Kyla begged.

"You don't argue with the results of what comes off of my grill," Raleigh drawled.

She rose to kiss his cheek. "That is absolutely true. Go man your steaks, love."

I leaned toward Alex. "I did mention he was from Texas, aye?"

THIRTY-ONE
ALEX

"I'm not going."

Ciara met my announcement with a patient stare. "Who's being feartie now?"

"I'm not afraid. But I don't like leaving you alone. We both know Brodie's behind this latest rash of petty shite."

"That's exactly it," she protested. "Petty shite. So I'm getting more junk mail and subscriptions. And there's that bit of identity theft that's already being dealt with. All things from a distance. It's annoying, but not dangerous. There have been no more direct threats from anywhere. There's no reason for you not to go to poker night."

The family dinner I'd attended last week had gone well, and Ciara's contingent of stand-in brothers had generally behaved. As we'd been leaving, they'd invited me to their monthly poker night. I knew what it really was—an opportunity to interrogate or intimidate me without the women present. I hadn't one hundred percent committed, but I hadn't clearly said no either. In truth, I'd expected more actual need of my bodyguard services, but there'd been no further attempts on her life.

"I can't justify asking Finn or Callum to keep watch on you just to go hang out and play poker."

"You don't have to. I'm literally going to be downstairs with my girlfriends. The Kilt Lifters are playing tonight, so the pub will be packed with women. I've loved spending all this one-on-one time with you, but this is all part of my normal life, Alex. I feel like I've let Brodie take too much of that from me already."

I couldn't argue with that. Despite my efforts, I'd dug up nothing further to suggest who might have been behind the sabotage of her car. My gut said it wasn't a one-off, but I knew I couldn't keep her under lock and key.

"Fine. I'll go. But I'm walking you down to the pub myself. And if you need *anything*—"

"I'll call or text you." She rose to her toes and brushed her lips to mine. "You deserve to have a night off yourself."

I wasn't sure this qualified, but I wouldn't put that on her.

As she'd predicted, The Stag's Head was absolutely packed full of women. I escorted her toward the back of the pub, where the tiny stage was set up. Saoirse, Skye, and Pippa had already commandeered a table in the corner with a direct view of the band.

"There now. I'm safely here. You can go."

I fixed her friends with a heavy stare. "You'll look out for her, aye?"

"If the deplorable Brodie shows up and causes problems, you can rest assured that we'll take care of it. I'm a vet. I know where all the pig farms are," Saoirse declared.

Satisfied with that, I hooked my hand behind Ciara's nape and pulled her in for a long, lingering kiss that was as much a display for any gents present who might get ideas about her availability, as because I needed my own fix to hold me over. Her blue eyes were satisfyingly blurry when I eased back.

"Something to think about while I'm gone."

The incoherent noise she uttered made me smile as I nudged her toward the waiting chair.

"I'll see you later, Hellcat."

"Later," she murmured.

Her friends were grinning like Cheshire cats, and I suspected she was in for her own interrogation the moment I was out of earshot. I was okay with that.

The drive out to Hamish's only took about ten minutes. He and Afton lived in a sprawling old farmhouse that had clearly been added onto repeatedly over the last couple of centuries. A barn sat off to one side with several goats milling about inside the fence.

Huh. Hamish hadn't struck me as the farm animal type.

I parked beside the cluster of other vehicles and headed toward what appeared to be the main door, though all the additions made it a little hard to tell.

Hamish himself answered my knock. "Come in. You're just in time. We're about to deal."

I followed him back to the kitchen, where a truly impressive spread of food was laid out on the counter. I glanced from it to Hamish. "Afton?"

"Aye. We're her grateful guinea pigs."

"You're a lucky man."

"Don't I know it. Beer? Whisky?"

"No, thanks."

Raleigh shuffled the cards. "Not a drinker?"

I started to say I never drank when on duty, but that would've brought up more questions than I cared to answer. I wouldn't consider myself truly off duty again until I knew the threat to Ciara was past. "Seems smarter to keep my wits about me with you lot."

"I hope you came prepared to lose," Connor announced from the table.

I grabbed an Irn Bru from the cooler and took a vacant chair. "Honestly, I came expecting to be interrogated."

Hamish dropped into the chair beside me. "We can do that and take your money, too."

"We're multi-talented like that," Raleigh added.

"Get to it, then," I prompted. "No reason to delay."

"You know Texas Hold 'Em?" Raleigh asked.

"I'm familiar with most forms of poker." It was one of the few forms of easy entertainment we'd had on deployment. But no need to mention that.

He began to deal.

"So, I've noticed you haven't actually been staying in the flat you're leasing from me," Hamish said. "You're spending all of your time—including your nights—at Ciara's."

I swept up the cards I'd been dealt and began putting them in order. "That wouldn't be anybody's business but ours. She's a grown adult." Aware they were all staring at me with various shades of disapproval, I continued. "And given all the harassment she's had from her ex and whoever ran her off the road, I'm no' particularly keen on leaving her alone to give someone another shot."

As I'd hoped, that effectively shut down any *What are your intentions?* lines of questioning.

"Do we need to have a... conversation with Brodie?" Raleigh asked.

The pause before "conversation" made it clear he intended to let his fists speak for him. I knew I liked this cowboy.

"I already did. Not sure it did any good." I didn't want to admit the fact that Ciara's crash had happened after that confrontation. I didn't believe I'd set him off enough to go after her like that. If the target had been me, maybe. But I didn't like the proximity of the two events.

Hamish started the betting and slid a stack of three chips to the center of the table. "We could file a non-harassment order."

"Probably not a bad idea." I checked my cards and added my own bet. This was an opportunity to get different perspectives on Brodie. "You were all around while Ciara was dating Drummond. What are your perceptions?"

"Never thought much about him at all, to be honest," Connor admitted.

"He was just kinda there," Raleigh added. "But we didn't see any red flags while they were dating. He seemed okay. He certainly didn't seem like the kinda guy who'd run somebody off the road."

"Officially, he has an alibi," I pointed out.

"You sound like you don't believe it," Hamish said.

"I'm no' sure what I believe at this point."

I'd done my deeper digging. There was no record of him owning or having access to a dark 4x4. And while the additional evidence of his continued obsession was worrisome, I couldn't find anything tying him to the accident. Which just supported my original theory rather than the paranoia my handler had suggested.

He hadn't come back with any information yet, and I was starting to wonder if he ever would.

We laid down our cards. Connor won the pot with an ace high flush. He gathered his chips, and Raleigh began to shuffle again.

I swirled my finger through the condensation on my drink. "Is there anybody else you can think of that Ciara might have got on the wrong side of? Someone who might hold a grudge for any reason?"

"Nobody who'd have the kind of grudge worth threatening her life," Connor said. "All I can think of is small, schoolgirl shite from back when she was in high school. She found out a group in her class had stolen the test in their chemistry class in order to cheat and outed them. Torpedoed their grade in that class and landed them with a mark on their records. But everyone involved is either gone or married now."

"That doesn't exactly sound like a smoking gun," I agreed.

"Are the police any closer to finding out who's responsible?" Hamish asked.

"I've kept in close contact with Constable Williamson. The police are still looking for the vehicle that struck her. They put a notice in the area asking people to report any dark-colored SUVs with damage to their front bumpers. So far, none of the leads have played out."

"Yeah, but there's a lot of empty stretches of land up here," Raleigh said. "Seems like plenty of places to hide something like an SUV, if you're motivated enough."

"That's one of my concerns. And until we have answers or confirmation that whoever is behind this has been neutralized, I'm sticking close."

Raleigh dealt the next hand. "Well, we can't rightly fault you for that. But aren't you worried about the code?"

"The code?"

"Ewan's one of your best mates, aye?" Connor prompted.

"Says the man who married his sister's best friend?" I asked.

"Not the same thing," he insisted.

"Look, Ciara is a grown woman who can make her own choices. She's not property. She doesn't need her parents' or brother's permission to date someone. More to the point, she matters to me a great deal. At the end of the day, regardless of how Ewan may end up feeling about it when he finds out—and she's asked me not to tell him because she wants to talk to him herself, so I'd appreciate it if the three of you would keep this to yourselves—that's the only thing that matters."

The three men exchanged a look, then nodded.

"Good enough for us," Raleigh announced. "Let's play some poker."

THIRTY-TWO

CIARA

Saoirse fanned herself. "I think I'm getting second-hand scorch marks from you two."

Skye laced her hands together and bounced in her chair with a squee. "I'm so happy for you!"

"To she who is clearly getting all the orgasms," Pippa lifted her glass.

My brain was finally coming back online from that public claiming Alex had laid on me. "I don't even have anything to toast with."

"Shut up. We're having a moment of silence for your good fortune," Saoirse intoned.

My friends clinked glasses and drank.

"Now, tell us everything," Saoirse insisted. "And don't spare any smutty details. Some of us are living vicariously through you right now."

I snickered. "Your love of smut is a source of never-ending amusement to me."

"I don't have time for an actual man in my life, so I get my needs met where I can," she said primly.

Pippa leaned in. "So tell us... is he as... intense as he seems? He seems like a very... focused individual."

"If I'm gonna say anything at all about his... focus or intensity, I am definitely going to need a drink. Be right back."

Their collective groans followed me as I made my way through the throngs to the bar. As was always the case when The Kilt Lifters performed, the pub was utterly packed. Some came lured by the name to find out whether they lived up to the inherent promise. Some came because—spoiler alert—they did live up to that promise. Jason and his two mates, Ollie and Cal, ended every show by flashing their bums at the audience. It never failed to bring down the house. But a surprising lot of people came because they put on a rip-roaring fun show doing bagpipe covers of boy band songs.

The band had already started their first set by the time I made it back to the table with my pint, so I was saved from the interrogation about my love life. Under normal circumstances, I wouldn't be averse to sharing something, but things with Alex were too new. We hadn't discussed any kind of long-term future. We'd only just sort of gotten to the acknowledgment that this thing between us was real, and we wanted a chance at the thing we'd both sensed three years ago.

It was good to be out and about, at least a little. Life had felt suffocating the past few months, as I'd started changing more and more of my habits to avoid Brodie. I knew the bodyguard routine Alex had been in for the past week couldn't last forever. At some point, I'd be getting another car, and going back to my life. Tonight was a tiny step toward reclaiming normal.

By the band's first break, we'd gotten several appetizers to split, and Pippa had retrieved another round of drinks.

Skye picked up the conversation as if a half hour hadn't passed. "So, it hasn't escaped our notice that Alex has basically moved in with you."

I choked on the haggis pot sticker I'd popped into my mouth.

"Aye, what's going on with that?" Pippa asked.

Washing down the food with the last of my original pint, I pounded my own chest until I could properly breathe again. "He hasn't moved in." Though his toothbrush had definitely taken up residence next to mine, and his kitten had made herself right at home, officially, he was still living out of a bag. "He's just staying with me right now out of an abundance of caution. He's playing bodyguard and chauffeur in the wake of my accident."

Their chorus of sighs was loud enough to be heard over the crowd.

"I knew he was a good man the moment he volunteered to keep that kitten," Saoirse declared.

"He's just got the look about him. So attentive. Not to mention he looks at you like you're his favorite flavor popsicle," Skye giggled. "Oh, sorry. Ice lolly."

I will not imagine him licking me. I will not imagine him licking me...

Saoirse hooted. "I'd say she is, and the consequences are well worth it."

Oh my God, my face was on fire.

"Right. On that note, I need to run upstairs and check on Saffron." I didn't need any such thing, but I pushed back from the table, anyway. Maybe a few minutes with my head stuck in the freezer would see me fit to be in other people's company again.

Pippa pushed back, too. "I'll come with you."

I waved her down. "No, no, there's no reason. Look, the band is starting the next set. Stay and enjoy the show. I'm just going to slip out the back. It's literally ten feet to my stairs. Back in a wee bit."

From the stage, the guys rocked out to their version of the Backstreet Boys' "Everybody." People got up and started to dance beside their tables. I slipped through the crowd with the ease of habit from all the time I'd spent here as waitstaff. Without hesitation, I pushed through the kitchen door into Dom Bassey's domain.

He looked up from where he chopped onions with precision at the prep table. "Ciara, my love. To what do I owe the pleasure?"

I paused to buss his bristly dark cheek. "I'm using the back exit to pop up to my flat for a bit."

"You stop in for a visit on your way back down." He let more of his native West Africa slide into his voice as he gave the order.

"I will absolutely do that."

Moving by him, I hustled down the short hall, past the cooler and the pantry, and out the back door. The moment it shut behind me, I paused and inhaled a deep lungful of the chilly evening air. A breeze blew down the alley that ran behind the businesses on this side of the high street, cooling my burning cheeks.

My lungs gradually expanded, and I realized I'd been more anxious about being out in public without my trusty bodyguard than I'd realized. Points to Alex for his concern on that front. But I'd done okay. And I'd be fine again after a few minutes alone. Guilt propelled me toward my stairs so my little fib didn't stay a lie. I'd just look in on the kitten, maybe get a few minutes of cuddles, then come back for the rest of the show.

The faint scuff of a shoe was the only warning I got before an arm snaked around my throat from behind. I didn't stop to think, didn't question, I simply reacted, falling back on the training my brother had drilled into me. I dropped my chin and reached for the arm with one hand to protect my airway, then stepped wide to drop into a riding stance. I drove my elbow back hard into my attacker's gut. Feeling his hold loosen, I spun, catching him across the nose with a ridge hand. Something crunched and my assailant screamed.

As he staggered back, clutching his face behind the dark mask, I could've run, but I was so over this shite. I closed the distance, catching him in the ribs with a roundhouse. When he snarled at me and reached toward me again, I grabbed his hand and torqued it in a direction that was entirely unnatural. The man dropped like a stone, screaming again. I kept twisting until he'd flopped over onto his belly, and I pressed a knee into his back. Maintaining the arm bar, I used my free hand to pull off my belt and tie his hands behind him. Then I yanked off the ski mask covering his head.

And though a part of me had expected it, I still stumbled back when I saw his familiar, if bloody, face. "Brodie?"

"You bitch! You broke my fucking nose!"

"You attacked me, you wanker!"

"You were *mine*," he snarled.

When he started to get up, I scrambled over and drove my knee into his back again, pressing him to the pavement. "You're not going anywhere."

Under a hail of invective, I dragged my phone from my pocket, relieved it hadn't flown out during the struggle. With a deep breath, I dialed 999.

"I'd like to report an assault."

THIRTY-THREE
ALEX

"I thought you said you were good at poker." Raleigh raked in his pile of chips, which put him tied with Connor for current winner.

"Perhaps I'm a wee bit out of practice." Or I'd let them win. I was down nearly twenty quid, but I'd managed to establish a reasonable rapport with the other men in Ciara's life. I considered that a worthy tradeoff.

"You should have more snacks. That makes the losing a lot more palatable," Hamish assured me.

"I wouldn't say no to more of those egg rolls." I was just heading to refill my plate when my mobile rang. Ciara's name flashed across the screen. "Hey. Are you all right?"

She hesitated before answering, and in that pause was every fear, every terror that haunted my nights. "Ciara? What happened?"

"First off, I'm okay."

Every thought of the game fled my brain as I shifted into mission mode. "What. Happened?"

"Brodie's been arrested."

For just a moment, shock overrode everything. Then logic caught up and my hands curled into fists. "What did that fucking wankstain do?"

She hesitated too long again before finally answering. "He attacked me outside the pub."

I held in the fountain of curses I wanted to spew about what the hell she'd been doing outside the pub at all when I'd expressly told her not to leave. We'd have a conversation about that later. After I'd finished burning the world down and sorted how to break into the police station to rip the bastard's arms off and beat him to death—angry-Wookie style.

"Where are you?" All other noise in the room had ceased, which told me everything I needed to know about the fact that my tone had dropped into I-will-fuck-up-someone's-shite territory. Every cell in my body shouted at me to move, to get to her, but my training stopped me from going off half-cocked.

"The police station. The girls are with me."

Which meant she wasn't in imminent danger and likely wasn't too badly hurt. That was something. "Are they okay? Were they also attacked?" Had there been multiple assailants? Or was Drummond foolish enough to go up against a group?

"No. They were inside when it happened. I was just running upstairs to the flat and got jumped in the alley behind the pub."

It didn't matter that I'd given her explicit orders. She should've been able to do that. She shouldn't have had to worry about any of this at all. But I hadn't done my job well enough to protect her. I hadn't managed to put a stop to the threat.

Self-recriminations had to wait.

"Alex, I swear I'm okay. I took him down myself."

That had me pausing. "You... did?"

"Aye."

I'd be proud of that later, but right now, I needed to lay eyes on her. To make sure she was okay. "I'm on my way."

When I ended the call, I turned to find the rest of my poker-playing compatriots on their feet.

"What happened?" Connor demanded.

"Drummond attacked her outside the pub. Apparently, she took him down herself."

Raleigh nodded in approval. "That's our girl."

"The police have him in custody. I'm going to pick her up."

As they all moved en masse toward the door, I held up a hand. "She swears she's okay. Either way, she won't want an entourage or a mob with pitchforks." And I didn't need any more witnesses if I lost my shite.

"Let us know what you find out," Hamish said. It wasn't a request.

I nodded and rushed out.

When I strode into the police station ten minutes later, I'd already come up with two dozen ways to ruin Brodie Drummond's life. What little would be left of it after I tore him into little pieces. All plans of vengeance faded as I spotted Ciara sitting in the visitor's chair across from one of the desks in the small station, surrounded by her girlfriends, who all wore shades of concern on their faces.

"Alex." She rose as I approached. I was already scanning her from head to toe, looking for even the slightest scratch or new bruise, but all I saw were the fading marks from the accident before she walked straight into my arms.

I curled around her, careful not to hold too tight in case there were injuries I couldn't see. "You're not hurt?"

"I told you, I'm okay. He took the worst of it."

"You fought back."

"Damned straight." She pulled back far enough to look up at me. "You've met my brother. He equipped me very early on, before I went to university, for how to defend against unwanted advances. I just choose to avoid that most of the time." One corner of her mouth lifted. "I broke his nose."

It wasn't death, but the idea of it gave me an unreasonable amount of satisfaction. Having any woman hand him his arse would have been demoralizing for Brodie. Having it be her? Aye, that was a step in the right direction in terms of retribution.

"It's better than he deserves," Saoirse sniffed.

Pippa wrung her hands. "I should have come with you."

"We all should have come with you," Skye added.

"If you'd come with me, he might not have tried this, and he might not have been arrested," Ciara argued. "And I almost certainly wouldn't have gotten to break his nose."

"Arrest isn't conviction," I warned. Far too often, men who raised their hands against women were released to do it all over again.

She squeezed my hands. "I already got them the footage from the security cameras you installed. He's going to get into legitimate trouble from all this."

"I can confirm that." Constable Williamson stepped out from the hall. "I've just gotten off the phone with the judge. Because of his alibi for the time of the accident, we couldn't get a warrant before, but we've got one now. We'll be searching his property for any evidence of that dark SUV or proof that he hired someone. Regardless of what we find there, thanks to that video footage, we've nailed him for assault. He'll do time for that, and I can promise you, if there's something else to find to buy him a longer stay behind bars, I will find it."

"Thank you, Constable. We really appreciate it," Ciara told her. "You'll keep us in the loop?"

"Of course." Williamson turned to me and flashed a fierce

smile. "You should be proud of your partner. She managed a hell of a takedown. His face is a mess."

I'd work my way around to proud once I got past the fact that he'd had a chance to get to her at all.

"Will he be released on bail?"

"That'll be decided at the hearing, but I intend to push for no. We've got proof of escalation, and God willing, we'll find more evidence by the time he sees the judge after the weekend. For at least the next few days, you've certainly got a breather," Williamson said.

Did we? Was Drummond actually behind it all, as my handler had suggested? Or would this search for additional evidence be some kind of wild goose chase because the local police didn't and couldn't know about the potential outside threat?

A door opened, and another officer escorted Brodie out of what must have been an interrogation room. He truly looked like shit, with bruising along his nose and across both cheeks. Bloody tissues were shoved up his nostrils.

"I want a doctor before I choke on my own blood. And a solicitor."

"We've got a call in to Dr. Donaldson," Constable Williamson told him. "You'll get seen when you get seen."

His attention jerked toward her and from there to Ciara.

"Fucking bitch. You've pushed me too far! Everyone will agree!" Despite the handcuffs, he squirmed in the officer's hold.

I was still mentally assessing whether I'd be liable for assault myself if he broke free and I "apprehended him" with excessive force when the officer hauled him down another hallway where I could just see the edge of a cell.

"Wanker," Saoirse snarled softly.

"May someone sneak him a laxative milkshake," Skye added.

"I hope that's all the excitement we get for a while." Pippa moved to Ciara and wrapped an arm around her shoulders. "I'm glad he's been caught."

"You and me both. Thank you all for coming. Sorry I put a bit of a damper on girls' night."

"Are you kidding? I think this is inspiring me to sign up for a self-defense class." Skye looked at me. "I figure you maybe know someone who can help with that."

"Aye, I can do that." Making sure they could all defend themselves would give me something active to do in the face of a threat I wasn't at all convinced was over.

Ciara turned to Williamson. "Are you through with me?"

"Oh, certainly. If we have any other questions, I know where to find you. Go enjoy a well-deserved rest."

I stood back as Ciara made her farewells to her friends.

I kept waiting for some kind of relief to hit, but my brain was still spinning, insisting it couldn't be this easy. Nothing ever was.

Ciara cupped my cheek, drawing my focus back to her. "Let's go home, Alex."

THIRTY-FOUR

CIARA

The moment Alex dragged open the front door of their building, we were greeted by the thunk of a nail gun and the thumping bass beat of eighties American rock.

His brows drew together. "Are you sure you'll actually be able to work in all of this?"

I was sure of no such thing. But I was still without a car of my own, I didn't have an easy way out to Ardinmuir, and after hearing about the assault, my business associates had banned me from today's event, anyway. None of them had appreciated my pointing out that they should see the other guy. I was ordered to rest. As if I had time for that with the Mullen-Vaughan wedding staring us in the face for next weekend. Three hundred people for an outdoor wedding in early bloody November. I still wasn't satisfied with our in-case-of-rain plan.

But all that aside, I didn't want to leave Alex on his own. While it was tempting to think that everything was over now that Brodie had been arrested, Alex hadn't been able to settle. There was at least a small element of feeling impotent that he hadn't been the one to stop Brodie, and a more sizable chunk of guilt that Brodie had been able to get to me at all. If sticking close to Alex would put his mind at ease, I'd make this work. This was why noise-cancelling headphones had been invented.

"It'll be fine. I can as easily write emails and work on event flows here as there. And God knows, you've prioritized my work over your own for most of the past two weeks. It's your turn."

I let Havoc off his leash and dumped my bag on the front counter. He immediately began sniffing his way around the perimeter of the front lobby. The renovation efforts hadn't yet extended out here, so my office for the day would involve a camp chair and my lap desk. Not the most comfortable, but I'd worked under worse conditions.

Alex pulled Saffron out of his coat and set her in the playpen, which she protested at impressive volume for such a wee thing. "Wheesht. I can't be having you in my pocket while I'm using power tools, aye? Keep Ciara company."

Evidently deeply unimpressed with this suggestion, Saffron yowled at him.

"I thought cats were supposed to be independent."

I snickered. "It's your own fault. You've set yourself up as her emotional support human."

"I mean, you're right here."

"Yes, but she sees me as a rival for your affections." To prove the point, I edged in close, wrapping my arms around him and peppering kisses over his cheek.

The kitten hissed at us.

"See?"

"She's usually fine in the pen."

"She'll settle down once you walk away." I hoped.

With a sigh, he headed for the door to the back. I followed, curious how much progress had been made since I'd last been here. The other side of the building had been transformed.

They'd effectively gutted the place, erecting walls where none had been to delineate office space. Beyond that, the big rolling door had been installed, and the walls divided into different sections I presumed would ultimately house gear. Callum and Finn appeared to be constructing more wall sections.

"What about The Flying Scotsmen?" Finn suggested.

"What are you on about?" Alex asked.

Callum secured a section of 2x4 with the nail gun. "Still brainstorming names. I think his suggestions get worse as he goes."

"You still haven't named your business?" I asked.

"Nope. We can't agree on anything," Alex explained.

"Didn't you have to have a name for legal paperwork?"

"Aye, but the legal name of the venture isnae the same as the name we'll be doing business as. We wanted time to think of something marketable." Callum pointed at a waiting stack of cut wood. "Hand me that next piece."

Finn positioned the 2x4. "We could cash in on the tourist love of the Mel Gibson film and call it Braveheart Adventures."

"And I suppose next you'll be having us film a commercial in our kilts, with our faces painted blue?" Alex snarked.

"It would certainly bring in a certain type of clientele," I ventured.

"No' the clientele we want," Callum argued.

"What all will you be offering as services?"

"Hiking, camping, abseiling, kayaking, mountain biking. That sort of thing. There are a lot of opportunities in the area."

"All activities meant to get clients off the beaten path," I mused.

Alex nodded. "Aye. That's the gist of it."

"What about Out of Bounds Scotland? It gets at that off the beaten path aspect and suggests you'll be taking clients on unique adventures they won't get anywhere else."

All three men stared at me.

"Yes! That!" Finn exclaimed.

"Why the bloody hell didn't we ask her to begin with?" Callum demanded.

"To be fair, you've been a lot more focused on my needing a bodyguard for the past several weeks. And in case I haven't made it clear before, I really appreciate it."

"Of course. You're Ewan's sister. That makes you family," Finn declared. "Though it sounds as if you're no slouch yourself. I heard you bashed the bastard's nose in."

"I'm a very even-tempered woman until I'm pushed too far." Brodie had pushed me miles too far. Maybe if I'd been less concerned with being nice to start, we wouldn't have reached this point.

"Things to remember, Conroy," Finn teased.

Alex just grunted and moved off to grab his tool belt.

I lowered my voice. "Maybe lay off a bit, aye? I think he's struggling with not getting to beat the shite out of Brodie himself."

At their confirmatory nods, I stepped back. "I'm going to get out of your way and get to work myself."

Hopefully, some time with his mates would help sort out whatever was bothering him. Out front, I found Havoc lying beside the playpen in some sort of stare down with Saffron. Satisfied they both appeared to be occupied for the moment, I set up my temporary workstation and dove into the backlog of admin waiting for me. If I couldn't be boots on the ground for today's event, at least I could get ahead for some of the others.

I worked straight through the morning, with only a couple of pauses to deal with the animals. As I was without a marker board, I co-opted a stack of index cards and tape and made use of the big blank wall. It always helped me to get my thoughts out in a way I could see them all in one place.

I was trying to figure out how we could structure the timeline to pull off both a rehearsal dinner and an engagement party on the same night in early November when my phone rang.

Spotting Constable Williamson's name on the screen, everything else fled from my brain. "Hello?"

"Miss McBride. I have news."

"Can you hang on for a moment? I want to get Alex."

"Of course. He'll certainly want to hear this, too."

Pushing through the door into the back, I waved at the guys. They immediately stopped what they were doing, their gazes sharpening, their postures shifting, ready for action.

Alex came toward me. "What is it?"

"Constable Williamson has news." I put the phone on speaker. "Okay, go ahead."

"First off, we found the SUV that ran you off the road. It's consistent with exactly how you described it. The front bumper is damaged, with paint that clearly came from your car. It was hidden in an outbuilding at a fishing cabin owned by Brodie Drummond."

"Brodie has a cabin?" Why hadn't I known that?

"According to property records, he was deeded it upon the death of his grandfather, about ten years back."

"What does that prove?" Alex demanded. "You said he had an alibi."

"Well, in light of this discovery, I went back and had a longer conversation with his coworkers. Turns out that the meeting he was in the middle of was a video conference, and he had technical difficulties during a sizeable chunk of it. They could hear him on the call, but allegedly his camera kept going out. He had the time to get out to the gorge road and back. That's means, motive, and opportunity. Obviously, at the end of the day, it'll come down to a judge and jury, but we have him. It's over."

Over. I waited for the relief to hit, but mostly, I just felt queasy. A man I'd cared for, one I'd spent time with, one I'd considered—albeit briefly—building a life with, had tried to kill me. How could I have gotten it so wrong?

"Thank you for letting us know, Constable."

"I'm sure I'll be in touch as things evolve, but I knew you'd want to know first thing so you can get back to normal."

Normal. I didn't even know what that looked like anymore.

"I appreciate it." I hung up the phone.

Alex and I stared at each other. His brow was knit in concentration, and I could see the gears in his brain, trying to make this new information fit.

I reached out to lay a hand on his arm. "This is great news. I mean... horrible, but also good."

He reeled me in. "I know you want to believe it's over, but I'm not sure I buy this. It feels far too convenient."

Was it convenient? Or was this a case of the most obvious answer being the right one and Alex not being able to accept that? And if he didn't, was that about his own paranoia because of what he'd been through? Or did he think that if the threat disappeared, suddenly I would, too?

Before I could figure out what to say, Havoc burst into a spate of excited barking. A big, broad figure filled the doorway to the lobby.

"What the actual fuck were all of you thinking?"

THIRTY-FIVE

ALEX

I'd known this was coming for weeks. Despite Ciara's wishes, we couldn't keep her brother in the dark forever, and if the forbidding scowl on his face was anything to go by, someone had certainly clued him in.

Ewan stalked into the room. "Do you lot want to tell me why, exactly, that not a single one of you saw fit to tell me that not only was my sister was being stalked, but someone tried to fucking kill her?"

Not cowed in the least by his thunder, Ciara stepped in front of all of us. "Because I asked them not to. Who finally told you?"

Ewan's hands were curled into fists. "Mum and Da. They called last night to tell me that your stalker had been arrested after assaulting you."

"Did they mention that all your training held up, and that I handed Brodie his arse? Because I can assure you, he got the worse end of that fight."

"Do you think that makes it better?" I recognized that low, lethal tone and knew to tread carefully.

Whether out of ignorance or the simple foolhardiness of being a younger sibling, Ciara didn't back down an inch. "I didn't want you handling it."

"Oh, but you could go to him?" He jerked a chin at me, along with a narrowed gaze that told me his parents had mentioned that my role in her life was more than simple bodyguard.

Isobel managed to get through the door, Havoc effectively glued to her side. "Ewan, we talked about this."

He only growled in response.

Time for me to step up. "I handled the situation."

"Is that what you handled?"

Ciara got in her brother's face. "Don't you bloody well dare, Ewan McBride. I am a grown adult woman who can make her own choices. Alex is one of your best friends, and prior to this, you'd have said one of the best men you know. You can't have it both ways, brother. You can't decide he's somehow not good enough for me when he's put his life on the line to protect me for weeks."

"Ciara, stand down," I murmured.

The glare she turned on me was a twin of her brother's. I'd handle that later. Ewan was the bigger problem just now.

"A private word."

"Fine." Ewan ground out the word as if he were imagining my bones.

We stepped out the front and circled around to the side of the building, into the trees, so we wouldn't offer a front-row view to any passersby.

"Sitrep," Ewan demanded.

Out of long habit, I delivered my report regarding Drummond, as brief and to the point as I'd been trained.

"You're involved with my sister."

"Aye."

I braced myself for some sort of lecture about getting involved with the target of my protective detail. Which, frankly, would have been a little pot calling the kettle black, considering how he and Isobel had gotten together, but I knew well enough I ought to keep that to myself.

He chewed on that for a bit, studying me. "This isn't just the past few weeks."

That observation shook me out of the just-the-facts calm. But I didn't want to lie. "We didn't just meet when I moved up here, no."

"Thought so."

"What gave it away?"

"My sister's an open, friendly sort. But I saw you two arguing the night Isobel and I left. Isobel insisted it was nothing I needed to get involved in, so I let it go. But it's been niggling at me all this time." He folded his arms. "Ciara was Edinburgh. The one you were all set to change your whole life for."

I'd wondered if he'd remember that. I'd been full of hope, with stars in my bloody eyes when I'd gotten up here after meeting her, and though I hadn't mentioned her name, I'd talked about making big changes to my life.

"Aye."

"You didn't change your life back then." Some of the animosity was gone from his tone.

"No. I made a choice. Perhaps the wrong one. But I had the opportunity to go after the men who ended my career. I didn't want any of that to spill over onto her. And despite my best efforts, it looks like it has anyway."

"Explain."

So I told him what I could without breaking confidentiality, all the way up through the bombshell Constable Williamson had just dropped.

Ewan listened without interruption until I'd finished. "You dinna think it's over."

He'd known me too many years not to be able to read me. "No. My handler thinks I'm being paranoid. The evidence seems to support this version of events. But my gut tells me Drummond wouldn't have done this. To me, maybe. Not to her. I can't stop thinking about what he said before we left the police station. That she'd pushed him too far. He was clearly speaking to Ciara. But she hasn't done a damned thing to push him at all. She's gone out of her way to avoid him."

"Could be he sees her moving on with you as designed to get back at him."

"Maybe. But what if there was someone else somehow manipulating him, making him believe it was Ciara? He's no' a particularly smart guy. He'd have been easy to manipulate."

"Have you uncovered anything to support that in your digging?"

When I went brows up, he just smirked. "I know you, mate. If you didnae build a full dossier on this wankstain, I'll be verra disappointed."

It was my turn to smirk. "Okay, aye, I went digging. I found a lot of evidence of obsessive behavior, but nothing that would back up my theory."

"But you think there's something else there."

"I could only access so much remotely. I'd need direct physical access to both of his computers—at home and at work, to go further. Not to mention the chance to search his place in case there's physical evidence of some sort."

"That should be easy enough to arrange between the four of us."

"Just a wee bit of casual breaking and entering as a bonding exercise?"

Ewan grinned at that. "Aye. Just like old times. Hopefully, with fewer bullets involved. We'll make a plan this afternoon."

He started to move back toward the front of the building.

"Wait. That's all you have to say?"

"I remember how you looked when you talked about her before. You wouldn't cross that line if you weren't serious, so I dinna have to break your face."

Something in his tone had my internal alarms pinging. "Did Isobel tell you that?"

Ewan's expression was caught somewhere between a grin and a grimace. "Aye. She made me promise to behave."

A tension I'd been carrying around for years finally let loose. "If I fuck things up with her again, I'll invite you to break my face myself."

He extended a hand. "Deal."

THIRTY-SIX

CIARA

"What if they get caught?" I paced another restless circuit around my brother's lounge, as if that would help expel some of the anxious energy coursing through me.

"They're not going to get caught," Isobel insisted. "They're all highly trained operatives, who've run missions together for years. They've invaded terrorist cells. Breaking into your ex-boyfriend's house will be a cakewalk. It's not even technically breaking in since you told them where he keeps the spare key."

"Somehow, I doubt the police would see it that way." I peered out the front window into the darkness, as if that would somehow force them to appear. "I can't believe Alex had the nerve to suggest I get some sleep while they were gone."

They'd been gone for what felt like days. Every minute that ticked by felt like an hour.

"Your tune about him has certainly changed," Isobel observed.

"You were right. He had a good reason, and he finally told me what that reason was." I spared a glance for my sister-in-law-to-be. "I suppose I have you to thank for the fact that Ewan didn't utterly lose his shite over the two of us."

"Partly. Though I want to make it very clear that it was your mum who spilled the beans, not me."

"Honestly, I'm amazed she sat on it as long as she did. It was truly insane of me to think he wouldn't find out before I got around to telling him. We've just... had a lot going on around here."

"Clearly. I'm sorry you were hurt. But I can't be sorry it finally brought the two of you back together. You're two of my favorite people. You deserve a chance at happiness."

I paced back to the kitchen counter and swiped a cracker and piece of cheese off the charcuterie board of snacks we'd made for when the guys got back. "I hope we'll finally get that chance once all of this is resolved. But I'm worried. I have no idea if Alex is right and there's someone else out there who wants to hurt me because of him. If he's not, I don't know that he'll ever be able to let this go. He's convinced his father died because of this. It's one thing to have a 24-hour bodyguard for a few weeks, but as much as I care for him, I'm not sure I can live like this forever. It's not practical."

"They're going to get answers," Isobel insisted. "I don't pretend to understand the details, but Alex is very, very good at what he does."

Havoc lifted his head from her lap, his ears pricking. I swung toward the window in time to see a vehicle bumping along the driveway. A gusty sigh escaped, leaving my knees weak with relief. The SUV parked out front, and doors open and shut. Then they were all spilling into the house. Each one of them was dressed in head-to-toe black, and they looked like exactly what they were—a lethal, clandestine strike force. Some part of my brain registered that was incredibly sexy, but I was far too concerned with how their mission had gone to chase the thought.

Alex came straight to me, pulling me into his arms as if he needed the physical reassurance that nothing had happened to me in his absence. I burrowed in, needing the same.

"Did you find anything?"

His jaw was hard. "Aye. We found a lot."

"We made food," Isobel said. "Fix yourselves a plate and tell us."

I barely managed to leash my impatience as they loaded themselves down with snacks.

"We started with the house, in the event something went awry. Figured it was more likely we'd find something there." Alex sucked in a breath. "There were surveillance photos. Dozens of them. Someone's been watching you—watching us— and sending physical photographs to Drummond."

I stared at him. "What? Do you think he hired someone to follow me?"

All those little things he'd said that had made me mildly uncomfortable. Stuff he shouldn't have known. Was this why? Had he had someone actively following me and reporting back on my activities?

"I suppose it's possible that was how it started. I can comb through his hard drive to search for evidence of that. But I think something else is going on." He shoved his plate aside and reached for my hand. "Remember what he said at the police station? That you'd pushed him too far?"

"Yeah, that made no sense. I didn't do anything to him."

"No. But I think it's possible he believes you were the one sending the photos. Rubbing in the fact that you'd moved on."

"But I would never—"

"No, of course not. But this is what was bothering me. It didn't make sense for him to escalate from all the petty shite to physically laying a hand on you. Not without someone dumping kerosene on that fire. And even if that's what this was —someone attempting to fan his obsession in something bigger, darker—I don't believe that Drummond was in that car. I don't believe he tampered with your brakes. It doesn't make logical sense. If he'd done it to my car, sure. But he wanted you back. He didn't want you dead."

"But what about the SUV?" I asked. "The police found it after he was arrested."

"They found it at a property you didn't even know he had. You were with him for a year. Unless the place was a total shithole, seems like he would have taken you out there for a weekend getaway at some point. Now, is it possible he did the deed and hid evidence of it out there? I suppose. But it feels too neat. There were none of his prints on your car. I don't know, but I suspect that there were none on the SUV either. I believe it was planted to frame him. He has no history of this sort of behavior. No priors. It is a big leap from stalking to murder. And even if he's responsible for more than I believe, someone sent those photos to him. That alone tells us someone else is involved. The likelihood of that person being someone from your life seems pretty slim."

"So what does all this mean?"

"I'm still working through the details, but this feels like personal retribution."

"What are you thinking?" Callum asked.

"There were several people who were taken down as a direct result of my mission. It's possible that someone connected to one of them found out that I was responsible and has decided to exact some form of payback against me through the people that matter to me."

Finn leaned back in his chair and popped a slice of salami into his mouth, chewing thoughtfully. "You dinna have definitive proof about your dad's accident. You do about Ciara's. So focus on that for a moment. They're going after your woman. That suggests an eye-for-an-eye sort of logic. Could be this is someone who was a spouse or a lover of someone put away because of your op."

"That's what I'm wondering. I need to do some more research into who's connected to all the actors who were put away. That'll just take some time."

I pinched the bridge of my nose. I hadn't really thought we were going to get clear answers from this lunatic mission, but I hadn't anticipated getting a whole new string of questions.

"So now what? What do we do in the meantime?" I was afraid of the answer.

"Someone went to a lot of trouble to set up Drummond. Not that he shouldn't have been arrested. He did assault you. He did stalk you and make a lot of other nuisance problems for you. But whoever was behind this needs to believe that setup worked. That we all believe the right person was put away, and we can go back to more or less normal."

"How's that going to work? Because I know perfectly well that you're not going to just leave me without a bodyguard."

"No. But you're conveniently still without a car, so my remaining on chauffeur duty doesn't look strange."

"That's all well and good, and I won't argue with whatever you think needs to be done to put an end to this. But I still have a job to do. We have a three-hundred-person wedding happening this weekend. I can't *not* be there for that. This is the part of the business that's my specialty, and I can't leave everyone else in the lurch."

"That's fine. We'll all help out at the event. You said significant others are usually put to physical work, anyway. With all of us there, you should be covered without a problem."

"How long do you think this will be necessary?" Finn asked.

"Hopefully not long. It'll take me some time to dig down and figure out who we might be dealing with. I'm going to put in another call to my handler to see if I can get some additional intel out of him. But we're on the right track. I can feel it." Alex's confidence was clear in his tone.

I could only hope that he was as good as everyone said he was, and that he'd find the answers we needed to put an end to this threat. Because it was about damn time we had an uninterrupted shot at that happily ever after.

THIRTY-SEVEN

ALEX

It had been three days since I'd enacted protocol and reached out to my handler, and I hadn't heard a word back from Cardinal. I was starting to wonder if I was being blown off. I'd started putting together a list of the known significant others and close relatives of everyone I'd helped put away. Unfortunately, it wasn't a short list. Working my way through their whereabouts was an unfortunately slow process. Some were also incarcerated. Some were definitively out of the country. And many I hadn't yet managed to track down. I just needed more time to find the information. It was out there, somewhere. I'd dig it up eventually, with or without Cardinal's help.

But my deep dive would have to wait until tomorrow. Today was the Mullen-Vaughan wedding at Ardinmuir, and Ciara had been in go-mode since yesterday. So far, the weather was holding. It was cold, but not rainy. A massive tent had been erected on the grounds, and the entire staff, plus all their significant others, were on hand and prepped to move the chairs, currently set up for the ceremony on the front lawn of the castle, at a moment's notice. Ciara was glued to her tablet, keeping an eye on the radar and communicating with other event staff via a headset as she bounced between the two ceremony locations and the reception set up in the Great Hall of the castle.

"So far, so good. Who has eyes on the bride?" She angled her head, listening to someone on the headset. "I'll take care of it."

She did an abrupt about face and stepped straight on my foot for about the fifth time today. Frustration flashed over her features, and I watched her try to reel it in.

"Sorry. Where to?"

She reached up to frame my face. "Alex, love, I appreciate everything that you're doing for me, but I need you to back off a bit so I can do my job. You can't go to the bridal suite. No men allowed."

I suspected she'd have been amped up today under normal circumstances, but my hovering wasn't helping. I didn't like the idea of letting her out of my sight, but I also understood that she needed a little more latitude than I was giving her.

"Okay. You do what you need to do. Just... don't go outside alone. There are a lot of people here today that we can't account for. Both extra event staff and guests. Be alert, aye?"

Rising to her toes, she brushed her lips over mine. "Promise. Go check the emergency tent to see that the heaters have been put in place, please. I need to go speak to the bride."

"On it."

As she disappeared up a stairway to the bridal suite, I reached for my own earbud. "Status?"

"Clear," Callum reported.

"Clear," Ewan echoed. "Guests are starting to arrive. Connor and Hamish have been pressed into valet service."

"There are some stupendous appetizers in the kitchen," Finn answered.

"Better not let Afton catch you sampling those, or she'll hand you your arse," I warned.

"I'm the guinea pig to make sure they're right."

"You're on duty. Stop thinking with your stomach." I knew I was unreasonably snappish, but I hated everything about this situation.

I understood Ciara had a job to do, but I hated how little control I had over the circumstances. If I'd had my way, I'd have done up a full dossier on every guest and extra event staff. And I'd have organized the event from a security standpoint. But when I'd proposed making some adjustments, I'd been summarily shut down. The bride and groom would get their way. Period.

There was no reason to believe anything would happen today. We'd done exactly as I'd proposed and continued on business as usual for the past three days. But my instincts were keeping me on edge.

My mobile vibrated in my pocket just as I stepped outside to go check the heaters as requested. I checked the readout, expecting Ciara or perhaps my mum. But "unknown number" flashed on the screen. Bracing myself, I answered.

"Hello?"

"The falcon can't find purchase."

With a relieved exhale, I continued the exchange. "When the cliff face crumbles."

"Leaving only the valley below."

"Or the open sky above."

"We still have a lot of ground to cover."

"And a long trail to blaze," I finished.

"This is Cardinal. What is your status, Echo?"

"Not secure. In public."

"That's fine. You can simply listen to what I have to say. I'm sorry for breaking protocol and for the delay. It's taken me a little longer to pull the information than I'd like, but I wanted to be discreet, lest I set off any alarms."

"I appreciate it. What did you find?"

"I've put together a packet and sent it via the usual channels. Inside is everything I can offer you about known close associates of everyone arrested or killed in connection with the operation. You can read through when you're able. But there's one I wanted to bring to your immediate attention. Andrew Davies."

My gut clenched. Andrew Davies was the high-ranking government official who I'd uncovered as the mole leaking information to the anarchist group.

"I thought his wife divorced him."

"Oh, she did when he went to prison. But it turns out that Davies had a lover."

This was the first I was hearing of a lover, though it wasn't surprising. A man willing to commit treason was hardly a poster boy for marital fidelity.

"Who?"

"Johanna Klein. She was born in Germany and immigrated to the UK in her early twenties. Actual age, unknown. According to her profile, she's highly intelligent and technologically savvy. She's suspected of involvement in multiple data breaches but has never been charged. Evidently, she met Davies through the anarchist group and became his lover. Because of him, she lived a comfortable, protected life, with access to insider information."

"A life she'd have lost when he went to prison."

"Exactly. By all accounts, it seemed like they had legitimate feelings for each other. So if anyone's targeting you for your role in the takedowns, she seems like the most likely option."

The situation he'd described had the ring of truth. It fit with what had been going on here. "Current whereabouts?"

"Unknown. There's more in the files I sent, but you should know this woman has a multitude of skills. Forgery. Hacking. Even bombs."

"Why wasn't she brought in before?"

"Never had enough to make anything stick. She's smart. Always manages to keep herself a few degrees removed from anything truly illegal. And she excels in manipulating others to do her bidding."

Someone like that would have no trouble at all manipulating an embittered, entitled ex-boyfriend.

"Thanks, Cardinal. This was the piece I needed."

"I hope you're wrong about all of this, but I wish you luck, nonetheless."

"I'll take all of it I can get."

The moment I hung up the phone, I bolted for the castle. I'd brought my laptop, just in case. It wasn't my full kit, but it'd be enough to hopefully get a look at any photos included in the dossiers Cardinal had provided. I locked myself in Sophie's office and logged in, working my way through the layers of encryption until I could open the files. There were seventeen in total. I went straight to Klein's folder.

There were multiple surveillance photos inside, obviously older, as she was with Davies in most of them. There was no question they were lovers. The only close-up had clearly been pulled from some government ID database—a passport or driver's license photo. She appeared to be in her late twenties or early thirties, with sharp cheekbones and Slavic blue eyes. Her hair was listed as blonde, but that was changed easily enough. I snapped a quick photo with my phone, then moved on to open the other files. I didn't have time to dig through any of them yet, but I took pictures of all the potentials. I'd share them with the others, so they knew who to be on the lookout for.

When I was through, I hailed the rest of my team. "Meet me in the family kitchen. I have updates."

THIRTY-EIGHT

CIARA

My low-heeled shoes clicked on the stone steps as I hustled up the tower stairs to the second floor, where we'd converted one of the bedrooms to a bridal suite for those brides who wanted the full castle experience rather than a shorter walk to the aisle in their finery. Christina Mullen definitely fit the bill. An American bride with Scottish heritage, she'd booked Ardinmuir almost a year ago, asking for the "most Scottish experience" we could give her. Kilts. Castle. Bagpipes. The full Jock. And they were paying a premium for it, so we were going to see that today went off without a hitch. That included stopping any imminent panic attacks from the bride.

I knocked lightly on the door to the bridal suite. The door swung open immediately to reveal Melissa, one of the bridesmaids, in a satin tartan robe, her hair still up in rollers.

"Oh, thank God. She's in here."

I followed Melissa into the main part of the suite, where Christina sat at the dressing table. Her mum was fanning her flushed face.

"What seems to be the trouble?"

Christina looked up at me with suspiciously shiny eyes. "What was I thinking choosing an outdoor wedding at the beginning of November in Scotland?"

This had been a question we'd all had, but she'd been very firm in what she'd wanted when she'd booked, so we'd simply rolled with it. What the client wanted, the client got.

"It's freezing outside. And what happens if the weather turns? My guests—"

I stepped forward to take her hands in mine and put a little more of the burr I'd lost when I went to uni back into my voice. "Breathe, Christina. In and out. Wi' me now. In... and out... Now, we have a plan. There are multiple outdoor heaters to combat the cold. You already elected to have a more abbreviated, non-traditional ceremony to limit the time in the weather. And in the event the weather changes, the entire backup tent is set up and ready to go. I've been monitoring the radar by the minute. The moment that anything looks as if it's going to shift, we're prepared to move everything. We'll run about half an hour later than planned, to allow time to transition the chairs and the guests. We have a veritable army of umbrellas available. Everything is going to be just fine. This is why you hired us, aye? So that we can take care of all the things to give you the wedding of your dreams."

Christina sniffed. "Everything's handled?"

"Absolutely everything," I promised. "Now, have you eaten today?"

"No. I couldn't possibly. I'm too nervous."

I reached into the bum bag of essentials I was never without on wedding days. "Here. Eat this protein bar. You'll feel better with something in your system. You dinna want to pass out on groom now. There's a lass."

The bride's mum took my hand. "Thank you so much. You

and your entire crew have put in so much work and everything is simply beautiful. You're giving my baby her dream wedding."

A glow of pride spread through my chest. I truly loved my job most days, but it was extra gratifying to hear true appreciation from those clients we worked so hard for. It was odd to think that I might not have ended up here if not for Alex. If I hadn't met him, hadn't taken his advice to heart, I might not have dared to step off the path I'd started down.

I hoped we resolved the current threat soon so he had the chance to find his own path with the adventure company. He hadn't yet had the chance to really let himself live this new life because he hadn't truly gotten closure on the old one. I knew he still felt a little rootless and unmoored. He'd done so much for me. I wanted to be able to ground him, to be his safe place the way he'd become mine.

Once assured that things with the bride were well in hand, I made my way toward the Great Hall to check on the reception set up, with a brief stop in the kitchen to make sure Afton didn't need anything and that she hadn't suddenly turned green. We didn't want a repeat of what had happened six weeks ago.

Afton's cheeks were flushed with exertion as she moved around the prep kitchen. Her sous chef, Megan Murtaugh, was occupied wrapping scallops in bacon.

"How's the bride?" Afton asked.

"Emotional and anxious about the weather, which we anticipated. I reassured her and made sure she ate something."

"I'll never understand the not eating," Megan insisted. "I'd faint dead away if I tried to go all day without eating."

"Everybody handles nerves in a different way."

"How are things on the weather front?" Afton asked.

"So far, it looks like everything's going to be okay." But I pulled out my tablet to check the radar for the two-hundredth time that day. "Oh. Oh shite. There is a bit of a something forming." I watched the build and spin of green and yellow on the screen. "It might miss us."

"Can we afford might?" Afton asked.

"Shite. I don't want to be the one to make this call by myself." I reached for my headset. "Kyla, where are you? I want you to look at the radar and see what you think. We may need to enact Plan B."

Kyla came back several moments later, her voice low. "How bad?"

"Tough to say. You need to see."

I heard a low curse before she sighed. "I'll meet you in the library."

"Headed your way."

With a salute to the chef, I dove back into the maze of halls and headed for the nearest set of stairs that would take me up a floor. If we needed to move things, better we do it now before the guests arrived en masse. We'd hired extra staff to manage today, and all the spouses and significant others were on deck to provide additional support. Afton would be tied up in the kitchen, and Sophie couldn't lift anything heavy, but everyone else could be co-opted to move chairs. They weren't that heavy. If everyone could carry two a time...

My brain was full of mental math, and I wasn't fully paying attention as I stepped into the upper hall, so I didn't catch the motion to my left before something hard pressed into the small of my back and a quiet voice said, "Don't make a sound."

THIRTY-NINE

ALEX

By the time I finished updating my team on what I'd been told by my handler, I was itching to get my hands on a keyboard. The information was just waiting, and in it I'd hopefully find some answers. Not the least of which were faces of prospective suspects.

"How do you want to handle this?" Ewan asked. "I know you want to dig into the data."

"We can cover the rest of the wedding for you. Keep an eye on Ciara," Finn said.

Despite the itch, I shook my head. "I'm no' leaving. It'll keep. Maybe it's my paranoia, but I have a bad feeling about today."

"What's pinging for you?" Callum asked. "Something in the research you've already done?"

"No. I think it's mostly all the elements we can't control. This entire event is a security nightmare. I say we stay and keep our eyes open for anything that seems out of place."

Munro strode into the family kitchen, where we'd

convened for the sitrep. "Look alive, lads. Rain's coming. It's all hands on deck to get the chairs moved to the backup tent."

With some sense of relief, I headed outside to the front lawn. The sky that had started the day as pale gray had darkened to pewter, and clouds were beginning to boil in the distance. Could be the rain would pass before the ceremony, but there'd be no way to dry all the chairs in time. More than a dozen other people were grabbing chairs and streaming toward the tent. I scanned faces, looking for Ciara. With such a last-minute change to proceedings, I was certain she'd be out here helping move chairs herself. But she wasn't among the group. Then again, I'd ordered her to stay inside, so perhaps she was still in the castle or inside the tent.

I moved to the nearest row and began folding chairs, tucking two under each arm and hustling for the tent. Inside, Sophie directed placement of the chairs. Neat rows were already forming on either side of what would be the aisle.

"Just over there, on the bride's side, if you please, gentlemen. Thank you."

Following Sophie's orders, I started a new row to the left.

Kyla rushed in, two chairs under her arms. Spotting me, she made a beeline in my direction. "Have you seen Ciara?"

My hands stilled on the last chair. "Not since she went up to the bridal suite, maybe half an hour ago. Why?"

"She was supposed to meet me in the library nearly twenty minutes ago to go over the radar and make the call, but she didn't show. I thought maybe she got sidetracked by some other emergency, but she's not answering her headset or her phone."

That bad feeling I'd had all day intensified.

"She was under orders not to leave the castle on her own."

Kyla's cheeks paled. "Did Brodie get released?"

"No, it's... there's no time to explain. I'll retrace her steps. Where's the bridal suite?"

"Second floor of the main castle, but she's not there. I already checked. Afton saw her in the prep kitchen after that, right before she was supposed to meet me."

"Okay." Without another word, I headed in that direction.

"I'm coming with you."

I didn't argue. It would only waste time.

"Maybe she's in the loo," Kyla muttered.

"For twenty minutes?" I asked.

"I mean... food poisoning?" But she obviously didn't believe herself.

"She was perfectly fine when I saw her earlier."

A few minutes later, I strode into the prep kitchen. Afton and her sous chef were moving in a well-choreographed dance, juggling prep of multiple courses to feed three hundred people in a few hours.

"Which way did Ciara go when she left here?" I demanded.

Afton's knife thunked against the cutting board and clattered to the table. "She was headed up to the library. She went out that door. Is something wrong?"

Yes. My gut screamed it, though I didn't yet have confirmation.

Hurry. Hurry. Hurry.

Without waiting, I exited through the door she'd indicated, pausing in the corridor as I tried to figure out the way to the library from here.

Kyla moved past me. "This way."

I followed her down a hall and through at least two doors before we found ourselves in a narrow staircase. I mentally added the new areas to the map in my head as I continued to scan for anything amiss. As we emerged into the hallway on the second floor, I recognized where we were. I'd had no idea there was a stairwell at this end.

As Kyla headed toward the library, I slowed my steps, looking for... something. The hair on my arms stood up seconds before I spotted something slim and white on the floor beside some sort of plant in a decorative urn. I crouched and lifted Ciara's headset.

"Kyla."

She turned, her face paling as she saw what I held.

Following instinct, I parted the leaves of the plant and found her bum bag. Her phone was inside it.

Shoving down the avalanche of terrified profanity, I activated my comm. "We found Ciara's headset and her phone. No obvious signs of a struggle, but she didn't ditch them herself. She's been taken. Spread out. Check the exits and the parking area."

"What do you mean taken?" Kyla's voice had risen two octaves.

"There's no time to explain." I yanked out my phone.

"What are you doing?"

"Pulling up video feeds from the surveillance cameras."

"We don't have surveillance cameras."

I spared her one brief glance. "Aye, you do." Because I was that guy, and I'd installed them myself in the past few days. Not as many as I'd have liked, but I had eyes on all the exits I was aware of and on the castle drive. If anyone left by vehicle, they had to go down that drive.

I scrubbed the feeds, checking footage for the past half hour. With every additional minute that ticked by, my panic rose because that was one more minute, one more mile further away she could be. I hoped beyond hope that I was wrong. That there was some rational explanation. But I knew I wasn't.

And then I spotted it. Two figures stepping out of one of the back doors on the formal gardens side of the castle. Because of the setup for the wedding, no one should've been using that door. It wasn't near the front or any of the staff areas for the event. Zooming in, I recognized Ciara moving very slowly, her hands raised. The other figure stayed close, something black clutched in her hand. A gun pressed to Ciara's back.

The blood drained out of my head.

This was no longer a hypothetical, no longer simply paranoia. Ciara had been taken. And I hadn't been able to do a damned thing to stop it.

I let loose a frustrated roar.

"Talk to me, Echo. Lock it down and talk to me."

Ewan's calm, steady voice came over the comms.

Sucking in a breath, I relayed the information to my team. "I've got a visual on Ciara, being led at gunpoint out a door on the west side of the castle. Target is female, dressed as waitstaff. Timestamp is eighteen minutes ago."

"Is it Klein?" Callum asked.

"Unclear, but probable."

What the fuck did this woman have planned? This wasn't anything designed to look like an accident. This was outright kidnapping.

Turning to a white-faced Kyla, I pointed to the screen. "Do you recognize this woman?"

"I... no. She's not part of the extra temp staff we hired for the event."

"Are you sure?"

"I vetted them all."

But there were so many extra people around, it would've been easy to pose as part of the staff to slip inside. Was that why today? Why here? Had she known about this massive event, or had she simply chosen a Saturday because there were usually weddings here then?

"Any video of what kind of vehicle they left in?" Finn asked.

It was a mark of exactly how rattled I was that I hadn't even checked the driveway feed yet.

"Standby, Nomad."

I rewound the footage and scrubbed through it again. But while multiple cars had arrived, no vehicles left in the relevant window.

"Negative on video. No sign that anyone's left."

"I've got the main drive covered," Callum reported.

"Then maybe she's still on the grounds." If she was still here, that was good. The longer Klein had Ciara, the further she could get, and the lower our chances of tracking them.

"The main drive isn't the only way off the property," Kyla said.

I swung toward her again. "Where else?"

"There's a gravel road out beyond the formal gardens, behind some of the outbuildings there. It's gated, but not locked."

I relayed the information to my team.

"On it," Finn answered.

"Is there video of the parking area?" Ewan asked.

"Negative, Sentinel. I didn't have that many cameras. There's no coverage there." We needed eyes. As many of them as we could get.

I swiped over to the photo I'd taken earlier of Johanna Klein and sent it to Kyla. "Spread this through all the event staff and guests. Have everyone on the lookout. But no one should approach. She's armed and should be considered dangerous."

I didn't think Klein would start shooting targets at random, but I wasn't putting anyone else's life at risk to test the theory.

"Shouldn't we call the police?" Kyla asked.

They'd take time to mobilize, and the force here was small enough that I didn't expect much. But they could put out an

APB. "Aye, do that. Ask for Constable Williamson. She's been handling Ciara's case. Send her the photo I sent you and have her put out an alert to area law enforcement."

"What about the rest of you? What if she has questions for you?"

"We can't afford to wait. We'll be doing what we do best. Going hunting."

FORTY

CIARA

The barrel of the gun jabbed into my back, just to the left of my spine. As my captor led me through the back halls of the castle, I hadn't been able to see for sure to verify that it was a gun, but I wasn't about to take the risk that it wasn't. I kept expecting to stumble upon someone—anyone—wandering around. There were so many extra people here for this wedding, so much extra staff, it seemed impossible that my captor could navigate us through the halls that I still occasionally took a wrong turn in, without getting lost or running into someone. But we hadn't encountered a soul, and when she shoved me through a door, out the back of the castle near the river, I knew I was in deep, desperate trouble.

She'd made sure I left my headset and bum bag behind, so there was no phone, nothing at all to help Alex track me. I was furious with myself for not simply letting him do his job as bodyguard. If he'd been with me, this would never have happened. But beating myself up about it wouldn't get me out of this situation.

"People are going to be looking for me. I was on my way to a meeting when you stopped me."

"We've time enough yet. Everyone's worried about the wedding, and they'll look in all the wrong places." She jabbed again with the gun. "Keep moving."

The accent was English, but I detected something else underneath. The cadence of some other language. Eastern European? German?

She force marched me along the river for two dozen yards to the side of the formal gardens that were one of Sophie's pride and joys. Since she'd become mistress of the castle, she'd poured all the extra time she had into restoring them. But this time of year, they'd already begun falling dormant, and the bride had wanted the showpiece of the castle as the backdrop for her nuptials. So no one was out here. And unless someone happened to look out one of the narrow windows on this side, the moment we hit the hedgerow that marked the garden boundary, we'd be out of sight.

The sky above was starting to boil with clouds. Surely, by now, Kyla had made the call. Everyone would be out front helping to move chairs into the backup tent for the ceremony. No one would be looking out this side. The grounds were so expansive, I doubted anyone would even hear me scream. At least, not before my captor could make use of the gun she kept pressed into my back.

When she nudged me toward the hedgerow and down the outside, I had to ask, "Where are you taking me?"

"No talking."

There was no direct line to the car park here. No way out. Was she actually going to drag me into the woods? If she did, could I find something to use as a weapon? I was at a disadvantage in my skirt and low-slung heels. They were sensible, thicker heels, too. Not a stiletto that could be turned against my captor.

I wiped sweaty palms against my pockets, checking for anything I could drop to show we'd come this way. Hearing the faint crinkle of paper, I remembered the list of last-minute seating plan changes the mother-of-the-bride had given me. If someone found it, would they recognize it had come from me? Would they understand what it meant?

At the far end of the gardens, my captor urged me through a gate I hadn't even known was here. A rutted, overgrown dirt road snaked toward the woods. Where the hell was this woman taking me? I'd expected to be shoved into a vehicle and driven out via the main drive. Maybe that had been a foolish hope, because someone would have been far more likely to see. Instead, we marched on toward the trees.

A couple dozen feet past the tree line, I spotted the faint glint of light reflecting on metal. A car.

Where did this road even go? Did anyone even remember it was here? It was clear no one had driven on it in a very long time. Grass had all but taken over the track.

"Get in the driver's seat."

Not knowing what else to do, I opened the door and did as she asked. But as I slipped into the seat, I managed to slide the paper from my pocket and let it fall to the ground.

"Hands on the wheel."

I did as I was told and got my first good look at my captor as she circled the bonnet, the gun with a wicked-looking silencer aimed directly at me. She was tall, with at least three or four inches on me. Her hair was blonde, her blue eyes the almond shape I associated with Eastern Europe. She was dressed as all the extra event staff, in black pants and a white button-down blouse. She wasn't one of ours, but with so many extra faces, it would've been easy for her to slip in unnoticed.

She climbed into the passenger seat. "Drive."

The car was a push-button start. I could only assume she had the keys somewhere on her person. Moving slowly, I started the engine. I needed to buy time. I knew from my brother that the chances of being located plummeted if a hostage was taken to a secondary location. We were already further from the castle than I wanted.

"Where are we going?"

"Just pull onto the track there."

Carefully, I put the car into drive and followed her instructions. The rutted road kept me from being able to build up any speed, which was good and bad. I considered gunning the engine and crashing us into a tree, but that seemed like a good way to get shot.

"Who are you? What do you want?"

"I wanted you to die. That would have made all this so much easier. So much neater. But you couldn't cooperate, now, could you?"

I spared her a glance but found it hard to look at anything but the gun still pointed at me. "My car. The brakes. That was you?"

"It was. I miscalculated. It's terribly unlike me. I thought for certain you'd go over the edge."

"Why are you doing this?"

"Do you know what it is to lose the most important person in your world?" Emotion vibrated through her voice.

I thought of how I'd felt in the weeks and months after Alex had disappeared. But I was certain she wouldn't consider that counted, especially as we'd found our way back to each other again.

"No. I'm sorry you lost someone. But what does that have to do with me?"

"You have the misfortune of being that person for the man

who took everything from me. So I'm taking you away, so he'll know exactly how it feels."

Alex. She had to be talking about Alex.

He'd been right. All along, he'd been right.

"Did you kill his father?"

The woman trilled a chilling sort of laugh. "No. But I saw how he thought it. That was what gave me the idea with your car. It was supposed to be simple and easy. Something that would burrow under his skin so that he suspected—but wasn't *absolutely* certain—that it was his fault."

I filed that away. At least it was something I could give him. If I survived this.

When, Ciara. When you survive this. Because Alex is coming for you. There are four highly trained Royal Marines who are bound to be looking for you now.

I glanced at the car's clock. I'd been gone for nearly half an hour now. I didn't have a good gauge of how far we'd gone, but the rutted track met up with a more well-traveled one.

"Turn left here."

"Where are you taking me?" I tried again.

"It's not too much further."

A few minutes later, we pulled up at one of the cottages on the Ardinmuir grounds. I blinked at the whitewashed stone building. "You're staying here? On the property?"

The woman laughed again. "I've been here for more than a month. Multiple reservations. A wig here. Some colored contacts there. No one was the wiser, because no one's looking for a woman as the threat."

By my estimate, I was within three miles of the castle. But that was still more than twenty-five square miles of territory for them to search. How on earth would they know to come here?

My captor gestured with the gun. "Out of the car."

I stepped out, giving a fleeting thought to running. But

there was insufficient cover between me and the nearest line of trees, and I couldn't run fast in these shoes. Maybe there'd be something in the house I could use as a weapon.

"Look, I'm sorry you lost whoever it was that you lost. But hurting me isn't going to bring him back."

"My dear girl, he's not dead. He's in prison."

"Oh." I didn't know what else to say to that.

"I'm still working on how to get him out. But no, I have no intention of hurting you. I intend to kill you so that Alex Conroy knows exactly what it feels like to have the person he cares about the most ripped out of his grasp."

If I hadn't already been terrified, I was now.

"Open the door. It's unlocked."

I did as she asked, desperately scanning for anything I could grab as I stepped inside. Spotting an iron candlestick— Connor's work, I was sure—I edged toward it.

"Where's the light?"

The moment she flicked it on, I lunged, grabbing the candlestick and swinging toward her gun arm. The gun fired, and I'd have sworn my heart leapt straight into my throat. But the shot went wide.

Fighting every instinct to run, I moved in close, trying for a palm heel strike to her face, using everything Ewan had taught me. But it was different fighting someone closer to my own size, who clearly had training herself. She grabbed my hand and twisted, using my momentum to drive me head-first into the wall. My skull hit with an audible crack, and everything went white.

FORTY-ONE
ALEX

"Anything?" I asked.

"Negative," Callum reported. "The rain has washed away any tracks there might have been. All I can say for sure is there's been no vehicle on this road in a long, bloody time."

Lacing my hands behind my head, I paced a half-dozen steps, willing my racing heart to slow. I was about two inches away from losing my bloody mind. I didn't know what to do or how to effectively mobilize the assets at hand. Because if I chose wrong, it could cost Ciara her life.

Ewan got in my face, gripping me by the back of the neck. "Shut it down. You're no good to her if you panic. Work the mission."

I didn't know how he could even look at me right now, when this was all my fault, but I nodded.

"Think I found something," Finn announced. "GPS tracker on the undercarriage of your 4x4."

My head came up at that. "Military grade or commercial?"

"Looks like commercial."

Commercial meant a subscription and user account. Those were things I could track.

"If I can get a device ID, I can hack the company's databases and trace the signal back."

"Headed your way."

"Meet me inside, in Sophie's office. I'll have enough signal there to do what I need to do." I began moving in that direction, Ewan close behind.

"I may have found something, too," Callum said. "It's a soggy note, just inside the tree line to the west of the castle. Can't really make out most of it, but the paper hasn't disintegrated yet. It's relatively fresh. Someone dropped it recently."

"Is there a trail to follow?" Ewan demanded.

"Hard to say, but it looks like there was a vehicle parked here recently, and this road continues on through the trees."

"Stick with it a ways. See what there is to see, while Echo hacks this tracker."

Finn came in dripping, one side of his back covered in dirt and grass stains from where he'd clearly slid under my SUV. He handed over the tiny device. I pulled the frequency scanner I kept in my bag—because, aye, I was that guy, too—and used it to identify the make and model of the tracker. Then I set to work. No one said a word as I accessed the company's website and began hunting for vulnerabilities that would allow me to hack into their database.

I couldn't consider that I wouldn't find one. This had to work, because it was our only way to narrow down where Ciara might have been taken.

My fingers flew over the keys, doing what I'd once done best.

"Gotcha."

Once I'd made it into the system, it took only a couple of

minutes to hone in on the proper account and trace the signal back to its receiver. And then I did something I could conceivably face charges for if I was caught.

"Did you just hack a satellite?" Ewan's voice remained neutral, but I could feel his brows at his hairline.

"It's better if I don't answer that question, so you have plausible deniability." Piggybacking on the receiver signal, I used the satellite imagery to narrow our search grid. "Signal's not moving. She's about five clicks northwest. Here." I pointed to an area on the map.

Ewan squeezed my shoulder. "Let's go."

We swung around, only to find our path blocked by Connor. There were more people in the hall. Malcolm, Raleigh, Hamish.

"What can we do to help?" When we only stared at Connor, he scowled. "She's my family, too, damn it."

"What weapons do you have on the premises?" I asked.

"Some hunting rifles. A couple of shotguns. A bow. Plenty of blades. Enough for all of us."

Raleigh stared. "You're all former Special Forces. Didn't you come prepared for this?"

"This is the UK, mate. We dinna have gun racks over our fireplaces," Callum growled.

"But we've got swords," Connor added. "Verra big swords."

Ewan shook his head. "We aren't putting your lives in danger. The four of us are trained for this."

"We aren't standin' by doin' nothin'," Raleigh insisted.

I motioned Connor inside and pointed to the screen of my laptop, where I'd overlaid a map on the satellite imagery. "Do you know where this is on the estate?"

"Zoom out a little." I did as he asked, and he squinted. "Aye, that's no' far. One of the rental cottages, I think."

"What's the fastest way there?"

When he'd told us, I nodded. "There are two potential points of egress by vehicle. If you all insist on getting involved, team up in twos and see that they're both blocked."

"Shouldn't we notify the police?" Hamish asked. "They ought to be here any moment."

"You should, aye. But maybe give us some lead time. We can get in quicker and quieter than they can. We just need them on hand to do the arresting on the other side."

Moving quickly, we mobilized, accepting the weapons offered and loading into Ewan's Land Rover. I brought my computer, knowing I'd probably lose signal under the circumstances. We stopped to pick up Callum on the way as we headed down the narrow track he'd followed from the formal gardens.

"What's the plan?" he demanded.

We laid out what we'd devised in the ten minutes since we'd left the castle.

I kept staring at the signal on my screen. "What if Klein didn't take her back to the cottage?"

Ewan glanced over at me. "Then she probably left something there that will tell us where she's going next. One thing at a time. We deal with what's in front of us, aye?"

It was how we'd been trained. No multitasking. Complete focus on only what was directly in front of us. One decision, then the next.

We parked far enough from the cottage that no one would hear us. The patter of the rain would also cover our movement as we closed in on our target. The cottage itself had two doors, one in front and one set of French doors off to the left side, leading out to a wee stone terrace. Light shone through gaps in the curtains, a pale beacon in the gloom beneath the trees.

Operating via hand signals only, Ewan and I crept closer, taking opposite sides of the house. I had the side with the French doors. Keeping low, I leaned over just far enough to peer through a gap in the curtains covering the French doors. Through it, I spotted a small lounge with a fireplace. Ciara was tied to a chair in front of it. Blood trickled from her temple, and I spotted fresh bruising.

Rage geysered through me. I gave it two seconds to boil, then I flipped that mental switch until everything was cold and calculated. Emotion had no place here.

Peering back through the gap, I scanned the room, instantly committing the layout to memory. Klein paced the space in front of Ciara, gun still in hand, evidently ranting about something. Ciara watched the other woman, temper shining out of her big blue eyes. Temper was a damned sight better than fear. It meant she still had fight left. Signaling back to Callum that I'd spotted our hostage, I took my position to the left of the door and waited for the distraction. We'd kicked around options on the drive, given we didn't have flash-bang grenades or any of the things we'd normally use under such circumstances. Initially, we'd planned to fire a warning shot into the sky, but spotting the car, Finn had offered another idea.

He crept out of the trees on the opposite side of the late model sedan parked out front. He tested the driver's side door. Keeping low, he tugged it open and laid on the horn. The sound blared over the muffling rain.

Inside, Klein startled and bolted for the front window.

The moment she was across the room, I breached. The doorframe shattered as I barreled through, coming in fast and low, knives already in my palms. From the opposite door, Ewan burst in as well. We moved with a synchrony honed over years of training and missions. I saw the gun lift in my direction and threw the knives I held. Klein howled as the first struck true. Her arm jerked, and the gun fired.

For two heart-stopping beats, I panicked because I didn't know which way the bullet had gone. Frantic, I looked to Ciara. But there was no spreading bloodstain on her clothes.

Across the room, Johanna Klein was face down on the ground as Ewan cranked her arms tight behind her back, securing them with some zip ties he'd had in his 4x4.

I ran for Ciara, whose eyes were wide and full of terror.

Gently, I dragged the gag down. "Where are you hurt?" I demanded. "What did she do to you?"

"Alex, you're shot!"

"What?"

"Your shoulder."

I glanced down to see blood seeping through the front of my shirt. "Well, shite."

"There's a hole in the back, too. Through and through," Finn announced.

"It'll keep." I took my tactical knife to Ciara's bonds, swiftly slicing through them to free her.

She tumbled off the chair and into my arms. Her hair had come loose from the careful twist she'd put it in that morning, and her suit was rumpled and bloodstained. But she was alive.

I held onto her for a long, long time, my face buried against her throat where I could feel the strong, rapid beat of her heart.

She was alive. She was safe.

The threat was over.

"What the bloody hell happened here?" This came from Constable Williamson, who'd stepped through the front door that dangled on its hinges.

Ciara lifted her head long enough to point toward our captive. "That woman kidnapped me. She's also confessed to tampering with my brakes and running me off the road."

"There's also evidence she's been in contact with Brodie Drummond, fueling his jealous streak." Finn jerked a thumb toward the bedroom. "Her laptop's in here."

For several moments, Williamson could only blink at us. Then she squared her shoulders and marched toward a glaring Johanna Klein. "Right. You're under arrest."

FORTY-TWO

CIARA

"You know, this is starting to feel uncomfortably familiar," Dr. Donaldson announced as she examined my head.

"There were no bullet wounds last time," I groused.

"Alex is being treated down the hall. He had full range of motion, and the bullet went clean through. He'll be fine."

"It's just a flesh wound, right?" I scowled at my brother, where he stood in the corner of the exam room, then wished I hadn't, as the pounding ache in my head got worse.

"If Doc Albright sees anything concerning, he'll make sure your man does whatever needs doing to rectify it," Dr. Donaldson assured me.

My man. I'd have felt better if I had eyes on him.

Once the police had arrived, my captor—Johanna Klein, I'd been told—had been arrested and carted off to the police station. Callum and Finn had followed behind as escort, to make sure she actually got there. Constable Williamson had interviewed us briefly at the scene to get the essentials, before Alex lost patience and insisted I needed medical attention.

Never mind the blood that had soaked through the makeshift bandage Ewan had fashioned out of some kitchen towels.

We'd all come into the clinic together, but I couldn't shake the sense that something was wrong. There was a remoteness to Alex I didn't like. Maybe it was to do with whatever switch he'd had to flip in order to do the job he'd done for so long, and maybe he'd snap out of it. But what if it was something more? I needed to see him. To reassure him—and myself—that everything really was fine. That this prolonged nightmare was finally over.

"I hate that this happened... well, at all. But I especially hate that it happened today. What actually happened with the wedding?"

Isobel spoke up from her perch on the visitor's chair in the corner. "Oh, actually, despite all the chaos, once we got word that you were safe, the wedding still went off fine. And Christina insisted on saving you cake."

"That's really sweet. A little weird, but sweet."

"I think she feels terrible that something like this happened in the middle of her big day."

"It certainly wasn't her fault. Nobody was expecting anybody to get kidnapped. If anything, I feel terrible that this interrupted her festivities. We've been planning this wedding for a year!"

"Well, she's married now," Isobel pointed out practically. "And she definitely has a story to tell her grandchildren someday that no one else will have."

"Well, you are, again, very lucky. Another concussion, and that's a hell of a bruise on your head, but it could be a lot worse." Dr. Donaldson tugged off her exam gloves. "It'll be the same routine as before. Let's see if we can avoid cracking your noggin again, aye?"

"That is certainly the goal."

"Since this is your second in less than a month, I want to see you again for a checkup in a few days."

"I'll do anything you want. I just want to rest and get out of this suit."

"Fair enough."

My parents rose from the waiting area as soon as I stepped out of the exam room.

"Oh my God, my baby." Mum folded me into her arms.

"It's okay. I'm safe. The person who did this is in jail and going to stay that way."

"Let's get you home, love," Dad insisted.

The last thing I wanted was to get taken home and smothered again. I needed Alex.

Spotting Doc Albright speaking to the receptionist, I called out, "Are you through with Alex?"

"Oh, aye. He's already gone."

I jerked away from my mother. "Gone? Where?"

"Home to clean up, I believe."

Could he even do that alone? Why wouldn't he have waited for me? That sense of disquiet grew stronger.

"Look, I just want to go back to my flat and get some quiet. I swear if I need anything, I'll let you know. But I need to check on Alex."

"We'll take her and see that she properly rests," Isobel assured them.

It was clear both my parents wanted to argue, but they held their tongues.

Isobel drove us the short distance to my flat. It took longer than I wanted to make it up the stairs, as my head was feeling extra swimmy with the throbbing. But I was relieved to spot Alex as soon as I stepped inside.

"How's your shoulder?"

"Fine." The word was clipped, and he barely glanced at me.

Something was very wrong, and I could only hope that I had enough functional brain cells to handle it.

Turning back to the door, I glanced at Isobel and Ewan. "Can you give us some privacy for a bit?"

Ewan nodded. "We'll run downstairs. I'm going to go check on some things at the pub."

"Great."

The moment they headed back down the stairs, I shut the door. "This wasn't your fault."

Alex looked at me from across the room. He'd changed clothes, into another long-sleeved T-shirt and fresh jeans. I could just see the edge of gauze pads peeking out from the collar.

"That's what you're thinking, isn't it? You're blaming yourself for someone else's actions."

"You canna dispute the fact that this wouldn't have happened if you hadn't been involved with me."

I suspected if it hadn't been me, it would have been someone else. But I didn't think that would help, so I kept it to myself.

"You cannot take ownership of the behavior of someone who's clearly unhinged. Think about all the lives you saved because of that mission. How many more names would have been leaked? How many more operatives would've been compromised? How many more missions would've failed? You saved lives, Alex. You saved mine today."

When I got near him, he paced away, restless frustration and anger rolling off him in waves. "You should never have been put in that position. I should never have started this up again."

"Okay, first off, you didn't start this up again. I did. I'm the one who asked for your help with Brodie. I was having problems with him before she ever came along and fanned the flames of his obsession." The evidence of her surveillance had been found in the bedroom. No question. The photos sent to Brodie had come from her. "He was harassing me all by himself. I asked for your help, and you gave it. After that, it was a mutual decision that this should turn real again."

Moving slower this time, lest I spook him, I laid a hand on his arm. The muscles beneath my palm trembled with tension. "Nothing needs to change here, Alex. You solved the problem. The threat has been neutralized. It's done."

"Aye. It's done. This won't happen again. I won't allow it."

As he stepped back, I looked past him into the bedroom and spotted the duffel bag at the foot of the bed, all zipped and ready to go. Suddenly frantic, I glanced around. The kitten and all her accoutrements were gone. He must've already taken them back to his flat.

Panic wrapped like a claw around my throat. "What are you doing?"

"I'm the problem. I'm what made you a target. So I'm removing myself from the equation." He shouldered the bag and moved toward the door.

"Alex, no. This wasn't your fault."

"Nobody else is going to get hurt because of me or anything else that I've done."

I tried to rush after him but had to stop when the room made a slow revolution. "Alex, stop. Please, let's talk about this."

He didn't slow. "There's nothing to talk about. My mind's made up. I won't endanger you or anyone else anymore."

Bile rose in my throat, and I gripped the back of the chair like a vise lest I slide like a puddle to the floor. "Alex—"

He finally looked at me, his hand on the door. "I made

promises to you last time, and I hurt you terribly when I broke them. The only promise I'm making now is that this is the last time I'll hurt you. You're better off without me."

"I'm not!" My voice broke. "Alex, don't do this."

"It's what's best. Have a beautiful life, Ciara. And don't wait for me."

"Alex!"

But he'd already shut the door. By the time I managed to get across to open it again, he'd disappeared like the ghost he'd been trained to be. I sank down onto the top step and wept as he broke my heart all over again.

FORTY-THREE

ALEX

I barely registered the bedroom door opening before something hit me in the face. Saffron yowled in protest from where her sleep had been disturbed on the pillow next to mine.

"Get up. You're coming with me," my brother ordered.

I dragged the jeans he'd tossed at my head away from my face. "The fuck is wrong with you? I've been shot."

Deeply unimpressed, Aidan just glared at me. "You already said it was a flesh wound. Get your arse out of bed."

I flinched as he slammed the door behind him.

Saffron padded onto my chest, where she proceeded to knead with her sharp little claws.

"Och, there's no need for that. I'm awake." With my good arm, I lifted her off and sat up, scrubbing a hand over my face.

I felt like warmed over death, less because of my injury and more because I felt as if I'd performed open-heart surgery on myself with a rusty spoon. It had been forty-eight hours since I'd forced myself to walk away from Ciara. Two days during which I'd mostly slept, trying to avoid my own misery. Evidently, my brother had decided I'd moped long enough.

Dragging on clothes, I headed downstairs to find Aidan's husband Charlie fixing breakfast for Niamh. My niece knelt in her chair at the kitchen table, a princess tiara perched in her jet-black curls and a Lightning McQueen toy in her hands.

"Uncle Alex!"

I mustered up a smile and bent to kiss her head. "Morning, Sprite."

"Will you be eating breakfast?" Charlie asked. "I'm making eggs."

I opened my mouth to say yes, but my brother interrupted.

"Later," Aidan snapped. "We have somewhere to be."

"Somebody woke up on the wrong side of the bed this morning, aye?" I muttered to Charlie.

"C'mon, brother."

I shoved my feet into the boots I'd left by the door. "Where are we going?"

"Just get in the car."

I wondered what the hell had crawled up his arse, but kept my mouth shut in front of his daughter. Let Charlie explain to her why her da was being an uncharacteristically surly bastard.

As Aidan backed out of the driveway, I wished I'd at least gotten a travel mug of coffee, because I was exhausted. I might've slept much of the last two days, but I hadn't actually rested. I hadn't answered any of the phone calls or texts from my mates, either. I didn't miss the fact that there'd been none from Ciara. But I'd ended things, hadn't I? That was the whole point. To cut things off clear and cleanly, so there'd be no question that things were over.

Would Ewan be tracking me down to put his fist in my face? I wouldn't stop him.

"I dinna ken what the hell is going on with you, but you came down here as a miserable son of a bitch, and this is no' acceptable. You have apparently torpedoed your life and expect us to pick up the pieces. I'm done letting you wallow."

Aidan wasn't the only one who could be a surly bastard. "Excuse me?"

"You were always the one of us who was destined for greatness. The things you did during your service—I know you've never talked about it, but it was major, life-altering, world-saving shite. And I know it absolutely killed you when you had to stop. I know, too, that you took on something to do with all of that off-the-books."

When I stared at him, he made a noise of derision in the back of his throat.

"I'm no' an idiot, Alex. I didn't need to be read in to understand what you were doing. Especially with how you behaved after Da died. You blamed yourself, as if it was somehow your fault."

My shoulders had hunched up by my ears. "It was my fault."

"It wasn't. And that's what I'm here to prove to you."

"What are you talking about?"

I realized we were turning into the lot at his construction company warehouse, where he kept materials and heavy equipment. "I found Da's car."

"You what?"

"It took a while for it to work through all the proper channels, but eventually, mum was contacted by the breakers' yard where it ended up, because there were a few things of Da's that the owner wanted to know if we wanted. So I hauled the thing back here."

He stopped in front of one of the big rolling doors and climbed out of the driver's seat. I followed much slower, eying the door as if there were an entire team of enemy snipers behind it. He unlocked the smaller door to let us into the warehouse and flipped on the overhead fluorescent lights.

I spotted the car immediately on some kind of lift in the far corner of the building. My breath wheezed out as if I'd been inside when the front end crumpled like a bag of crisps.

Aidan snagged a torch off a tool bench and waved me over to the vehicle. "Look," he demanded.

He shone the beam of the torch on the underside of the car.

This was the thing I'd wanted for the past two years. To be able to look at the evidence for myself. To see with my own eyes what caused the accident. Bracing myself, I stepped close enough to peer under the front wheel well, where Aidan pointed. The failed ball joint stood out as if it were wrapped in neon lights. The thick grease boot was split wide open and looked dry and cracked. I could see the loose lower control arm dangling freely, detached from the steering knuckle. The ball joint itself remained connected to the wheel hub assembly, but the vertical post it attached to was sheared off where it should have been seated firmly in the control arm. I realized there was no doubt the front wheel had separated at speed when the worn ball joint finally hit total catastrophic failure. This was no act of sabotage. It was simply an aged component giving out after years of metal fatigue and negligent maintenance.

"Why the fuck didn't he check it?" I muttered.

"You know he didn't have the mechanical sense of a field mouse, and he was always putting off maintenance like oil changes and the like. Foolish. Tragic. Horrible. Preventable. But truly, just an accident."

I loosed a slow breath, and with it, some of the heavy weight I'd carried for the past two years began to lift.

Aidan clapped a hand to my good shoulder. "Da's death was no' on you."

"That may be, but I still nearly cost the woman I love her life. Twice. That *was* on me."

"Did you directly endanger her?"

"She was targeted by someone because of the op I ran."

"You said nearly. Is she okay?"

"Aye, we got to her in time."

"And did you capture the bad guy?"

"Bad woman, as it turned out. And aye, she's been arrested." In fact, the one message I had responded to had been from Cardinal. The intel they'd gleaned from the laptop recovered at the cottage was enough to link Johanna Klein to a number of cyber terrorist attacks, so she was going away for a long time.

"Okay, so you eliminated the threat. Why the hell are you here acting like your best mate died?"

Temper kindled. Didn't he see that this was for the best? "I'm no good for her. It's not safe to be with me."

"Oh, get your head out of your arse. Do you really love her?"

"Of course I do. That's why I walked away."

"You're a fucking idiot. Do you think that, because of everything you've done, you're somehow not worthy of being happy? Is that what this is? Because that's what it sounds like, and it's a boatload of shite."

"No, I just don't want—"

Aidan rolled right over me. "Are you planning to bail on your mates you just went into business with?"

I hadn't actually gotten that far. My focus had only been on staying away from Ciara so she'd be safe. "Well, no." Fresh guilt settled over me that I hadn't gotten in touch with Callum or Finn to reassure them on that particular front since all this went down.

My brother continued. "And don't you think it would be pretty fucking awful of you to be up there, running that business, to be near her and not be with her? She's going to matter to you no matter where you are. There will always exist the potential for somebody to find out about that fact. Wouldn't you rather be there to stop it, like you were this time?"

"Her brother is there. Callum and Finn are there." But the excuses sounded half-arsed to my own ears.

"Are *they* going to keep as close an eye on her and make sure that she's okay all the time the way you would?"

"Well, no, but—"

"I rest my case. Look, Alex, you've been happier when I've talked to you over the past couple of months than I've seen you in years. This woman is good for you. And if she still loves you after the total horse shite that you've now pulled on her, then I say you go back to do some major groveling, because she is your One. You look about her the way I look at Charlie. That is rare, my brother. Don't be a fool and waste it."

I looked back at the car, my brain slowly wrapping around what he'd said. "If I agree to think about it, can we go back and get some breakfast?"

Aidan wrapped an arm around my shoulders. "If you're good, I'll even share the bacon."

FORTY-FOUR

CIARA

My head hurt. I was really tired of this whole recovering from concussion thing. As the doctor hadn't wanted me left alone and everywhere I turned in my flat reminded me of Alex, I'd ended up convalescing at Ewan and Isobel's in their guest room. The pain was slightly less than it had been, and I'd slept a lot once we'd passed the window when someone had to wake me up every hour. But the frequent crying jags had done nothing to help get past the headache portion of this process. Probably the only reason it wasn't worse were the endless cups of tea my sweet sister-in-law-to-be kept foisting on me at every opportunity.

She was who I expected when a soft knock sounded on the guest room door.

"Come in."

But it was my brother with a mug in his big hands. "More tea."

I resisted the urge to wipe at the tracks of recent tears. It wasn't as if Ewan didn't know I'd been crying my eyes out.

"Thanks." I accepted the cup and clutched it between my palms, soaking in the warmth.

Instead of leaving, Ewan dropped into the chair in the corner, bracing his forearms on his knees. "You want me to break his face?"

The casual delivery might have made me smile if I hadn't understood he was a thousand percent serious. "No."

"He hurt you."

"Aye, he did. Because he thinks this whole situation was all his fault, and it's the right thing to do. Idiot. He's blaming himself. He thinks if he stays away from everybody he cares about that they'll all be safe. That is not how the world works."

"Did you tell him that?"

"I would have if he'd given me the chance. My brain wasn't exactly in full working order when he walked out." I scowled and regretted it as the bruising on my head twinged. "He ran away, Ewan."

"You love him?"

"Yes. We have a connection." I glanced at him with a wry twist of lips. "That may squick you out."

He lifted a hand. "I'm no' thinking about any kind of 'connection.' We'll just stick with the fact that you love him." Ewan laced his fingers together. "I believe he loves you, too. I think he has for a long time."

That got my attention.

"I didn't know it was you he met three years ago. I'm no' sure what I'd have done if I had."

"Broken his face?"

"I'd have considered it, sure. But the way he looked when he talked about you... He was ready to change everything, and he's no' a man who does things on a whim. I can't speak to why he didn't follow through back then."

"Because he believed he was righting a bigger wrong. And

he believed doing so would put me in danger. Not an entirely untrue assumption, as it turned out. But there are a million and one everyday dangers that could happen to any of us all the time. I could get struck by a car when crossing the street in the village. And the self-sacrificing ass would probably find some way to blame himself for that, too."

Ewan's lips twitched. "You do know him."

"If he'd said he didn't want me, didn't care for me, that would still break my heart, but I'd move on. But he didn't do that. At no point did he say, 'I don't love you.'" That was really the sticking point for me. The thing that had been circling in my brain over and over for the past three days. So, in a sense, I was right back where I was three years ago, with no closure.

"Has anybody heard from him?"

"No. As far as I'm aware, he hasn't contacted Callum or Finn, either."

So he'd bailed on them, too. Probably not forever, but I wasn't the only one being impacted by this crisis of conscience Alex was going through.

Abruptly fed up, I swung my feet out of bed and rose. "Okay, that's it. I'm done with this shite. Give me his address. Somebody needs to go shake some sense into him, and it might as well be me."

Ewan arched a brow.

"Don't act like you don't have it. I know you know where he lives."

"There's no guarantee he went home."

"He was recovering from a gunshot wound. He either went to his brother's or his mother's. I'm guessing his brother, because his mum would smother him. He and I have that in common."

Smothering a laugh, he nodded. "Aye, you're probably right." Then he sobered. "What are you going to say?"

"I don't know, but I expect I have at least two or three hours of a drive to figure it out. I'm not done with him yet, Ewan. This is twice he's walked away from me without giving me a say, and maybe he had good reasons, but I deserve the chance to be heard."

"Aye, you do. But are you good to drive? That head's still aching, aye?"

Like a sore tooth. But I wouldn't let that stop me. "If I feel worse, I'll pull over."

"Okay." He gave me the address. "And for what it's worth, you were right in what you said."

"Which thing?"

"Alex is one of the best men I know—his current idiocy withstanding. I hope the two of you can work it out. I think you're good for each other."

"Thanks, Ewan." I gave him a big hug. "Now get out. I need to get dressed."

I did that, then registered I looked like exactly what I was—a woman who'd recently been in a fight. So I took the time to detour to my flat. I showered and changed and carefully applied my makeup, so I looked like less of a reminder of exactly what Alex feared. Then I packed an overnight bag. The drive might only be a couple of hours, but in my current state, I didn't think I could do the round trip today. If things went sideways, I'd grab a hotel room somewhere before coming home tomorrow.

Deciding I was as ready as I was going to be, I shouldered my overnight bag and marched to the door. Out of habit, I set the alarm to away, then opened the door to leave and found Alex standing on the other side.

I took a half-step back out of shock. "Alex."

"Can I come in?"

"Yes, of course." I stepped back and dropped the bag, punching in the alarm code before the countdown had finished.

His gaze fell to the bag. "Going somewhere?"

I lifted my chin in defiance. "I was coming after you."

"You were?"

The temper that had settled down to a simmer during my shower rose to a full boil again. "Of course I was, Alex. Three years ago, you disappeared from my life, and I had no recourse but to let you. But things are different now. We're different. Because this wasn't just one night. We have been through shite together. Traumatic shite. And you don't get to just walk away because you think it's best. Not without giving me a chance to say my piece."

He angled his head as if in permission and somehow that just made me angrier.

"Life is hard, and the world is dangerous. There are a million and one ways something could happen to any one of us at any time. That doesn't mean any of us are walking around with targets on our backs. And even if it did, we have something together, you and I. Something that doesn't come along every day."

Mindful of avoiding his injured shoulder, I poked him in the chest, emphasizing every point. "I love you. And I'll be damned if I'm going to let you sacrifice both our happiness because you're afraid."

"You're right."

I frowned at him. "I'm right?"

"I am afraid. I'm fucking terrified of anything happening to you. I went home and my brother read me the riot act about the whole thing. He also gave me a gift."

"What kind of gift?"

"He found our father's car. It wasn't sabotaged."

I pressed a hand to my head. "Oh, my God. That was the

other thing I needed to tell you. I got confirmation from Klein while she had me. I asked if she had anything to do with your father's death, and she said no, but that your guilt over it was obvious and that was where she got the idea. I meant to tell you, but then concussion. But it's not your fault. None of this was your fault."

His lips curved. "I'm working my way around to believing that. I might need reminders."

"Does that mean you'll be around for me to remind?"

"That depends. Are you willing to forgive me for being a fool and let me back into your life, Hellcat? Because the one thing that has remained constant through all of this, all these years, is that I love you."

My throat went thick. "Do you actually want that future we talked about?"

His arms slid around me. "More than anything in the world."

"Then maybe you could kiss me and prove it."

I caught the flash of his smile as he bent his head to mine and my world righted itself again.

EPILOGUE

ALEX

At the center of the room, Finn tapped his glass of champagne, gathering the attention of the assembled crowd.

"My business partners and I would like to thank everyone for coming out today. Your support over the past few months has been nothing short of amazing. None of us are originally from Glenlaig, but you've all made us feel welcome here. For three former military lads, that means everything. Thank you, too, to Ardinmuir Event Planning for helping us put together this open house so we can most effectively introduce our business to all of you. So please, enjoy the nibblies put together by Chef Afton Colquhoun and take a look at the adventures we have on offer. And if you'd like, please book your excursion, because Out of Bounds Scotland is officially open for business!"

A cheer rose up around our front lobby, where family and friends had gathered to celebrate with us today. The space bore no resemblance to the tiny, slightly sad, rough-around-the-edges room I'd walked into all those months ago. We'd vaulted the ceiling and installed larger windows all around to take advantage of sunny days when we got them. The long back wall dividing the lobby from our offices and warehouse was covered in large, framed action shots of all of us, demonstrating the assorted services and adventures we were offering. Ciara's idea and Kyla's photography. A new custom-built reception desk occupied one end, with clustered seating for those awaiting their excursion appointments or equipment rental. It all looked pretty slick and official.

Of course, we didn't actually have a receptionist. That was on the list we hadn't gotten around to just yet. God knew, none of us had the temperaments to deal with running an office full-time. We all preferred to be out and about. But as it was still February, our offerings were slimmer just now. Business would ramp up when spring fully hit, so we had time. More to the point, we needed income to pay for a receptionist or office manager. Meanwhile, we'd started taking future bookings on the website I'd built. Callum had believed if we built it, customers would come, and he'd been right. We already had trips booked well into spring and summer.

A familiar arm slid around my waist. "Hey, handsome. How does it feel?"

I tucked Ciara closer to my side. "It feels pretty fucking fantastic to have you here with me."

She gave a teasing pinch of my waist. "I meant the grand opening."

"Oh, well, that's nice, too." But my focus wasn't really on the party. I had bigger plans for later in the day. Plans that involved surprising her.

The past few months had been blessedly quiet. Brodie had been convicted on charges of assault and stalking, and had already begun his five-year prison sentence. Johanna Klein was likewise incarcerated, and for a lot longer. Ciara and I had both done a lot of healing, physical and otherwise, and I was finally ready to take the reins of our happily ever after. I just hoped it didn't backfire on me.

Somehow, I made it through the party, smiling and chatting with all our guests, answering questions, booking trips. But by 3:30, I was itching to get on with my plan. Spotting Hamish across the room talking to Finn, I managed to catch his eye and give the signal. He gave a subtle nod and paused to send a text.

The countdown had begun.

It took another half hour for the party to begin winding down and for people to start clearing out. I snagged the last of the spring rolls. "Are you ready to get out of here?"

"Don't you have to, you know, clean up?" Ciara asked.

I offered a smug smile. "I drew the long straw, so I'm not on cleanup duty." That wasn't actually true. Callum and Finn knew what I was about and were doing me a solid by letting me sneak out early.

"In that case, I've had enough of crowds. I say we thaw out some of the stew from the freezer and curl up for a *Dr. Who* marathon."

"Put a pin in that. I have something to give you first."

Her blue eyes brightened. "Oh? What is it? Not that I'm opposed to presents."

"You'll just have to wait and see."

We said our goodbyes and stepped outside.

"What's the occasion?" she persisted.

"A thank you for all of your help with the planning of the party and with all the other things you've done. Beyond anything else, just because you're you, and you make me happy."

"Aw, that's so sweet. Your odds of getting lucky tonight were already pretty maxed out, but this is even better."

I shot her a heated look across the center console. "Definitely put a pin in that for later."

When I didn't turn to park behind the pub, she straightened in her seat. "Where are we going?"

"It's at my place."

"I didn't know you had anything left at your flat since you basically moved in with me."

"Is that a complaint?"

"No, absolutely not. You know I love having you with me."

I parked at the kerb and led her up the stairs I'd barely used the past few months. All was quiet on the other side of the door, and for a moment I wondered if I'd given Hamish's daughter enough time to move things. But we were here now, so I unlocked the door and swung it open.

Ciara was looking at me as she stepped inside, but at the metallic jingle, she turned and spotted her surprise. "Oh my God!"

From inside the wire crate, the puppy stared at her out of mismatched eyes and wagged her wee tail.

Ciara sank down in front of the crate, curling her fingers through the bars. The puppy licked her knuckles. "She's adorable. But what are you thinking? We can't have a dog in the flat. There's not enough room! And what will Saffron think?"

"I was thinking that you've been wanting a dog for months, and you've been trying to hide how sad you were when Havoc went home to Isobel and Ewan. You deserve a pet who adores you without reservation." Particularly as Saffron basically just tolerated her. She was absolutely my cat.

"But where will we put her?"

"I have a plan. There's a second part to all of this."

"There's more?"

"All in good time. Let's take the wee girl out."

She opened the cage, and the puppy tumbled out, all brown and white fur, clambering into her lap and immediately standing up to lick Ciara's face. Their mutual love fest made me grin. Part one of this surprise was going exactly according to my plan.

"Oh, I love her. She's so sweet!"

"She could probably do with a walk. I'm no' sure how long it's been since she's been out."

"How about that, wee one? Do you want to go walkies?"

Ciara snapped on the leash that had been laid over a chair and carried the pup outside. I subtly steered them both down the street, toward the residential section of the village. Once we reached a grassy area, she let the puppy down and allowed her to sniff all the things. The smile creasing Ciara's face as she watched the wee dog was the best thing I'd seen in months. She was so enamored, she didn't even realize I'd stopped until I reached out to snag her hand.

"We've come to part two."

She glanced around the street at the quiet houses. "I don't understand."

"The past few months, we've been working on blending our worlds, building that life we talked about all those years ago. I think we've been wisely cautious, given everything that happened. But it's time for us to take things to the next level. So, I got us a house." I pulled out the keys and dangled them.

Ciara stared. "You bought us a house?"

"Well, I rented us a house with the option to buy, in case you hate it. But it's got enough room for us and our stuff, Saffron, and this wee pup here."

Stunned, she followed me up the walk to the three-bedroom cottage. I gave her the grand tour. Like any property, it would need a bit of work and customization. Paint, at the very least, as everything was stark white. Ciara listened patiently as I pointed out all the features, finally ending in the kitchen, which opened out to the back garden. "It's still close to town, but there's a garden space that's already fenced, and plenty of room for all your shoes. Though I expect you'll want to put them away while this one is teething."

She hadn't said a single word other than noncommittal murmurs as I led her through the house, and I was starting to think I'd made a major mistake. I couldn't read her expression. Maybe I was moving too fast. Maybe I was getting too serious.

Abruptly, she launched herself at me, and I staggered, managing to catch her without squashing the puppy in her arms. "I love it. And I love you. So much."

"So that's a yes?"

On a joyful laugh, she looped her free arm around my neck. "Aye, that's absolutely a yes."

As her mouth found mine, I wondered exactly how long I'd have to wait before she'd let me put a ring on her finger.

If I had my way, not long.

Not long at all.

STINGER

CALLUM

As soon as Alex and Finn got back from picking up the new kayaks in Glasgow, we were implementing a new rule for how we decided who got stuck staying back here at the office manning the phones. None of this equitable taking turns. We were going full on Fight Club. We were all highly trained, but I had sheer loathing on my side. The fucking phone had been ringing all bloody day. If I didn't know better, I'd think my mates had put out a billboard with our number and express instructions for potential customers to call today, when there was no one else here but me. Why the fuck couldn't people just book on the website? That was why we'd had Alex build the thing.

I hated people. And talking. And people.

I especially hated people who couldn't read readily available information. See also The Fucking Website, which listed the activities, packages, and pricing we offered, with an interactive booking system that even showed availability by date. Why the hell was I responsible for handholding people through that shite? It wasn't like I needed to walk them through how to tie a figure-eight-follow-through knot so they didn't plummet to the bottom of a ravine. It was a website. They just needed to read and click some buttons.

The phone rang again.

Grinding my molars, I considered hurling the entire unit at the wall. That would solve the problem. But then Finn and Alex would give me more shite and probably stick me permanently with the replacement.

Blowing out a breath, I picked up the receiver.

"Aye?" Belatedly, I added, "Out of Bounds Scotland."

"I'd like to book a custom tour with your company." The accent was unquestionably American. That could be good or bad.

"I can help you with that. What sort of tour?"

"What do you offer?"

I scowled at the phone. They had to have found our bloody phone number on the website that already listed our services. Taking a firmer grip on my temper, I struggled to stay polite. "That depends on the time of year. When are you considering your trip?"

"July or August."

"That's a grand time of year to visit the Highlands. We offer guided hikes, multi-day campouts, abseiling, kayaking…" I continued to reel off everything I could think of, though I was certain I'd forgotten something.

"I'd like to book something a little more custom."

My back went up. "What kind of custom?"

"All of that sounds fantastic, but I want to end each day at high-end lodging, with custom whisky tasting experiences and gourmet catered meals."

So this was one of *those* Americans. The entitled arseholes who believed the world would work for them for a price. Not that the US had the market cornered on privilege. I'd seen plenty of this sort where I'd grown up. Hadn't had any patience for them then, either.

All I wanted was to get out in nature, lead some hikes, take some people rock climbing. Maybe do a little hang gliding. I was not made for dealing with the likes of this gobshite.

"I dinna ken who you think you are, but I've never heard of such entitled—"

The front door of the shop opened, and a woman walked in. For a moment, I was struck absolutely dumb. She was fucking gorgeous, with a cascade of glossy ebony hair and big brown eyes that wouldn't have been out of place on a Disney princess. And it was very apparent from those widened eyes that she'd heard what I'd said. Or maybe that look of horror was just her reaction to me.

"Excuse me?" The wanker on the phone was headed toward insulted.

Before I could dispense with him, the princess marched right up and yanked the phone right out of my hand.

"Hello? Hi. I apologize. Someone answered the phone who shouldn't have. How can I help you?" Another American. But not the posh sort of upper crust accent of the guy on the phone. Her voice was softer, smoother. Southern?

I stared at her as she listened to the prick, making "Uh-huh. Uh-huh. I see," noises.

Ignoring me entirely, she grabbed a notepad and began scribbling notes.

"And do you have any dietary restrictions? Mmhmm. Yes, sir. I understand. Well, I can't make any promises, but I'll see that all this gets to the appropriate people for discussion. Uh-huh. You, too. And I'm sorry for your experience earlier. Uh-huh. Buh-bye now."

The woman hung up the phone with a quiet click and laid

down the pen before lifting her gaze back to me. "I am so sorry. I know that was overstepping and incredibly inappropriate of me, but you cannot talk to people like that."

That voice flowed out like warmed honey, wrapping around me and melting all the irritation I'd been carting around like luggage all day.

"You're hired." The words were out before I could think better of them, but I wasn't about to take them back. She was fucking amazing, and I'd pay her salary out of my own savings, if I had to.

Those big brown eyes widened still further. "I'm sorry?"

"As the new office manager," I explained. "When can you start?"

Her delicate brows knit together, clearly baffled. "I... what?"

"Do you already have a job?" *Please God, say no. I need you.*

"Well, no—"

"Do you need a job?" She hesitated, and I pressed. "Do you?"

"Yes, but—"

"Then you're hired."

She scooped a hand through all that thick, glossy hair, and I itched to do the same. Her peal of laughter held a slight edge of hysteria. "You don't even know me."

"I know you just saved my business a potential client, and you're apparently not afraid of me." Which, honestly, was kind of fascinating. Most people were afraid of me, or at least gave me a wide berth. They had even before the accident that cost me my eye. I was the poster boy for "Does Not Play Well Wi' Others." There were days since my retirement when I felt feral and barely human.

She angled her head and looked at me with the gentlest expression on her lovely face. "Everybody has bad days."

"Every day is a bad day for some." I had no idea what prompted me to say it. The truth of the words landed between us and vibrated like a missile waiting to detonate.

She didn't move. Didn't lay a hand on me. But somehow the energy between us shifted. I felt as if she'd wrapped me in a hug without touching me at all.

The door opened again, breaking whatever spell this southern princess had cast.

Alex shoved inside. "We've got ten new kayaks. Finn's pulling around back. We need to open the loading bay door." He stopped at the sight of our guest. "Oh, who's this?"

I didn't tear my gaze away from her. "Our new office manager. This is..." I paused. "What's your name?"

Flummoxed, she batted those eyes at me for several long moments before finally giving in. "Parker. It's nice to meet you."

Choose Your Next Romance

OOOO BOY! I hope you're ready for the grumpy sunshine goodness that is Callum and Parker's story. *Beyond Highland Sunrise* releases in early 2025 (right now it says May but it's getting moved up!).

Now, if you want one more look at Alex and Ciara's happily ever after, you can nab the bonus epilogue right here: https://books.kaitnolan.com/hci96y7wd6

If you want more of the residents of Glenlaig, you can go back to the beginning and check out the Kilted Hearts series to hear all about how that three-hundred-year-old marriage pact impacted a WHOLE BUNCH of folks when Afton decided to pull a runaway bride. It was A Thing. It starts with the prequel, *Jilting The Kilt* and *Cowboy in a Kilt* (*Book 1*). You can find a preview of Raleigh and Kyla's book on the next page!

SNEAK PEEK COWBOY IN A KILT

KILTED HEARTS BOOK #1

A cowboy without a home

Robbed of the family ranch that should have been his legacy, Raleigh Beaumont is a man with no roots and no purpose. When a friend drags him to Vegas, he figures he's got nothing to lose. But after a hell of a lot of whiskey and a high stakes poker game with a beautiful stranger, he finds himself the alleged owner of a barony in Scotland.

An heiress with a crumbling heritage

When her brother's bride disappears just days before the wedding that's meant to save their ancestral home from the mad marriage pact that's held their family captive for generations, Kyla McKean believes they've been granted a reprieve. Until she finds out about the new, single—male—owner of Lochmara and knows she's next on the chopping block or ownership of both their estates revert to the crown.

A modern answer to a three-hundred-year-old problem.

Raleigh's lost his land once. He's not about to lose it again. Not even because of some lunatic pact made centuries before he was born. Kyla's desperate to save Ardinmuir. She agrees to marry him on one condition: They wed for one year to satisfy the pact, then get a quick and quiet divorce. There's no stipulation against it, and they'll both get what they want.

But this displaced Texan and his fiery bride are about to find so much more than they bargained for.

"It always rains the day a good man dies."

Raleigh Beaumont felt a smile tug the corner of his mouth, because the weather was bone dry. They'd been in a drought for the past few weeks. "Mama used to say that. She'd also say not to speak ill of the dead."

"Your daddy was probably the only thing your mama and I really disagreed on." Charlotte Vasquez came to lean beside him on the split-rail fence bordering the north pasture, propping one booted foot up as they both looked out over the rolling hills of the East Texas ranch that had been in his family for generations. "Luther Beaumont was a bastard, and we both know it."

"You're not wrong." One corner of his mouth quirking,

Raleigh glanced down at the tiny Latina woman, who barely came to the top of his shoulder.

When Raleigh's mama, Lily, had been diagnosed with stage-four cancer, it had been Charlotte who'd taken a leave of absence from her job as a high-powered executive and moved in to care for her—and by extension, Raleigh. His daddy hadn't stuck around to watch Lily's decline as illness stole her vitality and vivaciousness, leaving her only a shell of the woman she'd once been. Luther had thrown himself into keeping the ranch running smoothly. At the time, Raleigh had convinced himself his father was only outrunning the inevitable grief. That he was protecting the legacy he'd married into.

He'd learned better since.

"I mean, come on," Charlotte continued. "He moves that little hussy—" Said hussy being Twila, Luther's second wife, who was a bare seven years older than Raleigh himself. "—into the house when your mama's barely been six months in the ground? She only married him for his money, and he married her for the trophy." Her tone rang with bitter judgment, though it had been nearly fifteen years.

Raleigh stretched an arm across her shoulders, tugging her in for a hug. In the wake of Lily's death, Charlotte had convinced Luther to let her stay on as housekeeper, so she'd be around as a mother-figure to Raleigh because, God knew, Twila didn't have a maternal bone in her body. Back then, he hadn't understood what she'd given up for him, but at sixteen, that link to the mother he hadn't wanted to forget had saved Raleigh. And though he was well grown now, somehow, Charlotte had never left. He'd once asked her why, and she'd told him that losing his mother like that had shown her there were far more important things in life than breaking her back to climb a corporate ladder, and until she found another of them, she was staying planted near him.

"You didn't have to be here today. I'm a big boy. I can handle the reading of the will."

She squeezed him back, her head only coming to his shoulder. "Of course, I did. You need somebody here who's an ally."

They both turned to see a black Ford F-150 pulling up in the circular drive in front of the house.

"Looks like you weren't the only one with that idea," Raleigh murmured.

A familiar lanky figure climbed out of the truck and headed in their direction. Ezekiel Shaw was one of Raleigh's oldest and best friends. The one who'd as often been the instigator of mischief as the one to help him out of it.

Charlotte shot him a knowing smile. "Hey, Trouble."

Zeke grinned and pulled her in for a hug of his own. "Hey, Charlotte. When you gonna run away from this place and marry me?"

"I can't marry you. Who'd be around to keep this one on the straight and narrow once he takes over the ranch?"

He clutched his chest in dramatic fashion. "Breakin' my heart, woman."

"Somehow, I think you'll survive." But a twinkle in her rich chocolate eyes softened the dry retort.

Turning to Raleigh, Zeke hauled him in for a back-thumping hug. "You holding up?"

"Ready to get this show on the road. What're you doing out here?"

Zeke pulled a flask out of his pocket and offered it. "Figured I'd be around for moral support, just in case."

Raleigh waved away what he knew would be bourbon. "You think things won't go well with the reading of the will?"

He shrugged. "Got no reason to think one way or the other. I just know you and Twila don't exactly get on."

"She'll be out of my life soon enough." And thank God for

it. Raleigh was itching to truly take over the reins and begin implementing the plans for diversification and modernization that his father had rejected.

"From your mouth to God's ear," Charlotte muttered.

A whistle sounded behind them.

Hamp Browning, the family attorney, waved from the front porch. "Come on! It's time."

They strode toward the house, where Zeke dropped into one of the rocking chairs on the porch. "We'll see you on the other side."

Charlotte squeezed his shoulder once. "We'll be right out here."

Raleigh followed Hamp back to Luther's study. Kitted out in lots of wood and leather, the room still smelled of his daddy and the cigar he habitually allowed himself at the end of the day. He could just imagine the old man leaned back in the chair behind the massive desk set in front of the picture window that framed their spread. But it wasn't his seat anymore. After today, it would be Raleigh's.

Twila sat in one of the two chairs in front of the desk, looking like she'd come dressed for a board meeting instead of the reading of a will at home. She'd never fit in around here, with her city airs and high-heeled shoes. He didn't think he'd ever even seen her on a horse, and the only time she'd come out to the barn was to track down her husband. God forbid she risk stepping in something in her Feragucci shoes. Raleigh figured she'd be lighting out of here almost as soon as the reading was over. Back to Dallas, to her high-society friends.

He lowered himself into the other chair as Hamp circled around to the opposite side of the desk. The old man sat with a creak of springs and leather, running a hand down the tie that fell to the paunch overhanging his belt, then back up to smooth his big walrus mustache. Not for the first time, Raleigh thought he wouldn't look out of place as an extra in a western. Maybe in a leather vest at a poker table or behind the bar in an old saloon. The thought of it had his lips twitching into a smile. His mama would've appreciated the image. She had loved her westerns.

On a sigh, Hamp opened the folder he'd placed on the blotter. "Let's get to it, shall we?"

As the lawyer fell into the drone of legalese, reading the last will and testament of Luther Alexander Beaumont, Raleigh's gaze strayed past him to the window. Just a little while longer, then he'd finally be free to speak to the hands and their families, giving them the reassurance that nothing would change. They wouldn't lose their homes or jobs. His mind shifted to what needed to be his first orders of action. He'd had plenty of time to consider that, but he had to think about the season and what expenses the ranch would have coming up.

Abruptly, Raleigh realized Hamp and Twila were staring at him.

"I'm sorry. I zoned out there for a minute. Can you break it down into layman's terms?"

Hamp glanced at Twila, then back at him, his expression apologetic.

What the hell had he missed? Fighting not to curl his hands around the arms of the chair as a bad feeling set up like Quikrete in his gut, he waved at Hamp. "Go ahead; spit it out. I don't care about the money. I just want the ranch."

The old man winced. "Your father left everything to Twila."

That couldn't be right.

Shock was the only thing that kept his voice level. "I'm sorry. What?"

"All of it. He changed his will a few years ago. The stock, the land, the house. It all belongs to her now."

Raleigh exploded up, sending his chair skidding several feet back as he rounded on his father's wife. "This is fucking bull-shit. This is my birthright. My mother's family's land. You have no right to it whatsoever. You don't want this place. You have no interest in running a ranch."

Unperturbed, she lifted her chin, somehow managing to look down her nose at him from where she stayed seated, her long legs crossed neatly in the slim pencil skirt. "You're right. I don't. Which is why I've already made arrangements to sell it."

The blood drained out of Raleigh's head. "Sell it? To who?"

She named a developer who'd been sniffing around for years with designs on turning their several thousand acres into cookie-cutter suburban houses.

As he let loose a string of profanity and began to pace, Twila examined her manicured nails. "You're welcome to try to beat the price." The figure she quoted was stratospheres above what Raleigh could afford.

When he said nothing, she flashed a smug little smile. "That's what I thought." She turned back to Hamp. "If that's all?"

At his short nod, she picked up her designer purse. "You have a week to clear out." Then she strode out of the room without a backward glance.

Raleigh scrubbed a hand over his head. "This can't be happening."

Hamp shoved up from the chair, looking about ten years older than he had when he'd sat down. "I'm sorry, son. There's nothing we can do."

"Can I take her to court? Contest the will?"

"You can try. But in my professional opinion, it's going to cost you more than you've got, and you're not going to come away with a ranch in the end. Luther was in his right mind when he changed his will. The bastard screwed you right and proper. There's no two ways about it."

The sucker punch of it had Raleigh swaying on his feet in a way the loss of his father had not. It threw him back to the devastation of his mother's death. He'd promised her he'd take care of the ranch. Take care of the people who worked there. Carry on their family legacy. And all of it had just been ripped away.

He didn't even remember leaving the room, not until he almost ran over Charlotte.

"Honey, what happened?"

Raleigh just shook his head and kept going. He needed out of the house, into the hot, humid air.

As soon as he hit the front porch, Zeke pushed up from the rocking chair he'd commandeered. "What the hell happened?"

"I got fucked, that's what happened. The old man left her everything. All of it. The entire ranch. My *mother's ranch*. She's selling it to fucking developers. It's gonna be a goddamn neighborhood here next year. My home is liable to be bulldozed or turned into some kind of clubhouse. Not to mention what the hell happens to all the hands and their families." Heart sinking, he scrubbed both hands over his face. "I promised them I'd look out for them, and there's not a damned thing I can do about it. She gave me a fucking week to get out."

His gaze caught on Charlotte's face. Her expression had turned carefully neutral, but she'd lost all color. He realized he wasn't the only one out of a home.

"Fuuuuuck." Zeke drew the word out. "Man, I'm sorry. I don't even know what to tell you. I mean, I could—"

Raleigh held up a hand, knowing what he was about to suggest. "Not an option. Thank you, but no."

"Alright. Well, in that case, I'm thinking the best option is gonna be for you to get the hell out of town before you do something you're gonna regret."

Raleigh had no idea what he might do if he stayed and

wasn't much inclined to risk ending up behind bars. And yet. "I can't just leave. I need to break the news to the hands. Do what I can to help them find other placements. And I should pull together the family momentos before that bitch tosses them all." The idea of losing anything else of his family history made Raleigh sick.

"I've already done a lot of that, setting things aside for you over the years," Charlotte assured him. "It won't take long to pull together the rest. We should probably hurry before that harpy gets it in her head you don't have a right to them."

Zeke pulled out his phone. "I'll make the arrangements for boxes and storage."

As his friend stepped away, Raleigh took Charlotte by the shoulders. "I don't know where I'm gonna land with all this, but wherever it is, you'll have a place there. Always. You're family."

She cupped his cheek. "You're a good boy, Raleigh, and you grew into a fine man. Your mama would be proud. Now, let's go get to work."

"MAYBE NO ONE WILL NOTICE."

Kyla MacKean briefly shot her brother some side eye. "Aye. Right. No one will notice the six-foot-wide chunk of plaster that's crumbled off the wall." The remains of that plaster lay in a heap on the scarred hardwood floors she'd only just waxed and polished for the wedding reception set to be held here in a matter of days.

Connor shrugged with his usual insouciance. "It's a six-hundred-year-old castle. We'll say it's part of the ambiance."

"Be serious, Con. This is important. We can't afford for anything else to go wrong. Too much is riding on this weekend."

The reality of living in a centuries-old castle in the High-lands of Scotland was nowhere near as romantic as books and movies made it out to be. It was cold, drafty, and often wet. Parts of the castle were fully uninhabitable. The estimates they'd received from various contractors for truly weather-proofing the place were astronomical. Every single problem they discovered was usually a sign of a bigger, deeper issue that called for bigger, deeper pockets than they had. The truth was, they were land rich and house poor, and without a massive influx of cash, the home they both loved would fall to ruin. And while Scots did love their ruins, Kyla wasn't keen on living in one.

She had a plan. One that involved using her brother's wedding as an opportunity to show the world that Ardinmuir could be a premier wedding destination. People paid big money for that sort of thing. But not if the bloody walls of the great hall were falling down around their ears.

"Dinna fash yourself. It's stood for this long. It's no' gonna crash onto our heads this weekend."

"So say you."

He swung an arm around her shoulders and squeezed. "Aye, I do."

"Oh good. You've got your line down." She teased him out of long habit, but in truth, she was worried.

"That's right. Until I do my bit as the sacrificial groom, your bit hardly matters."

Kyla spun into him, clutching his shirt. "You're not thinking of backing out, are you?"

His beleaguered sigh didn't make her feel any better.

"No. I know my duty. I've had a lifetime to accept it. This wedding will happen, and the terms of the marriage pact will finally be satisfied."

Then the axe hovering over all their heads because of an

agreement made by ancestors who'd long since turned to dust would be gone, and they could get down to the serious business of actually saving the estate.

"I hope you know how much it means to me that you're doing this. I know Afton isn't who you'd have chosen."

"I'm certain I'm not her first choice, either. But it is what it is. We're friends. That's a far better basis than many have in arranged marriages."

Afton Lennox was the remaining heir to the barony of Lochmara, the neighboring estate. Her legacy fell under the same threat as their own, and Kyla could only thank God that she was willing to adhere to the terms of the pact. Then again, if she didn't, both their estates were forfeit to the Crown. Kyla would never stop cursing their ancestors for the addition of that little failsafe to the agreement meant to ensure the alliance between their families actually happened.

Knowing there was no changing their situation, she shook off the frustration. "We need to get someone out to look at it to make sure it's not going to get worse before the wedding. I don't want to have this place full of guests only to have plaster crashing down onto plates at the reception." Already feeling the beginnings of a headache, Kyla headed for the door. There was no getting mobile reception inside three- to four-foot-thick stone walls. "Maybe we can have a quick patch job done to get us through, then deal with the more permanent repair after."

It wasn't ideal, but she simply didn't have the bandwidth to deal with more disasters right now.

Connor followed her out. "I'm gonna go check in on Uncle Angus. The latest iteration of the wedding cake should be about ready."

"But the cake was decided on weeks ago! Why is he mucking around with it?"

"He reckons it'll be good practice for his audition for the

Great British Baking Show, and who am I to turn down more cake?"

Kyla closed her eyes and prayed for patience. She loved her great uncle and her brother, both, but sometimes dealing with them felt like wrangling a couple of cheerful puppies rather than grown adults. At least if Angus was baking, he wasn't out getting into some other sort of trouble. And, really, she wasn't going to turn down more cake, either, given how the day was shaping up.

It took longer than she wanted to get ahold of Theo Gordon, the contractor who'd done the most work on Ardinmuir. And longer still to convince him to come out today, after he finished up the job he was working the next village over. If a batch of Angus's jaffa cakes had been promised as a bribe, well, she'd run into Glenlaig to pick up ingredients herself, if she had to. It wasn't like they could finish setup until this was sorted, anyway.

Satisfied that she'd done all that could be done for the moment, Kyla made her way down to the kitchen, which was housed in the newer portion of the castle. New being relative, having been added on in the nineteenth century, when James MacKean, head of the family at the time, had been flush with cash from a shipping empire that later collapsed. But at least that part of the house had been comparatively modernized.

As she stepped into the kitchen, Angus straightened at the heavy wooden island, lifting his piping bag in triumph from a truly lovely confection of swirls and flowers.

Kyla sniffed the air and caught the tang of citrus. "If that's a lemon chiffon cake, I just might fall to my knees and weep with gratitude."

Angus's blue eyes twinkled. "Then ready your tissues, lass. But you'll have to wait until I take a picture for my blog."

"We have a deal. Although you may take that back when I

tell you that the only way I could get Theo out today to look at the wall in the great hall was to promise him a batch of your jaffa cakes."

One white brow winged up. "And what'll you trade *me* in this bargain?"

"My undying gratitude." Kyla slid her arm around him, and pressed a smacking kiss to his leathery cheek, feeling a bit of a pang as she realized he'd gotten a little more frail over the winter. Other than Connor, Uncle Angus was the last of her immediate family. When had he last gotten a checkup? She added that to the never-ending list in the back of her brain. Something to address after the wedding.

Connor snagged an Irn Bru from the avocado green refrigerator and kicked back against one of the long stone counters, smirking. "That disnae sound like much of a deal to me."

She pointed a finger at him in warning. "You stay out of this."

Angus considered. "You do the second round of dishes, and we have an agreement."

"Done."

As they shook on it, someone knocked on the door.

Connor pulled it open. "Malcolm! Welcome. Did you come to help with the setup for the reception, or did you hear a rumor that there's more cake?"

The brawny, fifty-something man stepped into the kitchen, kilt swinging, his thick-soled boots thumping on the hardwood floors. His hazel gaze slid over the cake on the island, but his expression didn't change. There were some in Glenlaig who believed Lochmara's estate manager to be surly, but Kyla knew the truth. He just preferred animals to people. In social settings, he tended to be a man of few words. Still, the prospect of cake usually would have garnered at least some interest.

A frisson of unease traveled down her spine as she registered the tension in his burly shoulders and jaw. "Is everything all right, Malcolm?"

"No." His throat worked. "Afton is gone."

The words hit Kyla like a well-aimed stone to the gut. "Gone? What do you mean she's gone? The wedding is in less than a week. She can't be gone."

"I found a note."

"Saying what?" Connor asked.

"That she's sorry."

"That's it?" Kyla knew her voice was edging into the realm of shrill, but couldn't seem to control it.

"That's it."

Like a puppet with cut strings, she dropped into a nearby chair. "You can't be telling me what I think you're telling me. If she's gone... If she doesn't go through with this wedding, we're all screwed. The Crown has been watching since we filed the paperwork for the marriage. We have to find her."

"Her car is still in the village. I tracked her that far before I came here. But she's gone. She could be anywhere."

"What about the police?" Angus asked.

"Since she left a note, we have no reason to get them involved. She's not a missing person since she left voluntarily." Malcolm spread his hands. "Unless you want to pour money into a private investigator to track her down..."

That was money they didn't have.

This was terrible. Disastrous.

Connor tunneled a hand through his mop of blond hair. "Maybe she'll come back."

Kyla shot a hard stare in his direction. "Are you willing to wait until the eleventh hour to see? I'm not. We all need to turn our efforts to tracking her down. She has to go down that aisle if I have to march her there in handcuffs myself."

Grab your copy of *Cowboy in a Kilt* today!

OTHER BOOKS BY KAIT NOLAN

A complete and up-to-date list of all my books can be found at https://kaitnolan.com.

KILTED HEARTS
SMALL TOWN CONTEMPORARY SCOTTISH ROMANCE

- *Jilting The Kilt* (prequel)
- *Cowboy in a Kilt* (Raleigh and Kyla)
- *Grump in a Kilt* (Malcolm and Charlotte)
- *Playboy in a Kilt* (Connor and Sophie)
- *Protector in a Kilt* (Ewan and Isobel)
- *Single Dad in a Kilt* (Hamish and Afton)
- *Kilty Pleasures* (Jason and Skye)

SPECIAL OPS SCOTS
SMALL TOWN MILITARY SCOTTISH ROMANCE

- *One Fine Night* (prequel)
- *Before Highland Sunset* (Alex and Ciara)

- *Beyond Highland Sunrise* (Callum and Parker) Spring 2025

BAD BOY BAKERS
SMALL TOWN MILITARY ROMANCE

- *Rescued By a Bad Boy* (Brax and Mia prequel)
- *Mixed Up With a Marine* (Brax and Mia)
- *Wrapped Up with a Ranger* (Holt and Cayla)
- *Stirred Up by a SEAL* (Jonah and Rachel)
- *Hung Up on the Hacker* (Cash and Hadley)
- *Caught Up with the Captain* (Grey and Rebecca)

RESCUE MY HEART SERIES
SMALL TOWN MILITARY ROMANCE

- *Someone Like You* (Ivy and Harrison)
- *What I Like About You* (Laurel and Sebastian)
- *Bad Case of Loving You* (Paisley and Ty prequel) Included in *Made For Loving You* (Paisley and Ty)

THE MISFIT INN SERIES
SMALL TOWN FAMILY ROMANCE

- *When You Got A Good Thing* (Kennedy and Xander)
- *Til There Was You* (Misty and Denver)
- *Those Sweet Words* (Pru and Flynn)
- *Stay A Little Longer* (Athena and Logan)
- *Bring It On Home* (Maggie and Porter)
- *Come Away with Me* (Moses and Zuri)

MEN OF THE MISFIT INN

SMALL TOWN SOUTHERN ROMANCE

- *Let It Be Me* (Emerson and Caleb)
- *Our Kind of Love* (Abbey and Kyle)
- *Don't You Wanna Stay* (Deanna and Wyatt)
- *Until We Meet Again* (Samantha and Griffin prequel)
- *Come A Little Closer* (Samantha and Griffin)
- *Just Wanted You To Know* (Livia and Declan)
- *A Love Like You* (Juliette and Mick)

WISHFUL ROMANCE SERIES
SMALL TOWN SOUTHERN ROMANCE

- *To Get Me To You* (Cam and Norah)
- *Know Me Well* (Liam and Riley)
- *Be Careful, It's My Heart* (Brody and Tyler)
- *The Matchmaker Maneuver* (Myles and Piper prequel)
- *Just For This Moment* (Myles and Piper)
- *Wish I Might* (Reed and Cecily)
- *Turn My World Around* (Tucker and Corinne)
- *Dance Me A Dream* (Jace and Tara)
- *See You Again* (Trey and Sandy)
- *The Christmas Fountain* (Chad and Mary Alice)
- *You Were Meant For Me* (Mitch and Tess)
- *A Lot Like Christmas* (Ryan and Hannah)
- *Dancing Away With My Heart* (Zach and Lexi)

WISHFUL MOMENTS SERIES
BITE-SIZED WISHFUL ROMANCE

- *Once Upon A Coffee* (Avery and Dillon)

- *Once Upon A Rescue* (Brooke and Hayden)
- *Who I Am with You* (Dinah and Robert)

Wishing For a Hero Series (A Wishful Spinoff Series)
Small Town Romantic Suspense

- *Make You Feel My Love* (Judd and Autumn)
- *Watch Over Me* (Nash and Rowan)
- *Can't Take My Eyes Off You* (Ethan and Miranda)
- *Burn For You* (Sean and Delaney)

Meet Cute Romance
Small Town Short Romance

- *Once Upon A Snow Day*
- *Once Upon A New Year's Eve*
- *Once Upon An Heirloom*

Summer Fling Trilogy
Contemporary Romance

- *Second Chance Summer*
- *Summer Camp Secret*
- *The Summer Camp Swap*

ABOUT KAIT

Kait is a Mississippi native, who often swears like a sailor, calls everyone sugar, honey, or darlin', and can wield a bless your heart like a saber or a Snuggie, depending on requirements.

You can find more information on this *USA Today* best selling and RITA ® Award-winning author and her books on her website http://kaitnolan.com.

Do you need more small town sass and spark? Sign up for <u>her newsletter</u> to hear about new releases, book deals, and exclusive content!